Published by Turner-Bone Editions.

Also by Steven Turner-Bone

Friends and Enemies

The Enemy Within

Farewell to a Friend

In need of a Friend

***

The Firebird Inheritance

By

S C Southcoat

Invitation to a Murder

ISBN: 9781838147808

Printed by Book Printing UK
Remus House, Coltsfoot Drive, Peterborough, PE2 9BF

Invitation to a Murder

S C Southcoat

Acknowledgments

Many thanks go to

Maureen Stonehouse, Caroline Mitchell and Kris Egleton

my BETA readers.

Dedicated to

Geraldine and Jonathan Cant

Author's Note

Though this story is a work of fiction the following places do exist.

GCHQ Scarborough, Radio traffic interception station.

RAF Carnaby is now an industrial estate. But during WW2 it was an airstrip with three dedicated runways for stricken allied aircraft returning from Europe.

RAF Leconfield closed as an airbase in 1977, but is now a military vehicle driving school.

There is no such place as the Yorkshire Dales Spa Hotel in Harrogate.

Chapters

Chapter One	*1*
Chapter Two	*11*
Chapter Three	*19*
Chapter Four	*35*
Chapter Five	*58*
Chapter Six	*79*
Chapter Seven	*100*
Chapter Eight	*120*
Chapter Nine	*141*
Chapter Ten	*159*
Chapter Eleven	*173*
Chapter Twelve	*185*
Chapter Thirteen	*201*
Chapter Fourteen	*211*
Chapter Fifteen	*223*
Chapter Sixteen	*241*
Chapter Seventeen	*252*
Chapter Eighteen	*265*
Chapter Nineteen	*279*
Chapter Twenty	*294*
Chapter Twenty-One	*314*
Chapter Twenty-Two	*322*

Cast of characters

April Showers	Private Detective
Mr Charles Showers	April's Father
Mrs Hazel Daisy Showers	April's Mother
Violet Rose Birch	Dead auntie
Rex Barker	Friend
Mrs Sheltie Barker	Family friend
Mr Bernard Barker	Family friend
Jennifer Clark	Typist
Patsy Stave	Music teacher
Annabelle Page	Editor
Inspector Allswell	Harrogate Police
Sergeant Duffy	Harrogate Police
Rev Christian Warlock	Priest
Mrs Faith Warlock	Rev's wife
Ewan Ramsbottom	Sheep/cattle farmer
Corriedale Ramsbottom	Farmer's wife
Natalie West	Ex-Bank teller/waitress
Rocky Punch	Ex-boxer/celebrity security
Mrs Judy Punch	Boxer's wife
Ada Betterman	Ex-nurse/nursing home owner
Holly Starbrightly	Film Star (Real name Holly Wood)
Hector Boysack	Film producer/husband to Holly
Mrs Bonnie Stone	Housewife
Ralf (Roofus) Stone	Ex-builder/DIY Store owner
Mrs Heidi Steel	Housewife
Robin Steel	Ex-thief/architect/psychologist
Octavia Tone	Music teacher

Cast of characters

Henry Bunkhouse	Hotel Manager
Jack	the hotel pot washer
Scops	Night porter
Perkins	Hotel Receptionist
Usher	Hotel Receptionist
Mrs Downy	Night-time comforter
George	Driffield Postman
Mrs Chaperon	Ada Betterman's Secretary
Mr Visconti	Bridlington cafe owner
Mr Suitor	Headwaiter
Colonel Spion	East German spy commander
Elizabeth Milbank	name on invitation

Chapter One

Hello, my name is April Showers and I'm a private detective. A strange career for a young woman in her early twenties you might think, but I'm not your average 1950s woman. I like to dress smartly and professionally but keep up with the latest fashion. I'm five-foot-six with auburn hair and more than enough determination to make my business a success.

I left school just as the war was finishing and the men were coming home looking for work. During the war, women had worked in the factories; drove the busses, worked on the land or for the privileged few, managed businesses. Now, with the war over they suddenly found that they were expected to give up their jobs in favour of men. Oh, no; that's not for me. I intend to control my own destiny.

How did I get stuck with a name like April Showers? Well, you can blame my mother. She doesn't take anything seriously, except the welfare of her darling daughter, much to the consternation of my father. He's the manager at the Driffield branch of the East Yorkshire Savings Bank and has very little time for frivolity; but they love each other dearly, which means Mother gets her way most of the time. You see,

I was born in April when it was raining and with a family name of Showers – you get the picture.

'It is distinctive enough for no one to forget who you are,' she reminds me constantly.

The thought of being ignored, or worse forgotten, would be more than my mother could bear. She loves to be the centre of attention in any gathering. But for me, frankly, I hate my name and its association with the familiar saying. My name afflicted me throughout my school years which made it difficult for me to make friends, and because of my silly name and lack of friends, I was constantly bullied. But the bullying did me one favour; all that teasing toughened me up and taught me to stand up for myself.

After leaving school at sixteen with a few good O-levels, I had to find a job. Unfortunately, nearly every interview I went to would produce the same result. An interviewer sitting across a desk from me with an amused smile on their face each time they spoke my name. I ended up drifting from job to job, finding it hard to settle anywhere. If I didn't find the job boring there would be other problems such as older people making jokes about my name. I'd had to put up with that at school, but no more. However, being an independent sort of person, I soon realised that a regular job working in a factory, a typing pool, shop or heavens above, becoming a nurse, was not for me. Not that I've got anything against those kinds of jobs. It's just that, I wanted to do something different, more me, something more exciting, before I settled down to marital bliss.

Well, after reading one of Agatha Christie's detective stories, it gave me an idea. There had been a murder in

Driffield and I solved it. The case had run on for weeks leaving the police baffled. The local newspaper made a big deal about the lack of progress the police were making, and the talk of the town was of who the murderer could be. Well, what with the police getting nowhere with the case, I started my own investigation. It's amazing what a trim waist and a coy smile can weasel out of even the toughest of men. So, when I discovered who the murderer was, the newspaper made a big thing about me solving the case and how incompetent the police had been. That was the catalyst that changed everything for me.

Forgive me. I digress, so back to my story. I wanted to become a private detective in my hometown of Driffield. Daddy thought the idea of setting up as a private detective a little dangerous and wasn't keen on the idea at all, but Mummy thought it would be absolutely perfect for me. And she insisted that Father part with the money I would need to get started. Mummy is such a darling. So I borrowed a little money from my father and bought the house at 23A Exchange Street, along with a small car, a green Morris Minor. The car is a few years old and has one or two rust spots and dents in the bumper, but a private detective must have a car, mustn't one?

The house is old and small but it's on a busy road just of the Market Place and is situated between a solicitor's office and a pub. As soon as I moved into 23A Exchange Street, I knew I'd made the right decision. I don't know what it is but, it's as though, I have someone looking after me, a guardian angel or some guiding power that nudges me in the right direction now and then.

As I was saying earlier, I'm an independent person and able to stand up for myself, which's why being a private detective suits me so well.

To help offset the cost of the bills of running the house and car, I had to let out all the rooms in the house that I wasn't using, so I converted them into offices. I let out the other offices to three business-minded ladies like myself and their rent pays most of my bills. With most of the cost of running the house taken care of, it takes the pressure off my detective agency finances until I become better established and I can afford to live on the premises instead of at home with my parents.

My first tenant, Jennifer, has the ground floor office across the hall from my office; she's a freelance typist. Most of her work comes from various solicitors' offices in the town when their typists have more work to do than they can handle. She also does my typing when I need her to. Jennifer, with her connections to several solicitors' offices, has also proved to be a very useful tenant when I need a little background information on a suspect. Consequently, we have become good friends. She also has a spare set of office keys in case I'm late into the office for any reason.

Annabelle is an editor of manuscripts from budding authors. She has the office above Jennifer. When we all meet up for elevenses, she tells us about the plot of the latest novel she is editing. Some of them can be quite shocking and racy, but it doesn't stop us from having a giggle at the bedroom antics of the characters she reads about. Not that I have any practical experience in that department.

Patsy is the third and last of my tenants, she has the office above mine. Patsy teaches music. I've come to terms with the noise of her piano lessons, but having to listen to the little dears sawing a violin in half with a horsehair bow can, at times, get a little too much for even the most patient person to withstand. When Patsy has one of those pupils in for a lesson, I give up trying to work and I go make a pot of tea, take it into Jennifer's office along with a plate of biscuits, and we have a natter until the offending child leaves the building. On Fridays, all four of us get together in the kitchen for lunch. Friday is also the day we take it in turns to bring in sticky buns as a treat to have with our tea.

I didn't get very many clients at first. My jobs, more often than not, turned out to be quite boring. They were mostly ladies wanting to know what their husbands were getting up to when they spent too much time away from home. Most of the men, it was usual to discover, were escaping the house to spend time in the pub or on the golf course and simply keeping out of the way of their wives, though I have discovered two men who were having extramarital affairs.

However, one day, a few months back, events began to unfold that set me on a path that changed my forever and made my detective agency the respected business it is today.

I arrived at the office at eight-forty-five, as usual, to open up before the others arrived, when Jennifer arrived early and marched into my room sobbing her heart out.

'David's got another woman!' she blurted out as she shut my office door and then sank into the chair opposite me.

'What! Are you sure? What makes you think that?' I was somewhat taken aback by her outburst, as they had not been married for very long. I grabbed my box of tissues, got up, and went around my desk to comfort her and give her a hug.

'He's staying out late, regularly, and won't say where he's been. We keep having rows, and when I accused him of seeing someone else, he just laughed at me and said I was imagining things.'

'I'm sorry, Jennifer; I have to ask, are you imagining it?'

'No, of course, I'm not! He stays out late lots of times.' She blew her nose and took a second tissue.

'Well, is he spending more money than usual? Getting dressed up before he leaves the house? Does he come home smelling of someone else's perfume? Is he ignoring you in the bedroom department?'

'No, none of those. He just won't tell me where he is going and why. So, it has to be another woman.'

'Well, he doesn't fit the usual bill of someone who is having an affair. There must be some simple explanation.'

'Do you think so?' She gave me a hopeful look. I smiled back reassuringly, praying I was right.

'Yes, Jennifer. I'm sure everything is fine and he'll tell you what he's been up to in his own time. Just give him a little longer. You'll see. You'll have been worrying for nothing.'

This, believe it or not, was how most of my cases started. The trouble was I'd put a lot of commitment into starting my detective business, as well as Daddy's money, so I had to stick with it and make it work even if the cases were mundane and repetitive.

Now; to get to the point of the story I wish to share with you. Around about the time I was dealing with Jennifer's problem, I was at my desk that morning when I heard the front door slam, followed by a blood-chilling cry that could only have come from one person. I knew who it was instantly when I heard my name called in that familiar way.

'AAAPRIL! WHERE ARE YOU, GIRL?'

I looked up from my newspaper, dreading what was to come. What on earth was she doing here? I hadn't seen my mother's sister for at least two years. She was the last person I expected or wanted to seek me out. I hurried to the hall to greet her, and there she stood with a face that would make babies cry and grown men shudder. She was dressed in a tweed jacket, matching skirt and sensible shoes. She oozed superciliousness. As I led her to my office door and showed her my nameplate. She just sniffed when I told her, 'you could have just come straight in, you didn't need to shout, Aunty.'

There was no hug or kiss of welcome. She just barged past me, marching into my office to sit in the chair I kept for my clients.

'I don't expect you get many customers when they have to sit in a chair as uncomfortable as this one,' she complained, whilst looking around my office, eyeing up my second-hand furnishings, sparsely filled bookshelves and single print hanging slightly askew on the wall behind my chair. She gave me her disapproving look.

'Hello, Aunty Violet, how nice to see you. How long has it been? Would you like a cup of tea?'

'Are the cups clean? I only take fresh milk in my tea,' she screeched.

I cringed at the insinuation. I couldn't imagine why Aunty Violet had come to see me; I only knew she would get around to telling me when she was good and ready. Though I surmised it must have something to do with my work as a detective, or why else visit me here, and not at home.

So, after Aunty Violet had finished complaining about the office needing dusting and that I should put up new curtains at the windows, she finally got around to telling me why she had come to see me. She showed me the letter and invitation she had received. It was to a painting sale which was to take place in a Harrogate hotel. The letter explained that the hotel room had already been booked and paid for. The artist, she explained, was a favourite painter of hers, and attending the sale would allow her to meet the artist in person. As Aunty wanted to add another one of the artist's paintings to her collection, she would get the pick of the collection before it all went on sale to the public the following day.

I smiled politely and sipped my tea, waiting for her to carry on.

'I want you with me when I go. You can be my companion; don't worry, I will pay,' she said.

I was amazed by the offer. I couldn't recall her ever sending me a birthday card never mind taking me away for an all-expenses-paid weekend. It was as she finished speaking that I noted for the first time, ever, a hint of fear in her voice.

'Of course, Aunty, I wouldn't dream of letting you go alone. I would love to go with you,' I lied. That chink of vulnerability I'd seen in her hardened face was enough to demolish my defences. She showed me the letter she'd received. It invited her to the Yorkshire Dales Spa Hotel in Harrogate. The trip also included a Saturday visit to the York Castle Museum. This, I thought a little unusual but, never having been to a private art sale before, who was I to criticise what was included in the itinerary. I suspected it was all part of the special treatment art collectors received. As I examined the letter, the light from my desk lamp showed up the watermark within the paper; it was of a lion. The letter had been printed on high-quality paper and I wished I could afford such fine stationary.

I asked Aunty if she knew who the other guests were, and about the person who had invited her to the sale, but she didn't answer. The booking was set for two weeks from now and the letter was signed by Elizabeth Milbank.

Aunty Violet had done little else for me in my life; so I was curious. I wanted to know what could have made her make such an uncharacteristic decision as to pay for me to go along with her. I looked at the name on the bottom of the invitation, again.

'Who is Elizabeth Milbank?' I asked more pressingly.

'I don't know. That is the primary reason why I want you to go with me to the hotel. To my knowledge, I have never met or had any dealings with a person of that name.'

'Why would a perfect stranger invite you to an art sale?'

'That is what I am wondering. I will telephone you with the travel details later on,' she told me, and then she stood up to leave. Short and to the point as always, I thought, but she had piqued my interest and as I had nothing more pressing on my books, so I was keen to know what had got her so worried and what would compel her to go on the trip if she thought it was suspicious.

'Will you be visiting Mummy, Aunty?'

'No, I'm far too busy, maybe later. Call me a taxi. I will be in touch when I want you.'

And that is what she did.

Chapter Two

On Thursday, the same day April got her surprise visit from Aunty Violet: unbeknown to April, an old acquaintance was back and on his way to meet his new employer.

Memories of day trips to the seaside flooded back as newly commissioned officer Captain Rex Barker drove his father's car along the coast road towards Scarborough. On the passenger seat next to him was his briefcase and a copy of the Bridlington Evening News. The headline read 'Unidentified man found dead in town harbour; police investigation underway.'

The road sign he was looking for came into view, so turning off the coast road he drove into the village of Seamer, easing off on the accelerator as he did so. Driving along High Street, it all looked so familiar. The shops and houses he'd seen so many times before as a child hadn't changed; it was as though the village was trapped in time. There was no sign here of the dereliction still plaguing most of the big cities and towns elsewhere in the country. He stopped at the Belisha Crossing to let a pretty girl in her mid-twenties wearing a calf-length, summery flowery dress cross the road. He couldn't help but admire her well-defined figure in her snugly fitted bodice, which emphasised her waist before expanding over her hips into a billowing skirt.

Two minutes later the houses had given way to the countryside, and he was looking for his next turning. His mood changed, becoming more serious. Tapping the left breast of his jacket, he reassured himself that his identification card was where it should be in his inside pocket. Taking a deep breath, he gunned the accelerator; the car leapt forward with a roar and a puff of black smoke from the exhaust. Turning right at the end of the road, he got the first sight of his new base. It seemed smaller than he'd been told. It had only one brick building, no bigger than a village school and a few wooden huts set in neat rows to one side of it. No one would have given it a second look but for the tall radio mast, the double line of fences topped with barbed wire and the prominent 'Keep Out' signs surrounding it. Driving up to the main gate, he pulled to a stop as a guard in army uniform approached. His partner, rifle at the ready, blocked the entrance. Rex pulled out his I.D. and held it up. The guard took it off him and checked it against a list on his clipboard. He looked at Rex and then back at the I.D. resting on the clipboard, before returning it to Rex.

'You may park your car in front of the principal building, Sir.' He pointed in the direction Rex should go and waved to his partner to open the barrier.

The guard at the entrance to the brick building also checked Rex's I.D. before letting him through. Inside the building, he found himself in an empty entrance hall with no one to greet him. He was confronted with a set of green-painted doors. At the far end of the hall, he spotted the Commanding Officer's door. Rex walked over, gave two knocks and entered. A middle-aged uniformed woman with the rank of sergeant wearing round, horn-rimmed glasses looked up from her typing but before Rex could announce himself, she issued her orders.

'Take a seat, Captain Barker, the Colonel will see you in a moment.'

Even though he was not in uniform and without checking his I.D, she knew who he was, leaving him feeling at a disadvantage. He did as instructed and sat down. Looking around the Spartan, but neat outer office, the only concession to informality was a Busy Lizzie potted plant on top of a filing cabinet. The woman returned to her typing, ignoring him completely. He felt out of place not being in uniform. The minutes dragged by as he counted the number of pencils in the tin mug which sat on the secretary's desk, how many keystrokes she typed in a minute. He read all the labels on the filing cabinet drawers then a buzzer sounded on the woman's telephone, bringing his attention back to the woman at the desk. The sergeant picked it up without speaking. Then answered, 'Yes, Colonel?' Looking at Rex for the first time since he'd entered the office, she gave him his instructions.

'You may go in now, Captain.'

As he stepped up to the Colonel's door, he felt his stomach tighten. It was as though he was standing outside his old headmaster's door after committing a misdemeanour. Knocking twice, he entered.

The Colonel was also dressed in civilian clothes and stood alongside his desk. Stepping forward, he extended his hand for Rex to shake. Rex hesitated and then responded to the friendly gesture.

'Take a seat, Captain. Welcome to Scarborough, we need people like you who have local knowledge of the area.'

'Thank you, Sir.'

'I know this is not the posting you were expecting, coming from Signals and after your time in Kenya, however, you know this area and its people, and more importantly, I understand that you can think on your feet. What we do here is secret. As far as the outside world is concerned, you run and monitor radio news traffic here for the BBC. However, what Military Intelligence needs you to do is find out who is setting up East German spies with legitimate cover jobs in the North East of England. Just down the road from here at Carnaby, we have a missile base that we share with the Americans. The East Germans have the base under surveillance, and we watch the East Germans to ensure they don't learn too much. The Americans want us to arrest the spies, but we prefer to know who they are and what they are doing. That way we can control the information they send back home. If we pick them up, East German Military Intelligence will only send replacement agents that we'll have to waste time trying to find and investigate all over again. It's the bigger fish we are interested in and who they can lead us to; that's where you come in. We want to know who is helping and supporting the spies that are already here. You will report to me on a weekly basis, but for now, you have two weeks to catch up on the case, read the files your predecessor made and re-establish your life in East Yorkshire.' The Colonel rose to end the briefing.

'As you leave, my sergeant will give you a file on the people we want you to monitor. Any questions, Captain?'

'Yes, Sir. What happened to the previous chap who was doing this job?'

'Ah, yes, him. We found him floating in Bridlington Harbour with a knife in his back. The local police are still investigating the death, but I doubt they will get anywhere with the case. So be careful, someone knows we are on to them. Good luck, Captain. I will see you in two weeks.'

'Thank you, Sir. I will get right on with it.'

As Rex left the Colonel's office, the sergeant coughed and briskly slid a birch coloured file to the corner of her desk. Rex picked it up as he passed by.

'Thank you, Sergeant.' The typing paused for a moment, but as Rex said nothing more the sergeant continued with her work with no further acknowledgement of him being there, so he left.

Placing the file he had been given him in his briefcase, he drove out the base gate heading for home.

He drove the car onto the drive at his parent's house in Wetwang, grabbed the briefcase and made for the front door.

'Is that you, dear?' A woman's voice called from the kitchen.

'No, it's me, Mum,' Rex answered. He put the briefcase on the entrance hall table and went through to the kitchen.

‘That was a quick interview. Didn’t you get the job?’ queried his mother. She rested her hand on his arm as he kissed her on the cheek.

‘It wasn’t so much an interview; it was more about checking me over to see if I’d fit in. But they did give me the job. They have given me some papers to read and said I was to call them in a day or two if I want to take up the post.’

‘So they offered you the job, then; that’s nice. Will you take it?’

‘I think so.’

‘Tea?’ asked his mother.

‘Yes, please. Is there any cake?’

‘Yes, I’ve baked a chocolate cake. Go through to the lounge, I’ll bring it through. After all, it’s not everyone’s son who gets offered a job at the BBC.’

‘Thank you, Mum.’

With the file on his lap, Rex read each page, placing the finished pages face-down on the arm of the settee next to him before starting the next page. It wouldn’t do for his mother to discover what his actual job was, she would worry too much.

The file contained a photograph, name and address, along with background information on each of the known East German agents, how long they had been in the country and what their cover job was. As Rex read each person’s profile, it surprised him how many female agents were amongst them. He looked for any clue that might lead him to which one had killed his predecessor, but also considered the idea that there may be an agent unaccounted for. In any case, the known agents had an unknown handler not too far away.

How was he supposed to find anyone with so little information to work on? He quietly cursed his predecessor for his lack of progress, concluding that his best course of action would be to start a new file of his own design. Rex selected the first person from the list and made a separate note of his address. Getting a look at the spy and studying his movements had to be his first step in his investigations. It listed him as a waiter at the Bridlington Princess Royal Hotel, with an address of Flat 2, 38 St Hilda Street. Rex folded the note and slipped it into his jacket pocket, then re-compiled the file and locked it in his briefcase. Feeling pleased at having his first plan of action resolved, he thought about the second, a slightly more difficult problem. *Would Father keep lending him his car when he needed it?* He doubted it. His father had been obliging enough when he had asked to borrow the car to go for his interview, but Dad was a bank manager in Beverley and getting the bus to work each day so his son could borrow his car to get to work would be pushing his father a little too far. He'd have to buy his own car.

'Ready for another cup of tea, dear?' asked his mother as she stepped into the lounge.

'Yes, please, and another piece of cake?' Rex followed his mother through to the kitchen where his mother broke the news about the following evening.

'I forgot to tell you. We have all been invited to dinner at the Showers house tomorrow evening. Won't that be nice? You'll get to see April again after all these years. Didn't she write to you whilst you were away in Africa?'

'Yes, Mum; once or twice. Are you sure the invitation include me? I didn't know that they knew I was home.'

'Oh, yes. As soon as I knew when you were going to be home, I telephoned Hazel to let her know. April will be at the dinner too. You liked her, didn't you? Although; she has some strange ways about her, still, I suppose she will grow out of them when she settles down. Did she write and tell you she had been in the local paper last year?'

'No, what was that about?'

'She solved a murder case. Her mother, Hazel, was quite a celebrity at my branch of the W.I. group over that. For weeks, it was all the ladies wanted to talk about. April has set up a private detective agency in Driffield. If you ask me, it's no job for a lady. She has too much time on her hands and watches too many of those dreadful American gangster films at the cinema. She must have got her fanciful ideas from those, but I expect she'll give that up now that you are home.'

'April, a Private Detective! She never wrote about that in her letters. This, I've got to see. And, what do you mean, 'you expect she'll give it up now that I'm home?'

'Well, she is sweet on you, dear. Now you're home, I expect you will be seeing a lot more of her. Why else would she have written to you whilst you were in the army?'

Rex sighed in disbelief at his mother's reasoning and her obvious attempts at matchmaking.

Chapter Three

Friday evening: at the Showers home.
The Barker's arrived at our house bang on the dot of seven o'clock to be greeted by my mother. I peeked from my bedroom window as Rex followed his parents into the house, wishing my mother hadn't set up this obvious matchmaking evening. I suspected Rex had been told all about me and my new business and now he'd be looking forward to meeting the strange detective girl he'd last seen over two years ago. As they came into the house I crept to the top of the stairs to overhear what was said.

'Come in, come in, it has been such a long time since we've seen you. How time flies,' gushed Mummy.

Coming out of the lounge, Charles Showers greeted his guests, 'Sheltie, Bernard, how nice of you to come and Rex the army has made a good-looking man of you. You must be pleased to be home again. April will be down shortly.'

Rex cringed at the compliment and the obvious pairing with April. *Don't parents ever let their children grow up or are we forever doomed to be ten years old? he sighed.*

'Good evening, Mr Showers. Yes, I had a great time in the army. It turned out better than I expected,' replied Rex.

'So I hear; all that training in the Signal's Regiment has led you to a good job with the BBC. Well done,' said Mr Showers. 'Come through to the lounge and I will make us all a drink.'

I waited at the top of the stairs for a few moments to allow everyone to get settled and for drinks to be served.

'Good evening. Sorry to be late, my hair took a little longer to dry than I'd expected.' I lied, a little; because I hadn't wanted to be confronted by Rex at the front door and be expected to give him a greetings kiss. I'd decided not to wear anything special for the occasion, just a smartish looking dark green dress with short sleeves. It was decorated with a belt made from the same material as the dress, tied in a bow at the waist, and the bodice had heart-shaped white buttons up the front. I noticed Rex's mouth drop open when he looked at me, so I went to sit next to Mummy.

Bother, I must have overdone it, I thought, *or has two years in the army made him desperate for any woman?*

'Right,' said Mummy. 'Now that we are all here we can go through to the dining room.'

As I expected, they parked me next to Rex. Throughout dinner, all Daddy and Mr Barker talked about was their respective banks and well they were doing. Mummy and Mrs Barker's conversation centred on the Women's Institute with occasional quiet words and looks in mine and Rex's direction, whilst Rex and I barely said a word to each other. I asked Rex about his time in the army but, when he started getting technical about wavelengths, dials and valves, I lost interest, just nodding and smiling in what I thought were the right places. In return, I told him about my trip to Harrogate with Aunty Violet, tomorrow.

Eventually, the evening was over, and it was time for them to all go home. Rex tried to kiss me on the cheek as he left, but I managed to dodge it and he had to make do with me saying 'goodnight,' and a wave from the doorstep.

Saturday.

It was a cloudy morning with a threat of rain when I picked up Aunty and drove the two of us to Harrogate. We arrived at the hotel around eleven o'clock. After parking the car, we carried our bags to the short distance to the hotel. Flowers grew along the front of the hotel in narrow, well maintained, beds, with Pansies at the front, Geraniums and Lily of the Valley in the middle rows and the back of the flowerbed, Foxgloves reached tall and slender up to the windows. As soon as we entered the hotel, our bags were collected by a porter, who led us to the reception desk. Aunty gave her name, telling the receptionist that she had booked two rooms. When I signed the reception card, I noted that most of it had already been filled in, only leaving me with the need to sign it, showing that I had arrived and taken the room key. Though I noted the name on my card was Miss Violet Birch, my Aunty's name. I assumed that was because she had booked the room for me. Our bags were taken up to our rooms for us, and we were ushered from reception into a private function room where tea, sandwiches and cakes were being served. Aunty and I sat together away from the others in the room at her request. I watched her face as she studied each one of the other guests over the rim of her teacup, pausing occasionally to give an acknowledging 'um' as she recollected who each person was. I asked her to name the other guests, but she declined to answer, so I continued watching her and her reactions as she studied the people on the far side of the room. I recognised one of the other guests as the film star, Holly Starbrightly. She was getting rather a lot of attention from the other hotel guests.

At one o'clock, a hotel porter came announcing that a coach had arrived and that it was ready to take us on our visit to the York Castle Museum, as per the invitation. I was a little shocked to hear his German accent, but the war was over and I suspected he was a friendly German who had left his country before the war started. As we filed through to the hotel lobby the other guests from the function room seemed tense and kept apart from us, watching us suspiciously. So I was relieved to be getting out of the stilted atmosphere of the hotel into more relaxed surroundings. I was looking forward to the trip, even though I'd been to the museum before, but that was ages ago, on a school trip.

When we arrived Aunty declined to go into the museum with us, saying she wanted to be alone. Where she went, I don't know. I can only imagine, having recognised someone in the group, she preferred to keep apart from them. This, however, was my opportunity to find out who the rest of the party were. It is my habit when meeting new people to give them one of my business cards, as one never knows from where new clients will arise. To enable me to remember who

I have met, I numbered each business card and then made a note of to whom, when and where I had given it to them.

York Castle, I was reminded by our guide, was built by William the Conqueror in 1068 and was later famous for being the prison that housed the notorious highwayman, Dick Turpin. As our party was led around the museum, I found the prisoners' cells very daunting and claustrophobic, but the recreated Victorian street with its old-style shops in the museum's heart was a delight. As the group wandered from shop to shop, it gave me the chance to mix and speak to them. Without Aunty amongst us, they had relaxed and chatted with me. They wanted to know what I was doing with 'that woman.' I didn't go into detail; I just told them that I was a hired companion, which they accepted.

After leaving the museum, I found Aunty Violet already sat on the coach, unwilling to tell me where she had been or what she had been up to, so; we sat in silence, all the way back to the hotel where we had tea in the lounge. After our refreshment, we went up to our rooms to prepare for dinner. But before that, after walking Aunty Violet back to her room, I did a little exploring of the hotel. After checking all the ground-floor rooms open to the public, I spotted a sign on a door that said, Staff Only. It was too good to resist. Stepping through it, I found another world. There were no signs of the plush hotel on this side of the door, just bare painted walls and unpolished floorboards. Creeping along the corridor, I heard low voices coming from a room where the door had been left ajar, tiptoeing on, the temptation to see more of this hidden part of the hotel exciting. Reaching the door, I tensed before looking through the crack between the door and the doorframe, I couldn't believe what I was seeing, the hotel manager and the headwaiter embracing and kissing. Taken aback by what I had seen, I gasped with shock. They must have heard me because they separated, both of them looking towards the door. Spinning around on my heel, I flew back to the public side of the hotel and dashed up to my room.

After dressing for dinner, I went to collect Aunty Violet but received no reply to my knock so I went down to the dining room alone. We had been given a private dining room away from the other hotel guests. A large oval table dominated the room, with dumbwaiters and smaller tables set around the walls. The furniture looked late Georgian in design, matching the age of the hotel. Long, heavy curtains hung at the windows and the room was lit by two crystal chandeliers. The only person not in the room by seven o'clock was Aunty Violet. I wondered if she had also changed her mind about coming down to dinner.

The highly polished, oval table was set with pink carnations, bowls of fruit and bottles of red wine. Each place setting had a vast array of silver cutlery and a variety of glasses. Ice buckets on silver stands were lined up along one wall. Whoever was paying for this weekend away had spared no expense. Whilst listening in on various conversations, I learned, everyone was speculating over who our host might be. I had my suspicions. The lady in the fox-fur and perfect make-up looked like the most likely candidate to have the disposable income to lay on such an event, being a Hollywood film star. But, there were one or two others, judging by their expensive-looking dinner jackets, who could also afford to pay for this weekend away.

Once we were seated and the wine was flowing, the conversation got into full swing. Aunty was still missing and I wondered if I should try to find her, but decided to wait a little longer. Everyone else seemed to be at ease with one another now. The only interruption came when one lady knocked over her glass of red wine. The liquid ran off the table and over her dress, making her jump up and flick at her dress with a napkin. Her husband, the Reverend Warlock, looked most displeased with her as he helped her mop up the wine with his napkin.

I had expected to be seated next to Aunty, but I was at the opposite end of the table to the empty chair which was at her place setting. I soon realised that from my vantage point, I could see all the other guests, but the only person who I wouldn't be able to see clearly, due to all the table decorations, would be Aunty Violet, that is if she turned up. I turned to the lady to my right who seemed to have been left out of the conversation her husband was having with the person sat to his right, so I spoke to her. She smiled politely and immediately began talking about her husband and how wonderful he was. Judy Punch had very little of interest to say that didn't involve her husband and his business. So I introduced Judy to the lady sat on my left, which let me bring her into the conversation. Learning that she was a music teacher, allowed me to talk about my experiences with Patsy, back in Driffield, and the music lessons she gives. It seems like all music teachers have to endure the same mixture of tone-deaf pupils and over-enthusiastic beginners who fall by the wayside when the lessons get harder.

Thanks to the repeated topping up of our glasses by the waiters, the conversation became lively and friendly, centred on the day's weather and the visit to the museum, until Aunty showed up and sat down. Everyone fell silent. The sour look on her face as she searched the faces of everyone at the dining table was powerful enough to make anyone think twice about speaking out of turn. I'd almost forgotten that she hadn't been there up to that point. Now that Aunty Violet was seated at the head of the table, the waiters served the soup. The only sound in the room was the chink of soup ladles against china, as they served the tomato soup. Just as we were about to eat, all the lights in the room went out. The ladies around the table gasped, a profanity came from one of the men, but in less than a minute the lights came back on again. A murmur of disapproval rippled around the table. The head waiter came over immediately and apologised, saying he would investigate what had happened to the lighting. As we continued with our soup in silence, some of the waiters left the dinning-room with the empty soup tureens. The tension around the table was palpable as everyone waited for Aunty to speak first, and that is precisely what she did. We had all just about finished the first course when she abruptly stood up and announced to all present in her irritatingly shrill voice.

'I know at least one of you here wants to kill me!'

A volley of protests and questions erupted, all aimed in Aunty Violet's direction. But all she did was sit down and say nothing more. She looked at everyone, in turn, staring at them for a few seconds as if daring them to confess and give in under the pressure from her overbearing will. But no one broke as we waited for the soup plates to be cleared away.

I sat silently looking at the other guests, wondering who would want to kill the old bag. Yes, that's right, I didn't like her either. She had made my life hell from a very early age. Each time she visited our house, she took pleasure in telling me; I was not clever enough, or smart enough, I was too fat, too thin. Why didn't I go out to play, why didn't I read a book? Nothing I had done was right in her eyes and as I got older her pointed remarks got worse. My job wasn't good enough, I didn't earn enough money; I didn't work hard enough, I should give more of what I earned to my mother. But am I ready to kill her? No, I don't think so, not yet anyway.

I had already formed an initial impression of each person around the table from our time together at the museum. Though they had been reluctant to talk about their own dealings with Aunty Violet, they were keen to dish the dirt on what they had learnt about Aunty from other people. I soon discovered that the prim and proper face that Aunty put on for the family was only a facade. She had a much darker past than I had imagined. So now, I had some idea of who these people were, and their connection to my Aunty. To my mind, each one of them had a good enough reason for bumping off the old dear. I looked around the table, making a mental note of where each person sat.

Reverend Christian Warlock could have been Vincent Price's twin brother with his swept-back, thinning hair and penetrating eyes. The only thing missing was the neatly trimmed moustache. I could visualise him standing in the pulpit, thumping out a sermon of doom on all would-be sinners during his Sunday services. He was sitting with his wife, Faith, to the right of Aunty Violet.

Sitting to the left of Reverend Warlock and his wife was Mr Ewan Ramsbottom and his wife, Corriedale. They are or were sheep farmers, but now raise cattle.

Sitting next to Mrs Ramsbottom was Miss Natalie West, a small timid looking woman who had come on her own. When I caught up with her in the museum she'd been reluctant to talk to me at first until that is, I told her I was a private detective, secretly investigating Violet Birch. She hadn't told me much about herself just yet, only that she is a waitress at a cafe close to the harbour in Bridlington, and that Violet Birch had ruined her life. She refused to go into detail about her encounter with Aunty Violet, so I let the matter drop, and went to find someone else to question.

Next in line around the table was Rocky Punch, an ex-boxer and his wife, Judy. Apart from once being a professional boxer, I knew little about him yet. I was sitting next to Rocky's wife at the dinner table, so I planned to question her later during the meal about her husband.

Miss Octavia Tone sat to my left, a music teacher by profession, a quiet, private looking woman, with sharp eyes, which I noted, darted from one person to the next, following the flow of conversation, but not joining in with the others. She'd a nervous habit of fiddling with the corner of her napkin, which she held in her lap, each time she looked at Aunty Violet. Was she wanting to join in the conversation, but couldn't pluck up the courage. She, of all the guests, displayed the most nervousness. Maybe it was because she was on her own? Though, when I spoke to her in the York Museum, she seemed quite relaxed, or was she nervous because she is expecting something to happen?

I tried starting a conversation with her, but she was reluctant to converse, apart from one brief conversation.

'Oh yes, I remember you from the museum. I'm sorry, I'm always unsure of what to do in mixed company. I rarely attend parties and the like, but as this was all paid for, I thought it was an opportunity to get away for a little while. But now, I'm not so sure. I can't understand why Miss Birch invited me here. She frightens me. The last time we met we were not exactly friendly towards each other.'

'I'm sorry to hear that. What happened?'

'It's not something I want to go into right now.'

After that short confession, she went back to fiddling with her napkin and watching Aunty Violet. That was interesting, to my knowledge, Aunty hadn't invited anyone here except me and Aunty's invitation had come from Elizabeth Milbank. I also wanted to know why Miss Tone had accepted the invitation if she was frightened of Aunty Violet.

Seated next to Miss Tone was Robin Steel and his wife, Heidi. Roofus Stone and his wife, Bonnie, were the next couple around the table. Then came Holly Starbrightly, the actress, she's the one in the fox-fur. She met her husband, a film producer, in America. I knew of her from articles in magazines and newspapers. According to the magazine I had read, she was touring the country promoting her latest film, so what was she doing here, and what was her connection with Aunty Violet?

Ada Betterman was seated next to Holly's film producer husband, and to the right of Aunty. Ada used to be a nurse. The only other person was me; family, as you already know, not that there are many of us left who get on with each other. Single-handedly, Aunty Violet has turned one member of our family against the other, until none of my Aunty's, uncle's or cousins will speak to each one another, and are unlikely to do so, for some time, as Aunty Violet continues to interfere in everyone's lives; muckraking whenever she goes visiting. I can't understand why anyone puts up with her unless they fear being excluded from her will. My parents think there is a fortune to dole out when the old dear finally pops her clogs.

However, as I said earlier, I may not have enough courage to bump off the old battleaxe, but I am capable of investigating to find out who she believes is going to kill her, which will not be easy when so many people find it easy to dislike her. I was still pondering the wisdom of coming at all when Aunty Violet got to her feet again and began pointing her finger at people, making wild accusations about how they all hated her and had she known they would be attending the art sale she wouldn't have come.

'Someone around this table has summoned us all here for a reason,' she announced. 'But, I can assure you all, that whoever this Elizabeth Milbank maybe, she is unknown to me. She is playing a very bad practical joke on us all and me especially. I know this because, apart from one other, I am the only one here who knows every person at this table. I can therefore only assume that it is me, who one of you wishes to take revenge upon. Those of you not involved in this plot, will I suggest, also take pleasure in it when the person I am speaking of makes their attempt on my life. But I will disappoint you all; I am not an easy victim to take revenge upon. I am ready for you. Therefore, I plan to expose the perpetrator of this fiasco and report them to the police.'

There followed a further outburst of questions and accusations from all those at the dinner table. Aunty Violet was in her element, she had everyone's attention. Standing at the head of the table, soup spoon in hand; waving it about as though it was her baton and she was conducting an orchestra. She banged the spoon on the table, prepared to speak again but then suddenly, her face contorted for a second as she clutched at her chest. Everyone watched as she slowly slumped forward across the table, her head thumping down against the table surface with a loud thud. She lay still, her eyes wide and unblinking, a look of disbelief frozen on her face. The room filled with silence; no one moved. I don't think anyone could believe what had just happened. At first, I thought Aunty was playing some sort of prank on us all, but she remained where she lay with tomato soup staining her clothes. Then, as though on cue, panic set in; screams, shouts, questions; everyone speaking at once. People stood and moved away from the table. The lights went out again, followed by screams and then a few seconds later the lights came back on.

At first, I didn't notice him, but with all the noise and the lights going off and coming back on again, a waiter had come to the table to apologise and reassure us that all was fine. That is until he saw Aunty Violet face down on the table. He spent a second or two looking at her body, then; he looked around the dining room at all the panicking guests, before fleeing. I hoped he was going to fetch the hotel manager.

As people fled the table, they gathered in small knots or made for the dining room door to escape only to be stopped by the headwaiter.

'I think it best everyone remains here. Someone has already gone to get the manager and he will call the police,' he insisted.

The Reverend Warlock and his wife, having been sat next to Aunty, were standing over her. He pulled her soup plate from beneath her body and placed it next to his plate before I could stop him.

I made my way to the head of the table to examine Aunty for signs of life; there were none. I'm afraid I have to admit to being a bit flustered. Solving the murder of a stranger is not the same as being in the same room as the victim when it has just happened and for the murder to have been committed on a relative. Taking a deep breath, I forced myself to focus on Aunty Violet. I didn't know what to do. I couldn't bear to see her lying there so I tried to pick her up off the table and put her back onto her chair, but she was too difficult to move until the Reverend Warlock gave me a hand. Aunty's body flopped back against her seat with her head hanging over the backrest, mouth open. She looked very undignified like that and I wished I'd left her on the table. The Reverend, having knocked Aunty's soup spoon onto the floor, bent down to pick it up.

Was it a heart attack or maybe it was a stroke brought on by old age? I tried to put a more reasonable explanation to Aunty's demise, anything other than murder.

Faith Warlock fussed about her husband, helping him clean spilt red soup stains from his hands and trousers, which had splattered from his plate when he quickly jerked back to avoid Aunty as she fell onto the table. My attention was drawn away from Aunty Violet's body by the arrival of the hotel manager. He shut and locked the dining room doors behind him and announced to everyone that the police had been summoned and that we were all to wait here until they arrived and could take charge. The first person to protest about the locked door was Hector Boysack, the film producer from America who was accompanying Holly Starbrightly. She was on her first radio and televised publicity tour of Britain. Mr Boysack insisted that he had seen nothing and had nothing to do with the death of the woman. He insisted that Holly's name had to be kept out of the newspapers, as publicity connecting her to a murder in England would not do her career any good back in the states. The hotel manager stood his ground, promising nothing.

Rocky Punch was the next to try to escape the dining room. He barged between the diners, lambasting the hotel manager and pushing him up against the door, demanding the key or he would rearrange the manager's features. It was only thanks to the intervention of Judy, his wife, that the altercation didn't take place. She whispered something in his ear and took hold of the hand which was grasping the hotel manager's jacket, making him release his grip, then she led him away to a corner of the room where she spoke to him out of earshot of everyone else. The hotel manager straightened his clothing and continued to fend off questions from the frightened diners.

Finding myself left with the body of Aunty Violet, I looked at her with fresh eyes. Gone was the robust, malicious woman with a voice like fingernails scratching across a blackboard. All I was left with was a short, slightly overweight, white-haired corpse with a face that had softened for the first time that I could remember. I looked back towards the door. One of those protesters clambering to be let out was the murderer, and I was determined to find out which one it was.

Chapter Four

The sound of the dining room doors unlocking announced the arrival of the police. A plain-clothed detective strode through the open doorway with two uniformed constables at his back. It was like a scene from an old black and white B movie the kids watch at the cinema on a Saturday morning. All that was missing was the dramatic music and the close-up on the detective's face. Everyone in the dining room immediately took a step backwards as the tall man in the gabardine raincoat entered and waited for the murmuring to fall silent. His cold steely eyes searched the faces of all present before he spoke.

'Everyone, please retake your seats around the dinner table; just as you were before Miss Birch passed away.'

None of us moved until the uniformed police officers came forward intimidatingly, ushering everyone back towards the dining table. In one's and two's at first, everyone returned to their places, but only a few sat down. The Inspector took out a notepad and scribbled on it for a few moments.

Hector Boysack jumped to his feet.

'Look here, Inspector, I had nothing to do with the death of that old broad. She probably died of a heart attack. You can't hold me against my will, I'm an American citizen. I know my rights.' A constable placed a firm hand on his shoulder, suggesting he retook his seat, but he refused to do so.

'You must be Mister Boysack. Sir, please remember - this is not New York or Chicago or even the Wild West. You are in Harrogate. This is my town and there has been a sudden and unexplained death, so you will sit quietly until I have finished my initial investigation or I will take you down to the station and you will spend the rest of the night in a cell,' said the Inspector firmly but politely.

Boysack sat down only to be comforted by his young wife. I couldn't hear what she was saying to him, but she didn't look pleased.

The Inspector confirmed the name of everyone else around the table and their seating position relative to the deceased, making notes in his book as he did so.

'What was the nature of this celebration?' the Inspector asked no one in particular. There was a moment's silence before I took the lead.

'We all received an invitation to come here; to buy paintings direct from the artist. Except me, Inspector, I didn't, I came as Miss Birch's companion. She is my Aunty. She had concerns about why she had been invited on this weekend holiday, so she asked me to accompany her here.' My confession sparked another round of murmurings.

'If she was suspicious about the motives behind the invitation, why did she come?' asked the Inspector.

'My Aunty was a forthright and determined lady, she wouldn't allow anything to intimidate her, and besides, she was an avid collector of this artist's work.'

'If you were her companion, why were you seated at the far end of the table to Miss Birch?'

'I don't know Inspector, but as you can see, each place around the table has a name card. It predetermined where we were to sit.'

'Yes, I had noticed, but I suspect you didn't all arrive in the dining room together, which means anyone one of you could have rearranged the seating positions.' That insinuation raised a volley of protest from the rest of the group. The Inspector smiled, 'Now, now I am not inferring anything. At the moment, this is just the unexplained death of an elderly lady. Unless anyone knows something, I don't?'

The room fell deathly silent.

'I thought not,' the Inspector continued. A disturbance at the door heralded the arrival of the pathologist. A bespectacled thin man in his late forties, wearing a tweed suit entered the room. He ignored the Inspector and made his way to Aunty's body. He gave her a brief examination before signalling for the photographer to come forward and his two assistants to enter with a stretcher.

'You will have a preliminary report on your desk in the morning, Inspector. It is too early for me to give a verdict on how the deceased passed away, but there are no obvious signs of violence. I'll get back to my own dinner now, if I may?'

'Yes, Doctor, thank you for your time.'

As the pathologist left the dining room, the photographer began his work. He first took photographs of Aunty Violet's body as I had left it on the chair, then of the table, followed by the dining room. As soon as he'd finished with Aunty, the pathologist's assistants placed her body on the stretcher and took her away.

'Very well, Ladies and Gentlemen, once my officers have made a note of your names and addresses, you will be free to go. But, I may wish to speak to you again after I have read the pathologists report, so please, if you have any plans for leaving the country,' he looked directly at Hector Boysack, 'do not or I may jump to the conclusion that you have something to hide and be forced to have your local police arrest you.' While the police constables took down names and addresses, the hotel manager led the Police Inspector to one side.

'May I offer you a drink at the bar, Inspector; on the house, of course? Will your men be very long, only the other hotel guests are getting a little anxious at the police being on the premises? As yet, they have no idea what has happened here, and I'd like to keep it that way. If the other hotel guests see you in a more casual setting, it will ease their minds considerably.'

'I'm sorry, Sir, I cannot. Once my men have finished taking statements, I must return to the station. I am the only senior officer on duty tonight.' The Inspector glanced towards his sergeant. 'If you will excuse me, my men seem to be about finished.'

It was at this point that I took the opportunity to monopolise the Inspector's time.

‘Oh Inspector, may I have a word,’ I put on my best smile.

‘Yes, Miss, how may I assist you?’

‘Inspector, the lady who died this evening is my Aunty. I...’

‘So you have already said Miss. I’m very sorry for your loss; you have my condolences. You will be the next of kin, I take it?’ interjected the police officer politely.

‘Thank you, Inspector, and yes, I suppose I am, but that is not why I wanted to speak to you. Aunty Violet wanted me to come with her on this trip because she feared for her life. You need to know, I have learnt that each one of these people was known to my Aunty, and each one of them held a grudge against her. I believe she was murdered by someone in this room.’

‘In that case, you, Miss Showers, are just as much a suspect as any of the other guests that were sitting around this dinner table. More so maybe, as you may inherit from the lady’s estate. Do you have proof that she hired you to work for her?’

‘No, Inspector, she was my Aunty. She came to my office to ask for help. At first, I didn’t really take her seriously about an attempt on her life. I thought she was just being melodramatic. I thought she just wanted to take me on a holiday to make up for disagreements we’d had in the past.’

‘Disagreements, Miss, what kind of disagreements?’

I had dismissed the Inspector’s earlier remark about me being a suspect, but now, I realised, I had to take the Inspector’s remark more seriously. If I did stand to inherit from Aunty’s will, it would make me a suspect just like everyone else in the room. A shiver ran down my spine, *did I stand to gain anything from Aunty's death?* The thought had never crossed my mind until the Inspector brought it up.

'Miss Showers?'

'What? Oh, er, nothing much; just the usual family disagreements. She could be a bit direct at times. You know how elderly aunts can be, that's all. Nothing to want to kill her over, I assure you.'

The Inspector hit me with another question. 'What line of business is your employer involved in?'

'My employer? I don't have an employer, as such. Aunty Violet was my client. I suppose, you could say, Inspector, that she was my employer. You see, I'm a Private Investigator. As I said previously, Aunty suspected that she was in danger, which is the reason why she asked me to accompany her on this weekend trip.'

'In danger, from whom; did she say?'

'No, Inspector, but I intend to find out. All I have learnt so far is that she knew everyone around the table.'

'No, Miss, you will not. This is a police matter and you, until proven otherwise, are a suspect. So, you will leave the investigating to the professionals.'

'I am a professional, Inspector. Investigating is what I do. Ask the police in Driffield. Last year, I solved a murder which had had them baffled for weeks.'

'I don't doubt you may have had a lucky break in Driffield, Miss, but Harrogate is a much larger town. Leave the investigation to me. Is that clear? Now, Miss Showers, if there is nothing more?'

'No, Inspector, that is not all. When will I be allowed to take Aunty home? I will have to inform my family that she has died. They will want me to arrange for her to be taken back to Driffield as soon as possible.'

'Yes, I see. You may contact me at the station tomorrow. Ask for Inspector Allswell. After I have read the pathologist's report giving the cause of death and if it informs me that there are no signs of foul play, your Aunty's body will be released to you.'

'And if, as I suggest, she has been a murdered. What will happen to her?'

'In that case, we will keep Miss Birch's body for further examination. Now, Miss Showers, I must get back to the station. I will expect to hear from you tomorrow afternoon when I will be back on duty.'

'Until tomorrow then, Inspector.'

As soon as the police had finished and left the dining room, everyone started talking at once. Most were speculating and hypothesising over Aunty's death, some about a ruined weekend, but I never heard a word of sympathy over Aunty's demise. I wanted to start asking questions, but the other guests had begun to disperse. I needed some space, some peace and quiet, some time to think, somewhere private from where I could telephone my parents and give them the sad news about Aunty. I left the dining room to make my way back to my room.

The upper floors of the hotel seemed deathly silent compared to the clamour that had gone on in the dining room. The closer I got to my room, the more overcome with grief I became. Tears wanted to flow but I wouldn't let them, so I paused for a moment in the corridor to retrieve my handkerchief and room key from my handbag. It was then that I heard raised voices from behind a bedroom door. I looked to where the sound was coming from. It was room 222.

A male voice exclaimed, 'You did what?' It was followed by a distraught female voice.

'I had to. She deserved it!'

Shocked by the exclamation, I got closer to the door to listen to what was being said, but all I could hear was a woman sobbing. I wanted to knock on the door and ask if everything was alright, but had second thoughts. I was in no state to ask probing questions and deal with a domestic confrontation, so I continued to my room. I was about to phone my parents to tell them what happened and that I would be home tomorrow, but then stopped. My parents would insist on coming to collect me. I needed to manage this myself; I had to prove to them that I was no longer the child they once knew and that I was old enough and responsible enough to deal with what was happening.

Whilst removing my make-up in the bathroom and staring in the mirror, I stopped and took stock of the situation.

Come on, girl, you didn't like the old bag and you certainly didn't kill her. It may well have been a heart attack that finished her off, but if it wasn't, you are going to find out what did, and who was responsible. Despite what the Inspector had said to me about leaving the investigation to him, I wasn't going to. I was going to investigate Aunty's murder myself.

I washed my face, combed my hair and redressed in my day clothes. Returning to the private dining room, I found the other dinner guests had all left. The only other person present was a waiter clearing the table.

'Excuse me, Miss, the manager said I should clear everything away. I'm very sorry. Things like this don't usually happen at private dinner parties.'

'No, I don't suppose they do,' I replied. I continued to walk around the room whilst watching the waiter as he collected the silver cutlery from the table. He placed the item carefully on his tray, separating the cutlery into its different sizes of knife, fork and spoon before moving on to the next place setting.

'Are you normally this diligent when gathering up cutlery?' I asked him.

'Only when it's our best silver, Miss. The manager likes it all accounted for or he blames the staff for stealing it. Though all the waiters believe it is the guests who take most of it as a souvenir of their stay in the hotel. It's solid silver, you see, for special occasions like. Even though it hasn't been used, it all has to be washed and polished before I put it away.'

'Oh yes, I see,' now only half-listening.

'Funny thing is, though, Miss. There is an odd one, not from the same set as these others.'

My head snapped around to stare at the waiter. 'What do you mean? May I see it?'

'Sorry, Miss, It's already gone with the dirty soup plates and used cutlery to be washed.'

'Show me quickly,' I demanded. He hesitated.

'It was my Aunty Violet who died during dinner, and despite the police being involved, I'm conducting my own investigation into what has happened here this evening.' He continued to dither until I produced one of my business cards advertising my services as, April Showers, Private Investigator. It tipped the balance in my favour.

'Come this way, Miss.' He led me through to the pot washing room next to the kitchen.

'Hey, Jack, you washed the cutlery and plates from that private party yet?' A sweaty little man in a dirty, damp apron removed pink arms from a large sink filled with steaming water. He pushed his greasy hair back out of his eyes to look up at who was speaking to him.

'Why, what's up?' His unusually high-pitched voice took me by surprise.

'This lady is a private investigator, and it was her Aunty who died tonight. She wants to see the soup spoons.'

'What for?'

'Never mind that, where are the spoons?'

'I've already done them. They're over there, on that tray, ready for polishing. An old one's come back as well.' He crossed to the tray and held up a spoon. 'This one differs from the others; it's from an old set. The manager replaced the old set because too many of them had gone missing. There were only enough complete place settings left for seating six people. I suppose one of the staff must have had a guilty conscience and brought the soup spoon back.'

Taking the proffered spoon, I compared the odd spoon to the others. It was similar, but the shape of the handle was slightly longer and wider at the hand end. The hallmark on the reverse was different too.

‘I think the police may be interested in this,’ I told the kitchen assistant.

‘What, just because a member of staff has brought back a spoon, Miss?’ said Jack.

‘Yes; exactly. The question is, Jack, who brought the spoon back and, why now? May I take this and show it to the police?’

‘Oh, no, Miss,’ said Jack and the waiter in unison.

‘You’ll have to ask the hotel manager, first. He’d get really upset with us if we just let you take it,’ said the waiter. Jack nodded in agreement with his friend and then flicked his greasy hair from his eyes again.

‘Well then, I’ll just have to speak to him.’ I turned on my heel and left the two men to get on with their work.

‘Excuse me; may I speak to the manager, please?’ I asked the receptionist.

‘Is there something I can help you with, Miss?’ Replied the receptionist, looking a little worried.

‘No, thank you. I need to speak to the manager.’

‘If you have a complaint or require assistance, I can assure you, Miss, I can resolve the matter for you.’

‘My name is Miss Showers, Miss Birch, the lady who died this evening was my Aunty and I want to speak to the manager, now!’ Taken aback by my directness and that other hotel guests had overheard me; the receptionist dropped his pencil and lowering his voice said.

‘I will find him right away for you, Miss. Please, excuse me for a moment.’

He turned to a door stencilled with Hotel Manager in gold and knocked three times before entering. Moments later the door opened again and a tall, elegant-looking man in tailcoat and pinstriped trousers emerged.

'Miss Showers, won't you please come through to my office?' The receptionist lifted the hatch in the reception counter to allow me to pass through. I thanked him and followed the hotel manager to his office.

'Right this way, Miss Showers. Please accept my condolences; is there anything I can do for you?' The manager closed the office door and offered me a seat at his desk.

'May I offer you a sherry? I'm sorry, I didn't realise there was a family connection between you both, Miss Showers, or I would have come to see you sooner. I was under the impression that you were just a paid companion of Miss Birch.'

'That is what I wanted people to think. Thank you, no sherry. Mr?'

'Bunkhouse. Henry Bunkhouse,' said the manager. 'How can I be of assistance?'

'I believe my Aunty was murdered by someone in this hotel. She asked me to accompany her here because she was suspicious about the invitation. She didn't recognise the sender's name on the letter.'

'Miss Showers, you cannot go around claiming that a person from this hotel murdered your Aunty. You have no proof. If you make a false claim against the hotel or a member of its staff, we will be forced to sue you for defamation of character.'

‘I didn’t say it was a member of staff or the hotel’s fault. I believe it was one of the dinner guests. My Aunty was lured here by an invitation to an art sale by a famous Newlyn artist.’

‘Ah, the art sale, yes, but what has that to do with her death? It’s just a few local artists who have booked the conference room to show off their work. Nothing worthy of bringing a well-known artist up from Newlyn, I wouldn’t have thought.’

‘That’s strange. My Aunty was under the impression that there would be work for sale by the artist Gertrude Harvey.’

‘No, I’m sorry. No one of that name,’ insisted the manager. ‘What gave Miss Birch the impression there would be works by Gertrude Harvey for sale?’

‘It was stated on her invitation.’

‘Then, you should take it up with whoever sent Miss Birch the invitation.’

I withdrew the letter from my handbag and looked at the signature.

‘It is signed by someone who calls herself, Elizabeth Milbank. I can only assume it is someone who knew Aunty, only she didn’t remember the name. I assume it was Elizabeth Milbank who made the hotel reservation for us all?’

‘I don’t recall, but their name and address will be on the billing letter. I will check the files in the head receptionist’s office. Will you excuse me a moment?’ The manager left the room, returning a few minutes later.

‘That’s very strange. I’m sorry, Miss Showers, but I cannot find a letter in our files from Elizabeth Milbank confirming the booking for all the guests in your party, yet in the register, each room is marked as prepaid. I will have to run an audit to determine who and when the bookings were made and who paid for them.'

I made a mental note to investigate the name, Elizabeth Milbank, at a later date.

'Well, there is one thing you should be able to help me with. I was speaking to one of your waiters as he cleared away our table in the dining room. He noticed that there was a spoon that didn't match the rest of the cutlery set being used this evening, which he thought unusual. He told me you have to replace the cutlery every few years because people keep taking pieces of it as a souvenir of their stay. So, I asked myself why would someone return a soup spoon, why last night and what has it to do with the death of my Aunty. The return of the soup spoon on its own, I can put down to a guilty conscience, but for all three things to happen at the same time and in the same room makes me think that there could be a connection. Maybe, Aunty's spoon had been poisoned and when the lights went out someone swapped the poisoned soup spoon Aunty had used for one that they had brought with them, taken during a previous stay at your hotel, in the hope the switch wouldn't be noticed.'

'Very interesting, Miss Showers, I don't doubt what you are saying, but I can give you a more plausible answer to your riddle. A member of staff borrowed the old spoon for a while and has used the opportunity of last night's dinner to cover up the return of the piece of cutlery. The hotel staff do take hotel property up to their rooms from time to time, though as a rule, it is forbidden. However, it is generally overlooked, so long as it does not get out of hand. But what do you want me to do about it, it happens in every hotel? It is more likely that one of tonight's guests had taken the missing spoon as a souvenir, but without searching everyone in the hotel we will never know.'

'I would like to borrow the odd spoon so I can show it to the police. They may think as I do that it is too much of a coincidence, turning up at the same time as a suspicious death. It may be evidence and provide a link to the murderer.'

'Just a minute, Miss Showers, you can't go around saying things like that. I have the reputation of the hotel to think about. When I was speaking to the police Inspector earlier, he informed me that the death looked like a heart attack. What makes you think it was murder?'

'Aunty Violet hired me in my capacity as a private investigator, and a relative she could trust to accompany her on this trip because she feared for her life. Her fears have proved to be well-founded. She died in your hotel after being summoned here. I don't believe the spoon to be a coincidence. I will get to the bottom of this mystery, Mister Bunkhouse, for my Aunty's sake. There is history between my Aunty and the other guests staying in this hotel, unpleasant history, and I suspect one of them lured her here to kill her for a reason.'

'Your story seems a little farfetched to me, Miss Showers, but for the sake of a missing spoon, I will fetch it for you, myself. I cannot have the reputation of the hotel sullied with accusations of murder. Please remain seated, I won't be long.'

Whilst the hotel manager was out of his office, I took the opportunity to have a look around. There were a few filing cabinets, a set of bookshelves with a collection of Agatha Christy's first editions. *Yes, I suppose every hotel in Harrogate would have a set of these*. The hotel manager returned whilst I was still perusing the mystery novels.

'Sorry to keep you waiting. I'm afraid, Miss Showers, the spoon has gone missing again. When I asked the staff where they had put it, they went to look for it, but it had gone. I have left instructions for all the waiters to search for it and then bring it to me when it is found. I suggest we wait and see what tomorrow turns up. The police may give a perfectly innocent explanation for Miss Birch's death.' The hotel manager moved to the door and opened it.

As I rose to leave I asked one last question. 'Do you still think the spoon going missing is just a coincidence, Mr Bunkhouse?'

'Please, Miss Showers, have a nightcap on the house and try to get a good night's sleep. Perkins here will have whatever you desire brought up to your room.'

He was dismissing me as though I was a schoolgirl with an overactive imagination. I was furious. Marching from the manager's office I went straight up to my room. I was going to make sure Inspector Allswell knew about the missing spoon when I met with him the following afternoon.

In my room, I dropped my handbag on the chair and flopped onto the bed. I was exhausted and frustrated with the world and men. First, the police inspector and then the hotel manager; both of them had dismissed my opinions on

Aunty's death as an overactive imagination. The trouble was I had no means of proving she had been murdered as yet unless the autopsy report could show it. There was a room full of suspects, all of them according to Aunty, with a motive to want to kill her, but as yet, I had no idea of whom the killer may be. I could feel a headache coming on, so I took two aspirin tablets and went to bed, sure that a good night's sleep would help me think more clearly in the morning.

Sunday (only just).

I don't know what time it was, but I woke up when I heard a noise. Not a loud noise that makes you sit up instantly, wondering what is what it was, but that little noise that wakes you in the night and leaves you wondering if you heard anything at all or if it's just your overactive imagination playing tricks on you. I opened my eyes with my head still on the pillow and listened. Hearing nothing, I put the disturbance down to other guests in the hotel. However, the hairs on the back of my neck still tingled, keeping my senses alert. As I rolled over in bed to get a bit comfier, out from the shadows someone lunged at the bed, landing in the spot where I had just been laying. There was a tearing sound as I continued to roll over, falling out of bed as I did so. I screamed. The figure leapt from the bed; opened the door to my room and was gone. All I saw was a black silhouette framed in the light from the open door. I screamed again. As I sat on the floor disturbed hotel guests gathered in the open doorway to my room to stare at me. An older woman pushed through the gathering onlookers into my room and came to my bedside, helping me from the floor. She put her arm around my shoulder and introduced herself as Mrs Downy then, she asked what had happened. At first, I found it difficult to gather my thoughts. Trembling with fear, I found it hard to speak coherently, but finally, I managed to tell her that someone had come into my room and attacked me. A person standing near the door switched my room light on, and moments later the hotel's night porter arrived. He ushered the bystanders away, but Mrs Downy; I leant her name a little later, stayed to comfort me.

'What is going on here?' asked the night porter indignantly.

'This young lady has had an intruder in her room,' answered Mrs Downy.

'What do you mean; someone broke in?' The night porter looked a little more concerned.

'Yes; fetch the hotel manager and call the police, demanded Mrs Downy. This poor girl has been attacked.'

I was still shaking but re-gathering my composure now that someone was with me. The night porter had remained at my door, clearly perplexed by the demands placed upon him. I repeated Mrs Downy's instruction.

'Go fetch the hotel manager. This lady will sit with me until he arrives.' The second prompt for him to act changed the expression on the night porter's face. The idea of leaving this problem to someone else to sort out proving a good enough incentive to do as ordered.

Mrs Downy fetched my dressing gown from the chair by my bedside and draped it around my shoulders.

'Are you feeling a little better now?' she asked. 'What happened?'

'Yes, thank you. You are very kind. I'm sorry to have caused you all this bother.'

'Nonsense, do you know who it was that broke into your room?' She asked sympathetically.

'No, I heard a noise and then someone pounced onto my bed. When I screamed, they fled. Did you see anyone in the corridor as you arrived?'

'No, I'm sorry, my dear. By the time I arrived there was no one to be seen except other guests coming to find out what all the fuss was about. I expect you could do with a cup of tea right now, I know I could?'

'Yes. I don't think I'll be going back to sleep tonight.'

'Me neither, I'll get the porter to bring us up a pot of tea when he returns with the manager. Get dressed before he arrives. You don't want him to see you in your nightclothes.'

I smiled, 'Yes, of course.' So, as I slipped off of the bed to find my clothes, Mrs Downy closed my bedroom door.

'What is that doing there?' she pointed to the floor. My bedroom door key, which I'd left in the lock when I went to bed, was no longer in its place. She picked it up from the carpet and placed it on the nightstand. 'It must have dropped out when the door was opened,' she suggested.

I had no sooner finished dressing when Mr Bunkhouse and the porter returned, announcing their arrival with a knock on the door. I told him my story about the intruder, to which he looked somewhat sceptical until I pointed at the bed; there in the pillow, on which only a few minutes earlier, I had been laying was a large rent in the fabric, the torn material releasing small, white feathers onto the bedclothes.

'I insist you call the police. This proves beyond doubt that someone murdered my Aunty and is now coming after me.'

'Yes, yes, I am very sorry Miss Showers.' The manager turned to the night porter, 'Scops, call the police, tell them Miss Showers has been attacked!'

'And, when you come back, bring tea for two up to my room. I don't think this young lady will want to stay on her own in this room for the rest of the night,' interjected Mrs Downy. Mister Bunkhouse nodded his consent to the night porter.

'Yes, I agree with Mrs Downy. You go to her room and I will lock this room until the police arrive, I suspect they will want to examine it after what has happened,' said the Manager.

'Come along, my dear. You can tell me why someone would want to attack you in the middle of the night,' said Mrs Downy.

I looked at the old lady, somewhat taken aback by her assumption that I might know who my attacker was, and that I would be willing to tell her if I knew. However, on the other hand, I didn't feel like being on my own until the police arrived, so I accepted the offer of her company. Once settled on a chair in Mrs Downy's room, the shakes started again. The realisation that I had come so close to being killed had frightened me to my core. I was partway through giving Mrs Downy a run-through of the previous day's events when there was a knock on the door. The sound went through me like an electric shock, making me jump up.

‘Who is it?’ called out Mrs Downy.

‘Scops, the night porter, Miss; I’ve brought you some tea and brandy.’

Mrs Downy opened the door and the elderly night porter entered and placed a tray on the chest of drawers.

‘Compliments of the management, ladies,’ the night porter didn’t loiter, and we were soon on our own again.

‘Tea or brandy first?’ asked Mrs Downy.

‘Tea, please.’ We drank the first cup in silence then, as Mrs Downy poured the second cup, adding a dash of brandy. She asked me to continue recalling what had led up to my attack.

‘Shocking, quite shocking,’ she said when I had finished. ‘I’m sorry to say, I have to agree with you, your Aunty Violet sounds like a terrible woman, but she didn’t deserve to be murdered and neither do you.’

I found the old lady’s words reassuring. Feeling greatly relieved when she believed my account of what had happened. I guess it should have been obvious to anyone, but I was so befuddled by the attack, it felt unreal, like a nightmare.

‘I think I’m ready for that brandy now,’ I told her.

We each took our glass of brandy and sipped at it, but mine seemed to disappear quicker than expected. It was only when I awoke with a start at the sound of knocking on the door that I realised I had fallen asleep in the chair. Mrs Downy opened the door to reveal Inspector Allswell and the hotel manager.

‘Good evening, Ladies, or should I say good morning; may I come in?’ As the Inspector entered the room, the hotel manager attempted to follow him in.

‘That will be all Mister Bunkhouse; I will send for you if you are needed.’ The hotel manager looked disappointed at the rebuff but stepped back as the bedroom door was closed in his face. I rubbed the sleep from my eyes and repositioned myself in the chair, ready for a barrage of questions from the Inspector.

‘You, I take it, are Mrs Downy, the guest staying in this room. I was told that you were the first person to enter Miss Showers’ room after she was attacked?’

‘Yes, Inspector.’

‘Did you see the assailant who attacked you, Miss Showers?’

‘No Inspector, Just a shape in the doorway as they ran off.’

‘Was it a male or female shape?’

‘I don’t know; everything happened so fast, and I was lying on the floor at the time.’

‘I arrived just before the other guests, who had been disturbed by April’s screams,’ said Mrs Downy. ‘Her bedroom door was wide open, and Miss Showers was sitting on the floor looking terrified. So I went in to find out what had frightened her.’

‘Is that correct, Miss Showers?’

‘Yes, Inspector, as far as I can recall, that is what happened. I’m still trying to piece everything together and be sure I haven’t missed anything out.’

‘In that case, I think it better that we conduct the rest of the interview down at the station whilst our scene of crime investigation people examine your room for evidence,’

‘Do you need me as well, Inspector?’ asked Mrs Downy, somewhat hopefully.

‘No, thank you. As you didn’t see anything, I will contact you should I have any further question for you to answer. I have your home address from the hotel receptionist. Now, Miss Showers, would you like to come with me, please?’

Chapter Five

I took the seat offered to me in front of Inspector Allswell's desk. Before he took up his seat, he asked a constable for two teas to be brought in. His office was on the first floor of a three-story building set within its own extensive grounds, with a garden and double drive out front. His office was small, with only a single window overlooking the car park at the rear of the building. The early morning light was just breaking over the rooftops as I looked out of the window and accepted the seat the Inspector offered me. His desk was old and well worn, unlike the more modern ones in the main office outside. On one side of the Inspector's desk was a stack of paper files, on the other side an empty tray. A small wooden cased clock, a few pens and pencils in an old cup with no handle and a notepad were the only other items on his desk. His filing cabinets lined one wall, on top of which stood some amateur football trophies. A framed photograph hung on the wall depicting a married couple on their wedding day, in which the groom resembled a much younger Inspector Allswell.

'Well, Miss Showers, it appears you have had a very eventful night.' He pulled a paper file and a notepad from the top drawer of his desk and opened it.

'Yes, Inspector, one I would rather have avoided if I could.'

'No doubt.' He was just about to continue when there was a knock on the door. As I looked round to see who had interrupted us, a rather nice-looking young man entered carrying two mugs of tea. He set one down in front of the Inspector and the other in front of me; giving me a beaming smile as he did so.

'Thank you, Constable Beatty; that will be all.'

'I'm sorry Inspector, but I have a message from the desk sergeant. He asks if you could spare him a moment. There seems to be an issue with one of the prisoners in cells,' said Constable Beatty.

'Please excuse me, Miss Showers, I'm sure this will only take a moment.'

As soon as the Inspector closed the door behind him, I opened the file he'd got out of his drawer and made a note of all the names and addresses of the people at the dinner table. I'd only just finished and returned the file to the Inspectors side of the desk when he returned.

'Right, Miss Showers, I want you to take me through everything that has happened from when your Aunty Violet asked you to help her, to you being attacked in your room. You can take your time.' The Inspector's pen hovered over a blank piece of paper.

'Has the report on how my Aunty died arrived?' His eyes shot to the empty tray by his side.

'No, but I'm expecting a preliminary autopsy report later this morning. The pathologist will have to send blood samples to York City Hospital to be analysed and it will take time to get those results back. Without his full report, there is no evidence to suggest your Aunty's death was anything more than by natural causes. The attack on you may just have been a burglary gone wrong and not connected to your Aunty's death at all. However, I have to admit, I would be surprised if her death and the attack on you were not linked. Though as a senior police officer, I am not allowed to jump to conclusions. Until I get evidence to the contrary, there is no proof that your Aunty was murdered. For now, I only have your allegations of murder.'

Before I responded, I took a sip of my tea and cringed. It was very strong, with far too much sugar, so I left it on the Inspector's desk.

'I understand, Inspector. After all, I am a Private Investigator. I do know that it is evidence and not hearsay which makes a case and leads to a conviction.'

'Then you also understand that you must leave the investigation of what has happened to the police and not try to solve the case yourself?'

'So, Inspector, you admit that there is a case to solve?'

'A mere turn of phrase, Miss Showers; don't get carried away. Until I get reports from the pathologist and the scene of crime bods, I have only your word to work on. Now, please, take me through everything that has happened.'

It was over an hour later when I walked through the gates outside the police station. The taste of that horrid, strong, sweet tea was still present in my mouth. But added to that, I was also very hungry. I'd been up for hours, on top of which, I'd missed out on dinner last night. The Inspector had offered to have me driven back to the hotel, but I said I would rather walk and get some fresh air.

As I walked up North Park Road towards Albert Street, I was heading towards West Park, the better part of town, looking for somewhere to have breakfast and a proper cup of tea. My head was aching from lack of sleep and too many questions. I needed some sleep. The sound of a steam whistle told me I was close to the railway station. There had to be an early morning cafe there.

The smell of frying bacon wafted out onto the early morning street, tormenting people as they passed by. At the sweet and tobacconist's shop next door, I spotted a hoarding outside with the headline from the morning newspaper emblazoned across it.

'Death in Harrogate.' 'Hollywood film star spotted in victim's hotel.'

Below the headline was a photograph of the hotel and another of Holly Starbrightly. Aunty Violet's death seemed to be less important than the film star's stay at the same hotel. I turned my back on the newsagents and went inside the cafe, taking a seat and with just a cursory glance at the menu, ordered a fried breakfast, without the black pudding, toast and a pot of tea. As I waited for it to arrive, I felt my emotions building. I couldn't stop it, now, of all places, I wanted to cry. The feeling welled up in me like a bottle of fizzy lemonade about to pop its stopper. I snatched a handkerchief from my coat pocket and covered my face, sobbing into it. Moments later, I felt a hand on my shoulder.

'Are you all right, Miss?' I blew my nose and wiped the tears away to look up at the waitress.

'Yes, thank you. I've just had to say farewell to someone.'

'Oh, I understand, Miss, it happens all the time in here, loved one's departing; leaving sweethearts behind. Don't worry, I'm sure he'll be back again soon. I've brought your tea. A good cup of tea will make you feel better.' I watched her as she walked away. I didn't know whether to laugh or continue crying. In the end, I made do with blowing my nose again and pouring the tea before it stewed.

The waitress was right though, by the time I had finished my first cup of tea I had perked up a bit and then my breakfast arrived. I attacked the plate like a ravenous animal. If my mother had been watching me eat my breakfast, she would have been horrified at the un-ladylike way I tucked into the food. I finished the last slice of toast with a second cup of tea at a more sedate pace. Re-energised, I took a deep breath and felt calmer now, I was ready to go back to the hotel.

Back in my room, I packed my bags and then went to Aunty's room to collect her possessions. It was whilst going through one of her bags that I found a wad of letters. Pulling one free at random, I read the contents. The writer had written a list of hateful things they wished would happen to Aunty. I retrieved another one; it too swore that revenge would one day be taken upon her. I pulled out a third; the handwriting on all three was the same. Sitting on the bed, I read them all. The postmark and date on the envelopes showed they had been posted in various parts of the country and that they had all been posted some months apart. My eyes were drooping, so I took the opportunity to grab some sleep on Aunty Violet's bed. The chambermaid letting herself into the room woke me and I looked at my watch. At least I'd had a couple of hours of sleep.

Before leaving, I telephoned the police station and left a message for Inspector Allswell, telling him I was going home and that he could contact me there or at my office when he had the results of the post-mortem. I didn't mention the hate letters I'd found. I knew if I told the Inspector about them, he would take them from me as evidence and I would never see them again. I was going to follow up on those. When I returned mine and Aunty's room keys to the hotel reception, the hotel manager was waiting for me.

'Miss Showers, please accept my apologies for everything that has happened.'

'Thank you, Mr Bunkhouse.' He carried Aunty Violet's and my bags out to the car and loaded them into the boot for me.

'Next time you come to Harrogate, come and stay as my guest, please, as a way of allowing me, in some small way, to make up for what has happened.'

I smiled politely and thanked him for his consideration, but did not answer his request.

Alone in the car, as I drove out of Harrogate, I was glad to be leaving it behind, though I wasn't looking forward to explaining every detail of the weekend to my parents when I got home. But, I wasn't going to tell my mother about being attacked in my bed; she'd never let me leave the house on my own, again. It took me two hours to drive home with only one stop for petrol along the way. More tired than I'd ever been in my life, I pulled onto the drive at home just after lunchtime. As I stopped, the front door opened and both my parents came out of the house to meet me. Mother came rushing over and put her arms around me, holding me close, and firing a stream of questions at me.

'I've had the Harrogate police on the telephone asking for you. Whatever has happened? Where is your Aunty Violet? Has there been an accident? Are you alright?'

Father went straight to the car boot and retrieved mine and Aunty's luggage then followed Mummy and me inside the house. Facing my parents as they sat on the settee I broke the news of Aunty Violet's death. Father looked visibly shocked by my tale, but my mother stood up and took my hands in hers.

'You've been a very brave girl, having to deal with such a thing on your own. After an ordeal like that, you should have telephoned me and I would have sent Daddy to bring you home. After everything you have told us, you know when I think back, I had heard rumours of your Aunty Violet's goings-on, but I didn't realise she had upset so many people. She always was the black sheep of the family, but to die like that, and in public; how undignified. Come along, you look exhausted, I'm going to put you to bed.'

For once, I wasn't going to stop her fussing over me. The drive had finished me and even though it was only one o'clock on a Sunday afternoon, all I wanted right now was to sleep in the safety of my own bed, cosseted by my over-indulgent mother.

Monday.

The next morning I awoke early, very early. It was still dark outside. Looking at my bedside clock I could see that I had been asleep for a good twelve hours. I lay in bed enjoying the warmth and comfort in the familiar decor and smells of home. Having time to lie back and stare at the ceiling was rare in this house. It was more normal for me to get up at the last minute, with little time to spare, and rush off to the office, or at weekends, any chance of an extra hour in bed would be overruled by Mummy, insisting that I get up and not waste the day. I looked at the clock again, two-thirty, I couldn't believe it, I never got up at this hour. Well, not unless you count yesterday when an intruder tried to kill me. Thoughts about the weekend's events crashed and dance through my head. I was too alert to go back to sleep now, and I really fancied a cup of tea and a biscuit, so I crept down to the kitchen. I thought I was being very quiet, but just as the kettle came to the boil, Daddy put his head around the kitchen door.

'Making tea; is there enough for two?' I removed another cup and saucer from the cupboard and placed a plate of biscuits on the kitchen table.

'Is Mummy awake?'

'No. You could drop a bomb next to the bed and she wouldn't hear it go off.' We both had a little titter. He was right, Mummy was a heavy sleeper.

We were halfway down our cups of tea and the biscuits were disappearing fast before Daddy asked the question; I knew would come.

'April, what is it you haven't told us?'

All I could do was stare at him. Could he read all my thoughts? He was right about one thing though; I needed to tell someone the whole story.

'Promise you won't breathe a word of it to Mummy?'

He hesitated before answering, 'very well.'

'The same night that Aunty Violet died, someone broke into my bedroom at the hotel and tried to kill me.' I had to blurt it out plain and simple, or I wouldn't have been able to tell him at all. It seemed the quicker it came out, the easier it was to say. I waited for his angry outburst and the '*you are not going back to work, it's far too dangerous for a slip a girl like you,*' rant, but it didn't come. He simply sat back in his chair and pondered on what I had told him. I waited.

'What actually happened?' he asked calmly. I sighed with relief before replying.

'It's hard to say. I was asleep when it started. Then something disturbed me. I was lucky. I rolled over at the same moment someone lunged at the bed. I screamed; the intruder bolted. The next thing I knew, there were half the hotel's guests standing at my bedroom door. A kind lady took pity on me and invited me to her room to await the police. Most of what happened that night is just a blur. I guess that is what it's like for most victims of crime after the event.'

'Did the police catch the man that attacked you?'

'No. Everything happened so fast and in the dark, that I can't even be sure if it was a man that attacked me. I just assumed it was a man. I certainly couldn't identify the person if I met them again.'

'What are you going to do now?'

'Well, first, I'm going back to bed. Thank you, Daddy, I needed to talk.' I kissed him on the cheek. 'I'm a little more tired than I thought, now that I've had the chance to share what happened with you. Later this morning I'm going into the office to await a telephone call from Inspector Allswell. He said he would let me know what the autopsy report results are. I also need to find out when he will release Aunty Violet's body; there are funeral arrangements to make.'

'Don't you worry about those, your mother and I will take care of them. We will also contact her solicitor about her estate and will. There may be a clue to her death there.'

'Thank you, Daddy, what would I do without you?'

After arriving at my office a little later than I normally would and hanging up my coat, I was sorting through the post at my desk when Jennifer came rushing in.

'Well, what happened? Did your Aunty get murdered in her sleep or not?' asked Jennifer in a bubbly voice. At first, I was stunned by what she had said. Then I realised she didn't know. She thought it was going to be a fun weekend away. It should have been obvious to me soon that she would want to know what had happened whilst I was away. All three of my friends will want to know. I sat down, not wanting to relive the past two days again, but they needed to know what had happened. Looking up at her, the smile had gone from her face.

'Aunty died at the dinner table and later that night someone tried to kill me.'

'What! You are joking; tell me you are making this up.'

'No, it's true.'

'Oh, April; how terrible. Were you hurt? No, wait; I'll get the others. We all need to hear what you have to say.'

An hour later we were still sitting around the small table in the kitchen having had two cups of tea each and finishing the day's supply of biscuits when the telephone rang in my office. I expect that's the Inspector calling. I was thankful for the distraction; I needed to get away from all the sympathy that was being heaped upon me; it was becoming oppressive.

When I returned to the kitchen, my three associates awaited my pronouncement with bated breath. I stood in the kitchen doorway and waited a moment, still mulling over what I'd been told by the Inspector.

'The cause of Aunty Violet's death was heart failure brought about by reasons unknown at this time. Further tests are required. As for the attack on me during the night, the police have found a button trapped inside the slashed pillow, but have found no evidence connecting my attack to the death of Aunty Violet. As yet they don't know if the button came from my attacker or one of the chambermaids when changing the bed linen.'

A chorus of disappointed voices belittled the police report as being worse than useless.

'Your Aunty's death had to have been brought on by foul means,' declared Patsy.

'And, it's obvious the button came from your night-time attacker,' protested Jennifer.

'I was hoping to get the proof a murder had been committed from the pathologist's report, but it confirmed nothing except Aunty had died of heart failure. I feel cheated.'

'What are you going to do, April?' asked Annabelle. The others fell silent as they waited for my answer. I looked at each of their expectant faces in turn; knowing what they wanted me to say.

'I've already decided to investigate her death myself. I have the names and addresses of the other guests who were at the dinner. I shall start by interviewing them.'

My supporters cheered me on, then, they gathered around me, offering their support.

'All you have to do is ask,' they said, 'and we will do whatever we can to help you.'

So, there I was amidst the clamour of excited voices, not with one case to solve but two. All doubt about if I was up to the job had vanished. Just as we were all getting carried away with the excitement and had convinced ourselves that finding Aunty's murderer was a foregone conclusion, there was a disturbance in the hall. A lady with a little girl carrying a music case interrupted the party.

'Sorry, I did knock, but no one answered,' she said. 'The door was open, so I came. Is this the right place for the music lessons?'

Suddenly, normality returned. We all apologised for not hearing the knock on the door. Patsy ushered them out of my office and pointed them towards the stairs, taking them both up to her music room. Jennifer and Annabelle returned to their offices after arranging to meet me at lunchtime.

Back in my office, I started work by going through the names and addresses of the hotel guests. I sorted them into order, the closest address to Driffield at the top of the list, working down to the most distant. Holly Starbrightly and Hector Boysack, along with Rocky Punch and his wife, had addresses in London. The film star and her producer were staying at a London hotel, whilst Mr and Mrs Punch had a house in Kew. The telephone interrupted my thoughts.

'Showers Detective Agency, how may I help you?'

'April, is that you? It's Rex.'

'Oh, hello Rex; how are you? What a surprise, I wasn't expecting a call from you.'

'I'm great, thank you. I know it's a bit unexpected and short notice, but I was wondering if you fancied going out tonight. After meeting you at the party, I was wondering if you fancied meeting up again and going to a dance or the cinema?'

'Oh, I'm sorry, Rex, I'm on a case. I'm with a client right now. When I'm free, I'll call you to arrange something,' I lied.

That settled it; I would start the investigation tomorrow with a trip to London. Rex Barker is a nice enough chap but just because I'd met him at a party and wrote to him a couple of times, doesn't mean we are dating or anything. I'd forgotten all about him until he turned up with his parents the other night. I've never had the time for boyfriends, well, not that I've had many opportunities to find one, but it doesn't mean they don't cross my mind from time to time. At school, it was all studying and after that, it was a series of temporary jobs before starting my business. I suppose someone will sweep me off my feet one day, but not just yet. First thing tomorrow morning, I will get the train from Hull to King's Cross in London. I want to interview Holly Starbrightly and her producer husband.

Tuesday.

I was a little taken aback and disappointed when I arrived at the hotel. I was expecting something grander for an American film star. Instead, it was a modest place, still very respectable but lacking the panache of the Savoy or the Ritz hotels. Arriving early in the day meant I was more likely to find Miss Starbrightly at home, and so it was. I told the hotel receptionist that I was a reporter from Starbiz Magazine and would like an interview with their glamorous guest. The deception worked, and Mr Boysack invited me up to the film stars room to share breakfast with them. That's if you can still call it breakfast at eleven am. I knocked on the bedroom door.

'Good morning, Ma'am. Please, come in. Miss Starbrightly is ready for you,' enthused, Mr Boysack. 'Tea or coffee, would you like an English muffin? Take a seat just here.' I sat in a chair by the window as Holly lounged flamboyantly on the sofa.

'What is it your readers would like to know, Miss Showers?' asked Mr Boysack.

I started by removing a notepad from my handbag and asking, 'are you here to star in a British film or a stage play, Miss Starbrightly?' I planned to lead her into questions about

Harrogate and my Aunty later on, but my plans fell apart immediately.

The film star sat upright. 'I remember you from the hotel in Harrogate. You were asking questions there as well.'

I lay the notepad in my lap and stared at the film star before answering.

'The lady who died at the dinner table was my Aunty Violet. The police told me she died of heart failure. So, as a relative, I'm visiting everyone who was there that night to explain what happened and apologise for her outrageous outburst.' It was a weak lie, but the best I could come up with after being rumbled so quickly.

'So why did you say you were from Showbiz Magazine?' asked Holly.

'I didn't think you would see me if I told you the truth.'

'Now see here, Miss. Holly's time is precious. You will have to leave. We have real reporters to meet,' demanded Hector. I got up to leave feeling a complete fool, but Holly came to my rescue by asking me to stay. Hector protested, but Holly was having none of it.

'Okay, Miss Showers, tell us the real reason why you are here.' said Holly.

I was surprised by her insight and decided to risk telling her a half-truth.

'Well, as I said, my Aunty died that night, but the strange thing is after she got the invitation to attend the gathering in Harrogate, she contacted me and said she felt uncomfortable going on her own and would I accompany her. And then, when she died so suddenly, whilst saying the things she did, and the police turning up, I felt that everyone deserved an apology and an explanation of what had happened. You see, the family thinks she was mentally ill. I was hoping you'd be willing to tell me how you happen to know my Aunty.'

'Yes, I understand. Ah, well, let me see. We met at a small hotel in Stratford-upon-Avon. We were not friends. I was in a play and your aunt and I just happened to be staying at the same hotel near the theatre.' Holly went thoughtful for a moment, her face taking on a more serious demeanour.

'I believe it was your Aunty who got me fired from that play. She had asked if I could arrange for her to meet Ambrose Carmichael, the star of the show. I said I couldn't. I didn't know him that well as this was my first big starring role in the theatre. At first, your Aunty was a bit put out by my refusal, but the following evening she was all sweetness and light again. She bought me a drink as a peace offering just before I set off for the theatre. By the time I went on stage, I felt a little unwell, but it was too late to ask my understudy to take over. I muddled on but felt worse as time went by. I made a mess of my lines and ended up getting fired from the show after some terrible reviews in the newspapers. No other theatre would take me on after that so, desperate for work, I moved to America where I met Hector. He gave me my big chance in the movies and I got lucky with my first film. It was only a small part. However, it was enough. I was spotted and given a starring role in the next film the studios made. It was a box office hit. So now I'm back here in England promoting my new Film. You might say, Miss Showers if it hadn't been for your Aunty Violet, I would never have gone to the States and made it big. I owe her my thanks, though I didn't think so at the time. Now is that all, Miss Showers? The smile had left her face. Hector picked up on it too and stood up.

‘I think that will be all, thank you, Miss Showers.’ He walked over to the door, ready to open it for me. I knew there was more to this than she was saying, but I wouldn’t get it from her now.

I made a note in my diary to contact her again. My thoughts changed to thinking about the next person I wanted to interview, Rock Punch. What was his connection to Aunty? I looked at my watch. There was still plenty of time to get to Kew, speak to Mr Punch, and get back to Kings Cross to catch my train home later that afternoon. So I got the bus from the hotel to Victoria Station. I’d never used the London Underground and the thought of not being able to see where the train was going and the terrifying thought of it getting stuck in a tunnel with no lights was too much to contemplate. The overland train journey to Kew Gardens would be safest. I’d heard of Kew Gardens and was curious to know if I would have enough time to visit them after my interview with Mr Punch. From what little I had seen of him in Harrogate he looked like a rough character and I was a little frightened about meeting him, though I reckoned that if his wife was present, he would conduct himself more amicably.

I found their address in Ennerdale Road. It turned out to be a large detached property with extensions to each side. I walked up the red and black tiled footpath to the porch and knocked twice on the front door. I noticed movement through its glass panes, and moments later the door opened. The woman was wearing a floral apron and had her hair was wrapped turban-style, in a silk scarf.

'Yes, what can I do for you?' she asked in a strong Leeds accent.

'May I speak to Mr Punch, please?'

'He's at work. May I help you, I'm Mrs Punch?'

She looked more like the cleaner than the owner.

'Mrs Punch? My name is April Showers. Do you remember me from the hotel in Harrogate? I would like to speak to you, please.'

'Oh hello dear, I didn't recognise you at first. It was a right carry on at that hotel, wasn't it, what with that woman dying on the table? I am sorry. Do you want to come for a cup of tea; I've just put the kettle on?'

I followed her into the house and through to the living room. It was fabulously furnished in the latest style, similar to that which I'd seen in magazines. Everything looked expensive, spotlessly clean, and tidy.

'I love this room, you're very lucky to be able to live in such a delightful house.'

'Yes, not bad is it, considering me and Rocky come from the back streets of Leeds. He's worked hard has Rocky, things ain't always been this good. He got a lucky break, set up his own business and well, here we are. I have to admit though, sometimes I miss Leeds. They're a stuck-up bunch of snobs around here, but Rocky finds it handy for getting into London where he gets most of his work. So, what can I do for you?'

'I've come to see you about my Aunty; she was the lady that died on the table. The police have told me she died of heart failure. But, what with that astonishing outburst she made right before she died, I thought I'd come and apologise in person for what she said.'

'You needn't have bothered; Rocky's told me all about your Aunty. We've both been through hard times in our past, failed relationships and all that. That's how we met. Rocky saved me from my last husband. He came across my old man when he was beating me up outside a pub in Leeds. Rocky dropped Charlie with one punch. I was in a right state; battered black and blue. Trouble was, I couldn't go home, not after what Rocky had done to Charlie. He would have killed me. So Rocky took me back to his flat. He cared for me until I was better. A proper gentleman, he was. Well, one thing led to another. I ended up divorcing Charlie and marrying Rocky.'

'May I ask how my Aunty got to know Rocky?'

'Rocky told me that your Aunt Violet had gone into a sports shop to buy some new golfing shoes and while there completed a free to enter competition form. The first prize was a ringside seat at a major boxing contest. Well, your Aunty Violet won and went to see the boxing. Well, Rocky won it, didn't he? Anyway, part of the prize was getting to meet the winning boxer. So enraptured was your Aunty with Rocky that they had a brief affair. They were both much younger back then. Trouble was Rocky said that Violet wore him out. So much so, that he lost some of his aggression and lost his next big fight and the title that went with it. But what Rocky didn't know was that some unsavoury characters had been betting on the outcome of the boxing match and expected Rocky to win. They weren't happy with Rocky.

When Rocky got knocked out in the second round, they thought he had thrown the contest on purpose. Later, he got another beating from the thugs who had been betting on him. The beating was so bad it put him out of the boxing game for good, which also meant it was the end of the relationship with your Aunty.'

'I am sorry,' I said, 'my Aunty seems to have been a real dark horse.'

'You can say that again. Anyway, Rocky recovered and got work as a labourer doing anything for a bit of cash. It was during that time when he met me. We'd not been together very long when one night when we were at a club, Rocky broke up a fight. It just happened that the man he saved from a severe beating was a musician from a rock-and-roll band. This fellow offered Rocky a job protecting the band members from drunks, and the like. So Rocky took the job. They paid him better than his labouring job. That's when Rocky got the idea of setting up a business, supplying personnel protection to singers, bands and film stars. It worked so well he opened an office in London. Only now, he hires retired boxers to do the protection work for him and he runs the office. So you might say, if it hadn't been for your Aunty Violet, we wouldn't be here now; funny how life works out, isn't it?'

'I'm very pleased everything has worked out so well for you both. But, doesn't Rocky feel any animosity towards my Aunty Violet after what she did to him?'

'No, he knew his professional boxing career wouldn't last long. Rocky was a good boxer but not that good that he could have made big money out of it. In the end, boxers with genuine talent would have just used him to gain experience as they moved up the ratings. He knew he would have just become a human punch bag for other boxers, improving their careers. In reality, your Aunty saved him from a lot more beatings and injuries.'

I looked at my watch, I'd spent a pleasant couple of hours with Judy as she openly told me about her life with Rocky and showed me around their lovely house, but I couldn't help feeling that Judy Punch felt lost here in leafy Kew; a northern girl in a middle-class suburb of London and didn't quite fit in with her neighbours. Time was getting on; I couldn't risk missing my train from Kings Cross, so I forewent the visit to Kew Gardens with a promise to return one day when I had more time to spare.

Chapter Six

Arriving home in time for dinner, I knew I'd find Mummy in the kitchen so I went to let her know I was back.

'Hello, April, did you have an enjoyable time in London? Did you get to see Big Ben and the changing of the guard at Buckingham Palace?'

'No, Mummy, I was working. I went to London to interview two suspects.'

'Oh, yes. Well, did you have time to do any shopping; there are some wonderful shops in London?'

'No, Mummy, I was too busy. I was there because of work; I didn't have time to look around the sights.'

'That's a shame. Daddy and I will go with you next time. We'll show you all the best places to visit. Dinner will be ready any minute. Go freshen up, but don't be long.'

'Yes, Mummy.' I was too tired to explain to her that I took my career seriously enough to not want to spend it strolling around London as a tourist. After taking off my day shoes and putting on my slippers, I washed my hands and face and felt ready to go back downstairs. The smell of meat pie and vegetables wafting through the house from the kitchen made my stomach rumble. In the dining room, Daddy was reading the evening newspaper, flicking over the top half of the newspaper to look at me as I sat down.

'Good day?' he asked, his glasses almost hanging off the end of his nose as he looked at me over the top of the rims.

'Yes, interesting. I went to see Holly Starbrightly and her husband in the morning and then to Mr and Mrs Punch's in the afternoon, but only Mrs Punch was in, though she gave me a lot of new information. Both Miss Starbrightly and Mr Punch had suffered at the hands of Aunty Violet, but over time, their fortunes have taken a turn for the better because of their encounter. They still disliked Aunty, but from what I was told, I cannot see why they would risk all they have to do her harm now.'

'Um, are you sure? Some people bear grudges for a long time. They're simply unable to shrug them off. Just because they may find themselves better off now, doesn't mean to say they still don't feel the pain of an encounter from years before. You still don't know if one of them has been lying to you about anything being in the past. People lie all the time. I see it as a bank manager. Customers come to ask me for a loan. They tell me all is well with their business and that all they need is a small amount of money to make some improvements and they'll be able to make even more money, or that they have a good job, well-paid job and want a large mortgage to buy a dream house. People will tell you what they think you want to hear so that they can get what they want. It takes time to learn how to spot a liar. You have to have evidence from them to show that they are telling you the truth. Be careful, my dear, people will pull the wool over your eyes if they get the chance.'

'Yes Daddy, I understand.' I knew what he was saying was true. In my short career as a detective, I had come across many liars and people with pasts they wanted to keep hidden; only this case was proving more difficult. It had happened to a member of my family, even if Aunty Violet was a bit of a rotter. So far, there was no evidence to say that she had been murdered, only the say-so of a corpse and the attack on me. Even my suspects seemed to have put the past behind them. I had scant real evidence to work with, but I knew that there was more to her death than I and the police had discovered so far.

After dinner, I went up to my room to write up my notes while everything was still fresh in my mind. Tomorrow, I'll consult my list of suspects again and choose who to question next. I heard the telephone ring in the hall. After overhearing Mummy exchange of pleasantries with the caller, Mummy came up to my room.

'It's for you, dear, it's Rex. He is a nice boy; you ought to invite him around one evening.'

'Mummy, I hardly know him. He's been away for two years. What does he want?'

'He wants to speak to you, dear.' I slammed my notebook closed and went downstairs.

'Yes?' I said when I picked up the receiver.

'Hello April, I was wondering if you fancied a night at the cinema on Friday?'

'Oh, I'm sorry, Rex, I'm really busy right now. I'm on a new case and I just don't have the time. I promise to call you when I do.' Putting the phone down before he could respond, I spied Mummy standing at the top of the stairs. I could see the disappointment on her face because I'd given Rex the brush-off. As I returned to my room, I kissed her on the cheek.

'I'm tired. I'm going to bed now, it's been a long day.'

Wednesday.

I arrived at my office on Exchange Street before nine o'clock the following morning to find Jennifer making tea in the kitchen.

'Morning, you must have a lot of work to do if you're here this early.'

'Morning April, may I see you for a minute, no, it's not about work. I need to speak to you in private about a personal matter before the others arrive, I have a problem.'

'You'd better come through to my office or should we go to yours?'

'No yours. You can put the, In Conference, sign on the door so we are not disturbed.'

'Oh, I see. You'd better come through.' As soon as Jennifer was seated, she burst into tears. I couldn't get a coherent word out of her for the first few minutes. All I could do was console my distraught friend until the crying ceased. Finally, she was able to tell me what her problem was.

'Are you sure your husband is having an affair? How do you know?'

'David's been coming home late every Friday night for the past few months and he won't tell me why. He just tells me, he is working late. Each Friday is the same, he comes home smelling of cigarette smoke and drink. So, last Friday, I telephoned his office and asked to speak to him, but they said he wasn't there and that he had left at his usual time. I didn't know what to say. I tried talking to him about it last night, but he wouldn't tell me and we had a row. April. I love him, but he won't talk to me about what he's doing. Will you help me, please?'

What else could I do? 'Yes, of course, I will help you. Leave it to me.'

Jennifer opened her handbag and removed a photo of the two of them on their wedding day.

'It's a wonderful dress, you look absolutely beautiful.' I'd clearly said the wrong thing because Jennifer burst into tears again.

'Let me make you a fresh cup of tea, this one has gone cold.'

When I arrived in the kitchen, Annabelle and Patsy were waiting for me. They looked at me expectantly without saying a word.

'What?' I asked as innocently as possible.

'What do you mean what? What is the matter with Jennifer?' asked Patsy.

'What makes you think I have Jennifer in my office?'

'Her office door is open.' 'Jennifer is missing,' 'Her coat is hung on the door.' 'Her shopping bag is next to her desk.' 'Your door is closed and we can hear someone crying,' they'd taken it in turns to give me the evidence. I was beaten by their detective work.

Before I could stop them, they'd pushed past me and they were heading into my office.

‘Wait!’ I called, but it was too late, they were in. By the time Jennifer had finished telling them her story of an unfaithful husband, Annabelle and Patsy were ready to sign up as vigilantes in an all-girl assassination squad. It was only the arrival of one of Annabelle’s clients that broke up, ‘The Evils of Men Tea Party’ and brought us all down to earth. It was time to get back to work. I promised Jennifer that I would find out what her husband was up to this coming

Friday.

Alone in my office, I returned to the list of addresses for my suspects. The next person on my list was Natalie West. She had been sacked from her job as a bank clerk two years ago and was now a waitress in Bridlington. I chose to interview her next. I could spend part of my day speaking to her, which would leave me time to buy a train ticket to Edinburgh for tomorrow. I’d been to Bridlington many times on day trips to the coast; summer and winter, it was only ten miles from my hometown of Driffield.

The cafe where Natalie worked was in the centre of Bridlington, on Cross Street close to the harbour. Its red leatherette seating, espresso coffee machine, jukebox and the best knickerbockers glories in town made it the place to visit on a day out to the seaside. Then, during the evening, it was a popular meeting place for the local teenagers, so it was always busy. As I stood outside, looking in, I could see Natalie flitting from table to table taking orders from customers and dashing to the counter to return with a tray full of food and drinks. I watched her for a few minutes. She didn’t give me the impression that she was a person who had lost a trustworthy job and had been reduced to taking any work that she could get. She looked like she was enjoying her role in life. A couple with two children vacated a table, so I nipped inside and sat down before anyone else could take the empty seat. As Natalie cleared away the dirty dishes left by the family, I said, ‘Hello.’ She smiled at me, the automatic smile she probably gave all customers, ‘Hello, I‘ll be back in a moment to take your order.’

As she placed the dishes behind the counter, she looked back at me over her shoulder; the smile had gone; she had remembered where she had seen me before. When she came back to my table she glared at me with cold eyes, ‘Yes?’ was all she said, with her order pad poised in one hand, and a pen twitching from side to side in the other.

‘I need to speak to you,’ I said, smiling as pleasantly as possible, ‘in private.’

‘What would you like to order, Miss?’

‘Just a coffee, please.’

‘Espresso, Cappuccino, Americano, would you like cream or milk with your order?’

‘Er, Cappuccino, please. I need to speak to you,’ I repeated. She didn’t respond, she just turned her back on me and went to get my coffee. When she returned, she placed the cup and saucer on the table along with the bill and went to attend to another customer. I stayed to drink my coffee, hoping to catch her eye and try to explain why I had come to see her, but she looked away each time she passed my table. Not wanting to make a scene by forcing her to speak to me, I finished my coffee and left. As I closed the cafe door, I made a note of the cafe's closing time. In the meantime, I bought a train ticket to Edinburgh.

I returned to the Bridlington cafe ten minutes before closing. The café was empty and the closed sign was already showing in the window. Natalie was mopping the floor. I pulled back out of sight and waited in the shop doorway next to the café for Natalie to leave. The seaside town seemed to die before my eyes as I waited. It was dark; the day tourists were on their way home, the gift shops had turned out their lights and locked their front doors. The strong aroma of frying fish and chips wafted along the streets, making me feel hungry, but I couldn't leave my post and risk missing the waitress. Eventually, she came out, buttoning up the collar on her overcoat as the nip of cold air contrasted with the warmth of the café. Stepping forward, I ambushed her. She jumped back, looking frightened.

'I'm sorry to have startled you. Natalie please, I need to speak to you.' She paused for a moment, staring at me as recognition registered. She turned and walked away. I trotted up alongside her and started again.

'Please, Miss West, I'm learning what a horrid person my Aunty really was; it would help me enormously if you would explain what she did to you. I already know the basics of what happened, but not your side of the story.'

She stopped once again, 'what good would it do telling you? It wouldn't get my job back at the bank or restore my reputation,' she snapped.

'Then, why did you go to Harrogate for the weekend to meet her?' Natalie didn't answer but carried on walking.

'What did she do to you? Let me put it right if I can.'

'You can't!'

'Please, Miss West, Natalie. I believe my Aunty was murdered; and right now, you are the only person I've interviewed who is refusing to talk to me. You've got a choice, talk to me or the police!' She stopped again, the look of hate in her eyes making me think I may have pushed her a step too far. She turned away and walked on, saying nothing. I followed and we walked in silence for a while. We arrived at a large Victorian-style house and from the number of name-plates attached to the door frame, I could tell that the house had been converted into flats. She held the door open for me. Natalie had one half of the upstairs of the house. After hanging her coat on the back of the door, she switched on a two-bar electric fire, its plastic coal effect base illuminated by a red light bulb, before sitting in an armchair next to the fire and warming her hands. She hadn't offered to take my coat or asked me to sit, so I just sat in the other armchair with my coat on.

'I'm sorry that my Aunty hurt you; will you tell me about it?'

'I'm not sorry she's dead. I went to Harrogate to get my revenge, but when she died at the dinner table, I felt cheated.'

'What did you have planned for her?'

'I'd borrowed a kitchen knife from work. I was going to arrange a meeting with her in her room and then kill her. I hoped the kitchen knife would make the police think it was someone from the hotel.'

'You mean, you would blame an innocent person?'

‘No, not really, I reckon the staff could prove they were all too busy to have done it and that they had no motive. In the meantime, I would have made a getaway.’

‘Was it you who attacked me during the night?’ She looked at me for the first time since arriving.

‘No, I left the hotel after the police had interviewed me. I didn’t want to get searched and have to explain why I had the kitchen knife in my bag.’

‘Please, tell me the details of what my Aunty did to you.’ She looked across at me as though trying to decide whether to throw me out or tell me her life story.

‘Would you like a coffee? I only have instant,’ she asked.

‘Yes, please.’ I unbuttoned my coat and waited for her to return from the kitchen. A few minutes later she returned with a tray with two steaming cups of black coffee a jug of milk and a bowl of sugar. As I sipped my coffee, she began her story.

‘I come from Sterling in Scotland. I was a bank clerk in one of the smaller branches. The man I fell in love with also worked in the bank. He was offered a promotion, the job of Assistant Manager at the branch in Driffield. It was a long way from Sterling; however, the bank said they would pay his expenses for the move. I followed him down here and he saw to it that I got a job in the same branch. We kept our affair secret. The bank wouldn’t have approved of us living together and not being married. Everything was fine for a year, and then Angus was killed while crossing the road. I was devastated. I moved out of our rented house and got a flat so I could stay on at the bank, I didn’t want to go back to Scotland; I liked it in Driffield. Then one day your Aunty came in. She deposited some money with me and left, but came back minutes later claiming I had defrauded her of some money. The amount I had written in your Aunty's passbook was lower than she thought it should have been. She said I had taken twenty pounds of her money. The bank manager made me balance the money in the drawer of my teller station. It was correct. So he took us both into his office and he made me empty my handbag and purse onto his desk. I had twenty pounds in my purse. When your Aunty saw the money, she claimed that it was hers. I tried to explain that the money was for paying my rent, buying me a new outfit and doing my grocery shopping. But she continued to kick up a real fuss; accusing me of stealing the money. She threatened to tell the newspapers about the theft if the money was not returned immediately, so the bank manager, wanting to maintain the good name of the bank, sacked me on the spot. But, I heard later from a friend at the bank that your Aunty returned a couple of weeks later. She had discovered the missing money in a second handbag. She told the bank manager she had forgotten to pick it up before leaving the house. I hoped to get my old job back, so I telephoned the bank manager, but he refused to take me back, explaining that someone else had taken my job, though he returned my twenty pounds to me. It was no good the news of me being sacked had got out. I couldn't get a job in Driffield. The bank manager wouldn't even give me a reference because it would mean he would have to explain his mistake in sacking me. I never regained my reputation. I came to Bridlington and got a job as a waitress. I'm saving up to go back to Scotland; I'm going to stay with my sister until I can find a job up there.

‘I’m sorry for what my Aunty did to you. If you wish, I will go back to the bank and speak to the manager. I’ll explain what my Aunty was actually like and that I will inform his area manager about his miss-handling of the whole affair?

‘No, don’t. I’ve made up my mind; I’m going back to Sterling as soon as I can. That bank has too many sad memories for me now.’

‘I’m sorry, I hope things work out better for you in Scotland.’

After leaving Natalie, I went down to the seafront and bought a bag of chips, eating them whilst looking out over the harbour, wondering how many people have had their lives ruined by Aunty Violet and if I would ever get to know her full life story. Dropping the greasy newspaper in a bin, I walked back to my car thinking about Miss West. I had misjudged her when we spoke in the York Museum. Back then, she had given me the impression that she was too weak and small to have done Aunty Violet any harm, but the woman I’d just interviewed had turned out to be someone completely different. I tried to think of a reason for her to have attacked me during the night, but I couldn’t think of a good enough answer. However, she was not telling me everything. Whilst in her flat I’d noticed a man’s coat hanging on the back of the door. Who was she living with and why wasn’t he there waiting for her to come home from work? She’d never mentioned him; I had to find out who he was and why she never said anything about him.

Arriving home, Mummy was waiting on the doorstep. 'I heard the car coming up the drive. I thought it might be the police who'd come to tell me you'd been in a terrible accident. You know I don't like you driving in the dark. Why didn't you telephone and say you were alright and that you would be late?'

'Sorry Mummy, I was interviewing someone and lost track of time. I'll remember to telephone you next time.' She had made me some sandwiches for supper. I didn't want them, though I didn't have the heart to tell her I'd already eaten, so I forced them down with the aid of a cup of tea. We talked for a while and I told her about Natalie West, after which she went very quiet and thoughtful before saying 'goodnight.' I don't think she liked hearing about another one of Aunty Violet's victims.

*****

Unbeknown to me at the time, Rex was doing some investigations of his own.

From the dark recess of an alley near Bridlington harbour, Rex watched the entrance to a Bridlington café, waiting for it to close so he could follow the waitress home. The pubs had begun to empty and the residents and holidaymakers filled the street as they returned to their lodgings. Alerted by loud male voices, he suddenly realised his observation post was being invaded by a late-night reveller, looking for a private place to relieve himself. The man staggered into the alley, then stopped when he saw someone lurking in the shadows, Rex gave a discreet cough, the man changed his mind about using the alley and scurried away to rejoin his friends. Rex smiled, as he wondered at what that young man must have thought was a close shave with a dirty old man in an alley when he saw the dark shape of Rex watching him? Rex turned up the collar on his overcoat and leaned against the wall, getting impatient now, wondering when the last customer would leave the cafe. He could hear rock-and-roll music from its Juke Box playing an Elvis Presley song. The smell of the freshly brewed coffee drifted across the street, mingling with that of the fish and chip shop around the corner. His stomach rumbled, and he contemplated buying a bag of chips whilst he waited. Just as he was about to give in to temptation, the music in the café stopped and the red neon sign in the window blinked from open to closed. He watched as a late customer ignored the closed sign and entered the café. The late customer re-emerged moments later. But instead of walking away, she waited outside. The woman stood in the shadows of the unlit shop next door to the cafe, making it impossible for Rex to see her face.

'You're not *who I expected,*' he hissed. 'Who the hell are you? Just a girlfriend or another East German we don't know about?'

The last few customers left the café. The lights inside dimmed and the man behind the counter began to dismantle the coffee machine for cleaning. The waitress put on her coat and stepped outside, joining the woman waiting at the door. After a brief conversation, they walked off together. Rex kept a discrete distance as he followed them. After a short walk, they stopped outside a house, talked for a moment, then, both went inside. A light at an upstairs window came on and he watched as the waitress closed the curtains. Rex crept along the path up to the front door where he found two doorbell buttons; one marked Flat 1, the other Flat 2. He made a note of the address in his book, and the time at which they had arrived. Rex checked the time on his watch. Frustrated at not getting a good look at the woman who had waited for the waitress and not having enough time to wait for her to come out of the flat, he decided to return to the cafe the following night to see if she came back again.

Thursday.

I arrived at Driffield railway station very early to catch the train to York, where I needed to change for a train to Edinburgh. These early mornings on cold railway platforms were an aspect of detective work I seem to have overlooked in my appreciation of a private detective's career choice. The great black monster puffed, hissed and wheezed its way to a stop and I clambered aboard, already wishing I'd put more sensible shoes on. I shared a compartment with a young married couple, newlyweds I suspected, as she kept fiddling with her wedding ring as though unused to the weight of it on her finger. There was also a gentleman in a business suit reading The Times newspaper and a soldier in uniform. He smiled at me as I sat down, and I couldn't help thinking of Rex. I pulled an Agatha Christie novel from my coat pocket and read. I liked the Hercule Poirot detective stories, but I saw myself more as Tuppence, in the Tommy and Tuppence novels, only I didn't have a Tommy at my side to watch my back.

I'd never been to Scotland before, so I was looking forward to my visit, hoping that I would get the chance to visit the famous castle on the rock which overlooked the city. Octavia Tone had given her address as Albany Street, which turned out to be a row of late Georgian style, terraced houses built from granite, in a more upmarket part of the city. I rechecked the address that I'd written; I hadn't expected a music teacher to live at such an expensive-looking address, so it was with some trepidation that I knocked on the door. I don't know which of us was more surprised when the door opened as we recognised each other.

'Miss Showers, what a surprise. What are you doing here?'

'I'm sorry to just call on you like this; may I come in and talk to you?' She hesitated for a moment before stepping back and opening the door further for me to enter.

'You've come a long way. What would you have done if I'd not been at home? You should have made an appointment before coming all this way.'

'It's a risk that goes with the job, I'm afraid. If I telephone ahead to arrange an interview, people tell me they are too busy to see me, or I find they have gone away for the day when I turn up to see them.'

'Well, now that you are here, how may I help you? Though I must warn you, I am expecting the arrival of my next pupil in about an hour.'

'Yes, I understand. It is good of you to take the time to speak to me and hopefully, I will not keep you long. I am a private detective investigating the death of the lady who died in Harrogate. The police say she died of natural causes, but

I'm investigating why you, she and all the other guests had been summoned to a gathering at that hotel.'

'Oh, yes I see, but I didn't know anyone else who was there, only that Miss Birch had invited me. Her letter was most insistent. So, I went to rub her nose in it you might say.'

'Would it surprise you to learn that my Aunt did not send you that invitation? She too received an invitation to the hotel, only, her was from someone called Elizabeth Milbank; do you know the name?'

'No, sorry, I've never heard of her.'

'May I ask what it was that my Aunty did to you?'

She ruined me as a music teacher when I was living in Driffield, so much so that I was forced to return home to Scotland to live with my sister. That is until my fortunes changed.'

'Are you willing to go into detail?'

'Ah. Well, I suppose it started when she came to me for piano lessons. Your Aunty didn't have an ear for music. Though, I tried to help her as much as I could. She could read music well enough, but she wasn't a gifted student. Had she come to me when she was much younger, things may have been different. After one tortured lesson, I made the mistake of suggesting she give up. She was furious with me for making the suggestion. And so, she persisted, undaunted in her lessons. She refused to be beaten, she said and insisted that she would master the instrument given a little more time. I needed the money, so I continued to give her lessons. Progress was very slow, but she was enjoying her lessons, so I encouraged her. Then, during one lesson, she told me she had been invited to a dinner party, and that she had volunteered to give a piano recital to those attending. I tried to tell her she wasn't ready for an audience and that she may find they expect more from her than she could give, but she wouldn't have it. She accused me of trying to spoil things for her. She didn't turn up for her next lesson. In fact, she stopped coming altogether. After a few days, my other clients began cancelling their appointments. Then, I learned through a friend, that your Aunty was going around accusing me of being a poor teacher and that it was my fault that she had made a fool of herself. Apparently, during her recital, some guests had sniggered at her lack of playing ability. It was so bad that one or two of the guests left the dinner party early, upsetting the hostess.

By the time Miss Birch had turned away most of my clients, I couldn't afford to keep my business going, so I returned to Scotland. Before I left Driffield, a friend told me that the hostess of the dinner party was still being mocked by the ladies of the town for allowing Miss Birch to play her piano. It seems things like that take a long time to live down and your Aunty no longer got invited out to dinner parties by the socially privileged of Driffield. I'd lost all my pupils, but your Aunty lost a lot of friends. I believe she moved out of Driffield about the same time I did. With no income, only the money from the sale of my house, I went back to Scotland to make a fresh start.

Shortly after my arrival, my sister came home from work one day and mentioned that a friend of hers, who was very poor, had a son who wanted to learn to play the piano, but his mother couldn't afford to pay for lessons. My sister asked me if I would mind helping him out. I didn't feel like giving lessons ever again, but as I was living with her and had no job, I agreed. He came to the house, and I gave him a few lessons. I quickly discovered that he was very gifted. He learned everything I could teach him at an incredible rate. By the time he entered his school recital competition he had become very good, and he won the competition. His schoolteacher was so impressed with him she entered him for the town music competition, and he won that too. That's when I received a letter from a parent asking me to teach their child to play the piano. The fee they were offering was three times my normal price for a lesson, so I took the job. The child turned out to be the son of a high court judge, and soon I found myself giving music lessons to lots of wealthy children and adults. Almost overnight, my fortunes were turned around. As my reputation grew, I invested some of my time and money in two music academies for less well off children. Now I employ music teachers to do most of the tuition, but I keep the most gifted and wealthy clients for myself and teach them here at my home.

So you see Miss Showers, I couldn't resist going down to Harrogate to inform your Aunty about how well I was doing and rub her nose in my good fortune. I only wish I'd got the chance to do it before she died. So you see she cheated me out of that pleasure as well.'

I thanked Miss Tone for her time and left. As I walked back towards the centre of Edinburgh thinking about what Miss Tone had told me. It was clear from how she had spoken to me that she was still feeling very bitter towards Aunty Violet. She had a motive for killing my Aunty but, I don't think she did it. I wouldn't need to speak to Miss Tone again.

It was lunchtime, and Miss Tone hadn't even offered me a cup of tea during our chat. So, I went to find a cafe and got something to eat and drink. With a little spare time to kill before my train left, I went for a walk along Castle Hill to look at the shops, before making my way up to the Castle.

I found the streets of the old town narrow and overpowering. They were covered in black soot, no doubt from the many steam trains that ran to and from the station, which was not far away. It was also cold and damp; the high walled buildings shielded the streets from the sun, keeping them in perpetual shadow. The streets and shops which led up to the castle were busy with tourist and the incline of the long walk, deceptive. I stopped frequently, as much to rest and catch my breath as to look in shop windows.

By the time I'd reached the entrance to the castle, I had lost all interest in visiting the place. This was not my busy, friendly market town of Driffield. I felt lost and out of place, even more than I had done when I was in London.

It was with a sigh of relief that I took my seat on the train back to York. During the journey, I jotted down all I'd learnt in my notebook. When I put down my pencil, I stared out of the window and for the first time; I wondered if I was doing the right thing, Aunty Violet was turning out to be a horrible person. Maybe she deserved to die, but then I had second thoughts. No. No one deserves to die, certainly not like that. For a short while, I wondered if her death really had been the result of natural causes and not murder. I dismissed the doubt. If that was true, why had someone attacked me during the night at the hotel? No, the investigation must go on.

By the time I got home I was physically and emotionally drained after the long train journey. Supper was over, but Mummy had made me up a plate of ham salad. As I sat down with my cup of tea, and salad, my parents asked about my day in Edinburgh and Octavia Tone. I replayed the day's events to them and finished by telling them that I didn't think Miss Tone was the person I was looking for.

Chapter Seven

Friday.

Arriving at work still tired from the day before, I hung my coat on the back of the door, put my handbag in the bottom drawer of my desk and laid my notebook on the desktop. Staring at it for a moment, I sighed and gave up before even starting. I needed a cup of tea before writing up my notes from the previous day in Edinburgh. Going through to the kitchen, I knew what the real problem was. It wasn't yesterday or the tiredness that was bothering me; it was what I had promised to do this evening for Jennifer. Just as the kettle came to the boil, she also arrived early and came into the kitchen to find me, she closed the door behind her.

'Did you have a nice day in Edinburgh?' she asked. I knew what she was leading up to. 'You haven't forgotten about tonight, have you?' she continued without looking up in my direction whilst she poured herself a cup of tea. 'About David, I mean?' She finally turned to look at me. I desperately wanted to refuse her, to make any excuse I could think of to put her off, but the fearful look in her eyes broke down my defences, I couldn't let her down. If I said no to her, she wouldn't understand and I would lose a friend. If I reported back to her with the news she dreaded, I risked ruining her marriage and again losing a friend. I had seen firsthand what this kind of work did to couples and families when it tore them apart. All I could do was console myself with the view that I was bringing about the inevitable, sooner rather than later. Only, this time it was different, Jennifer was my friend. I had met David. He didn't seem the type of man who would cheat on his wife, but what do I know.

'Yes, don't worry, I haven't forgotten. I'm sure there is a simple explanation for what he is doing.' I told her, in my most reassuring voice. 'You'll see; you'll have been upsetting yourself over nothing.'

'Then why won't he tell me what he is doing? Why does he always come home smelling of drink and cigarette smoke? We haven't been married for very long, and he's fed up with me already, I know it. What am I going to do?' The desperation in her voice was palpable.

As Jennifer sobbed into her handkerchief, the kitchen door opened and Annabelle entered. 'I guess this is about David?' she said. I nodded in response.

Annabelle put her arms around Jennifer, 'don't worry Jen, I've read so many books about murder, I know just how to deal with him and how to get away with it. We'll stick by you and give you an alibi.' Jennifer pushed Annabelle away, 'I don't want him dead, I love him,' she squeaked.

I scowled at Annabelle, 'you can't say things like that. No one knows what he's up to yet.'

'Men,' Annabelle tutted, 'you know what they are like!' I was about to protest but stopped myself just in time. I'd never had a serious boyfriend, never mind a relationship. What could I add? Patsy arrived at that point and joined in the to-do. ‘David’s still at it then,’ she said.

‘Patsy!’ I scolded, shocked by her bluntness. ‘Come through to my office, Jennifer, we can’t stay here. I’m sure these two have work they can get on with!’

‘Not me,’ said Annabelle, ‘I’m all up to date. I have a client coming in later to collect his latest chapter, but that’s ready for him.’

‘Me too,’ added Patsy. ‘It’s Friday. I don’t have anyone booked in for lessons this morning, only this afternoon when I go to the Senior School to instruct class 4a in their guitar lessons.’

We decamped from the kitchen. With tea and a tin of biscuits in hand, we headed for Jennifer’s office instead of mine. Annabelle was unstoppable, reciting some of the murder plots she’d read from the books she had edited. She explained how we could all help Jennifer dispose of her husband’s body after I’d discovered him in the arms of his secret lover. Then she described the even grislier fate that would await the woman he’d been having the affair with. The idle boasts soon descended into the ridiculous, and, as they got more and more outrageous, they reached the point of farcical. The injections of outrageous revenge on the evil femme fetale did the trick. Jennifer began to laugh along with the rest of us, joining in with suggestions on what she would like to do with her husband’s lover. We were all laughing together and before we knew it the teapot was empty. I took the opportunity of there being no more tea in the pot as the excuse to return to my office, saying I had work to do. I looked at the clock; it was just after ten.

I closed my office door, settled at my desk, and retrieved my list of suspects ready to choose who to visit next. Looking down the list, I made a plan for the day. If I spent some of today interviewing a person who lived close by, I could be back in time for five o'clock and be outside David's place of work to follow him to his secret rendezvous with his unknown floozy. Ada Betterman's address was in Scarborough, less than an hour's drive away. I could be there and back in time for my evening job for Jennifer. All I knew about Ada Betterman was that she used to be a nurse. An interview with her would fill the day nicely. The address was Ocean View Retirement Home, Sea Cliff Road. If all went well I'd have time to buy an ice cream and enjoy a walk along the seafront.

The retirement home turned out to be a sizeable house, in a well-to-do area, on the southern edge of the town. Close enough to the cliffs and beach to enjoy a stroll on a warm summer's day, but far enough away from the clifftop not to be disturbed by the crashing waves on a stormy night. As I pulled onto the drive I read the small print at the bottom of the retirement home sign, Owner, Ada Betterman, S.R.N. Well, here was another one who seemed to have benefited from an encounter with Aunty. I was eager to hear her story. I'd hoped it would be easy to find a person with a clear motive for killing Aunty, but so far, most of my suspects, though having gone through a rough patch after their characters had been maligned by Aunty Violet, had benefited in the long run from their encounter with her. I couldn't understand it, Aunty had done so many bad things to people, but my suspects had risen above it all.

I stepped up to the front door. A sign next to it instructed callers to ring the bell and enter, so I did. From a door marked private, an elderly looking lady came into the hall. She was neatly dressed in a white blouse and black skirt and wore wire-rim glasses which were perched on the tip of her nose.

'Yes, may I help you?' she asked.

'Hello, my name is Miss Showers. Would it be possible to speak to Miss Betterman, please?

'Miss Betterman is very busy, I'm Mrs Chaperon, her secretary; may I be of assistance? I removed a business card from my handbag and gave it to the secretary.

'I'm a private detective. I would like to speak to Miss Betterman on a private matter, if I may?'

The elderly secretary pushed her spectacles back up her nose and read the card. 'Oh, well, err, I hope this is not a complaint from a disgruntled relative, they don't understand how confused some of our guests can get before they fully settle into their new surroundings.'

'No, it is nothing like that. I'm here on a different matter. Is Miss Betterman available?'

'Please, take a seat.' She indicated to a chair beside the wall. 'I will enquire if Miss Betterman has time to see you.' She disappeared back through the door marked private, so I did as I was bid and waited. From my seat I could see other doors leading off from the hall, all clearly marked as to their use, Dining Room, Library, Sitting Room, Kitchen and one with the letters, W.C. At the far end of the hall, next to the stairs, was an open arch with a sign, 'Ground Floor Bedrooms.' It looked as though the house had been extended to the rear, making it even larger than it appeared to be from the front. It was very warm inside the house, even though it wasn't cold outside. As I sat and waited, the excessive heat made me feel uncomfortable. We didn't have central heating at home; we still relied on an open fire and an electric heater for hot water. My office on Exchange Street did have the new style of heating, however, not set as high as this. The heat was making me feel quite drowsy. Just before my eyelids got the better of me, the door marked private opened and Miss Betterman emerged. She was dressed in a crisp blue matron's uniform, but without the cap. It made her look older than her mid-thirties, which I knew her to be.

'Miss Showers, I hope this will not take long?' I snapped out of my stupor and got to my feet.

'Thank you for agreeing to speak to me. I apologise for dropping in unexpectedly, I didn't have your telephone number.'

'What is it exactly you are investigating?' Her bluntness amazed me. Had she forgotten the death in Harrogate already?

'It's about the death of Violet Birch in the hotel in Harrogate.'

'Surely, that is a matter for you to take up with the hotel. Why have you come to me?

'Please, Miss Betterman, if we could go through to your office, I will explain.'

The office was cooler than the hall. It contained two desks, one for Miss Betterman and one for her secretary.

'Now then, what is all this about?' She directed me to a chair with the sweep of her hand.

Once seated, I began my explanation.

'Violet Birch, the lady who died, was my Aunty. She'd asked me to accompany her to the hotel because she feared that someone there wished to do her harm. You heard her statement before she collapsed and died in front of us all.'

'Yes, I did, but I hope you are not inferring that I had anything to do with her death?'

'No, in fact, the cause of death, according to the police pathology report, was heart failure.'

'Then why are you bothering me?'

'It's just that Aunty pre-warned me she was in danger. I know she wasn't an easy person to get along with. I have also discovered that several people bore grudges against her. I'm trying to discover, what she did to each of them, to earn their animosity?'

The retirement homeowner eyed me suspiciously for a moment before speaking.

'I have nothing to hide. It's all on record and in the past now. I had been working as a nurse for five years at the Royal and General Hospital in Driffield when your Aunty Violet was admitted with severe pain from uterine fibroids. She had a hysterectomy and had to stay in hospital for two weeks. One day, when we were short-staffed, your Aunty needed a bedpan. I was a little slow in fetching it, and your Aunty wet the bed. It was her fault for leaving it so late before asking for help. She played hell with me and then complained to the ward sister and I got a serious telling off from her too. She was a real dragon and wouldn't listen to anything I said. She even threatened to report me to Matron for being negligent. I was so upset over the incident, that later that day, I made a mistake with the medication for another patient and nearly killed the woman with an overdose. That was it, the end of my career. After I left the hospital, I came here to work. I was an assistant helping the guests feed themselves and go to the toilet, etc. But, there was one gentleman with whom I got on very well. He liked to tell me about his time as a soldier during the war, the first war that is. He'd been a colonel. Well, to cut a long story short when he died I discovered he had made a will and left all he owned to me. It was a substantial amount. So I bought out the owners of this place and improved it. It is now twice the size it was when I arrived and with a staff of my own choosing, who I treat far better than I ever was. I only take on the best clients. I even have a waiting list for vacancies. I went to Harrogate to tell your Aunty that she'd actually done me a favour, not to kill her.'

'Thank you for your honesty about why you had to leave nursing, it couldn't have been easy.'

'I hated my time as a hospital nurse; it was like being in the army. You can't do this, you can't do that. I became a nurse to help the patients, but the ward sisters were little Hitlers. Now, I'm my own boss. I can please myself how and what I do. I believe I give my guests a better service than they would get at more expensive establishments and so long as my guests appreciate what I do for them, I am happy to continue providing a service to them.'

'Thank you for your time, Miss Betterman, I'll be on my way now.'

I returned to my car feeling frustrated; Ada Betterman seemed like a nice lady. I found it hard to believe a nurse would be the sort of person to deliberately hurt anyone, but on the other hand, she would know the best kind of drug to use to kill someone, how to administer it and more importantly, have access to it. She had to be a contender for the murder no matter how nice she came across in that interview. As I put the key in the ignition, I remembered the ice cream I'd promised myself earlier, so I drove down to the promenade to buy one.

The cool North Sea breeze felt refreshing after the stuffiness of the retirement home. I licked at the edges of a cornet filled with soft dripping ice cream with a squirt of raspberry syrup on the top and a chocolate flake sticking out of it. Walking along the harbour promenade, I thought about the suspects on my list. I was only halfway through them with no serious contender to the murder jumping out at me. I reminded myself to be patient, it was unrealistic of me to expect to come across the murderer straight away and that if the job of a private detective was an easy one, everyone would be doing it. I had to keep faith in myself. I'd solved one murder, I would solve this one.

When I arrived back at my office, Jennifer was waiting for me.

'I'm sorry, I needed to see you before I went home,' she said. 'I know you don't want to do this for me and that I should go to someone else, but I can't. You are my friend, and I trust you to find out the truth for me. I would follow him myself but I don't want to see who it is that he is meeting just in case I know her. The embarrassment would be too much for me to bear.'

'It's alright Jennifer, I've done this sort of thing before, remember. I will be discrete; at least you are not asking me for photographs of the person.'

'Oh, I couldn't. I would never get her image out of my mind.'

'Go home and wait for me to come and see you. If David is seeing someone else I'll soon know and I will have plenty of time to come to your house and tell you about it before he gets home.'

At half-past five, I was sitting in my car on West Gate, outside the clothing distributors offices where David worked. I didn't have long to wait before he came out. He was alone and he hadn't waited for anyone else, he just made his way towards me. As he crossed the car park, he looked left and right before crossing the road, still heading towards my car. Had he seen me? Oh, no; what was I going to tell him, what reason could I give for being parked outside the place he worked? Then, just as I expected him to tap on the car door window, he passed me by, stepping onto the path just in front of my car. He hadn't noticed me after all. He marched on, not towards his home but up West Gate, heading towards North Street. I got out of the car and followed him, keeping far enough back so as not to be noticed, but close enough to see if he turned left or right or stopped outside someone's house. He left West Gate and crossed North Street and entered the Bay Horse pub. I stared at the pub, 'so,' I said to myself, 'he either has a bad drinking habit or this is where he meets his lady friend.' I continued to stare at the pub; I didn't want to go in. Nice Girls don't go into public houses on their own; and anyway, he would see me and wonder what I was doing there. I reconciled myself to my fate, I didn't have any choice. I had to go in after him. I went in and went through to the lounge bar; it was empty, so I went through to the main bar. David was nowhere in sight. There was just a young woman behind the bar pulling pints for two men in overalls. One whistled at me so I went back to the lounge. After a couple of minutes the barmaid came through, 'Yes love, what can I get ya?'

'Nothing, just yet, thank you. I'm looking for a Mr David Clark.'

'Davie, what do you want with our Davie?'

My heart sank. So it was true, he was having an affair. 'I just need to speak to him, it's important, it's about his wife.' The barmaid didn't answer me, she just turned and left through a door at the end of the bar. I heard her yell David's name and a few moments later he came through to the lounge.

'Yes, may I help you,' he asked all innocent like as he tucked his shirt in the waistband of his trousers. He didn't know who I was at first, but the light of recognition soon crossed his face.

'You're April, Jennifer's friend from work, what are you doing in here?'

'I'm here to ask you the same thing,' I blurted out as though he was my husband I'd caught red-handed doing something he shouldn't. The smile dropped from his face. He looked shocked at what I'd said.

‘I’m sorry, I didn’t mean it to come out like that; it’s just that Jennifer’s worried.’

He quickly put two and two together. ‘You’d better come through here.’ He lifted the hatch in the bar and I followed him through to the back. The back room was a mess and another man was working in there ripping up the floorboards.

‘Pete, this is April. She wants to know what we are up to.’ Pete turned around to look at me and I immediately realised my mistake. They were brothers, almost twins they were so alike. David lifted a dustcover off a chair and asked me to sit down.

‘What’s up, why is she here?’ asked Pete.

‘She a private detective, working for Jennifer, I’m afraid she’s caught us.’ Pete looked even more confused, and my face was growing redder by the second.

‘I’m sorry, it’s all been a terrible misunderstanding,’ I blurted out. Pete didn’t seem any the wiser.

‘What’s going on,’ asked Pete.

‘I’d better explain,’ said David.

‘I’ve been coming here each Friday night to help my brother, Pete, fix this place up. Friday is one of the busiest nights of the week in the pub, so he’s needed behind the bar. He’ll have to stop work soon when more customers come in. The rest of the week he can manage with just Debbie serving drinks. I come and help Pete with all this lot.’ He held his arms open to emphasise the state of the room. There’s woodworm in the floorboards and dampness in the joists. He’s paying me to help him fix up the pub. With the extra money I get, I’m saving it to take Jennifer on a holiday for our wedding anniversary. I wanted it to be a surprise for her.

Has she really been that worried about what I've been doing?'

'Yes. I'm sorry,' I kept repeating.

'Don't worry, I'll tell her when I get home,' said David.

Pete laughed, 'I told you she would find out what you were doing. You know you could ask her to come and help. If Jennifer served drinks behind the bar on a Friday, I could spend more time helping you in here. That way you would both get paid a bit extra towards your holiday.'

'That's a good idea,' I volunteered. 'I'm supposed to meet up with her later and tell her about this floozy you've been seeing on the side. I could tell her about your suggestion.'

'Thanks, but no,' said David, 'I'd rather explain that bit to her myself. You go home and tell her what you've found out. She must be worried stiff.'

I brushed a thin film of dust from my dress before leaving. 'Have a drink before you go, tell Debbie I said it was on the house,' said Pete.

I took him up on his offer and had a glass of cider before going back to my car. The lounge had filled up with people enjoying an end of working week drink. It was such a relief to know I could go back to Jennifer and give her the good news and tell her all was well with her marriage.

By the time I left the pub it was getting cloudy, daylight was fading, and the streetlights had come on. The two men I'd seen in the pub earlier were at the bus stop. As I walked past them, they whistled at me again. Ignoring them, I started to cross the road, but I had to jump back to the kerb to let a car go by before crossing. I was halfway across the road when powerful arms grabbed me by each elbow and whisked me off my feet. I screamed, looking from side to side I saw the two men in overalls from the pub were the culprits. At first, I was simply angry at them and wriggled to be set free. It wasn't until I found myself trapped against a wall on the far side of the road, with them blocking my escape, that I became frightened.

'We've heard about girls like you plying their trade in the pubs. Didn't expect to see one in Driffield mind,' said the older looking one.

'Do you do it just for drinks or do you expect to be paid?' asked the second one.

'Let me go! I'm a private detective out on business.'

'Aye, sure you are. A sweet little thing like you could tease the best out of any man,' said the first one.

'Please, let me go. I won't tell anyone what you've done if you let me go now.'

'Done, we haven't done anything yet, sweetheart,' said the second one.'

I kicked the first one in the shins, and he hopped back in pain. The second one slapped me across my face, his voice taking on a sinister tone.

'Settle down, we are just having a bit of fun, we'll pay you for our time.'

As tears of pain stung my eyes from his slap, I swung my handbag at the head of the second man, only he easily blocked it with his arm. The second man returned, and together they dragged me towards the park. I tried to scream, but one of them had his hand over my mouth. What happened next is a bit of a blur. All I remember clearly is seeing Rex standing before me asking me if I was alright.

Confused, frightened and shaking so much I could barely stand, I put my arms around him, grateful for someone I knew to be there. The reassurance of him holding me close and the feeling of being safe again was overwhelming.

'Let me take you home, I'll call the police,' said Rex. Hearing the word police seemed to bring to my senses.

'Not yet, I have a job to finish first.'

'What, are you mad?' protested Rex. 'You intend to let them get away with what they've just done.'

'You don't understand; I'm working; I'm on a job.' I looked down at the two men on the ground, one tending a bleeding and misshapen nose and lip, the other groaning in the street gutter.

'How did you know I was in trouble?'

'I was in the car that passed you while you were trying to cross the road. When I saw you, I got my friend to stop and let me out. Good job I did,' said Rex, looking pleased with himself. 'I saw the men follow you and then grab you as you crossed the road.'

'You did this,' I said stupidly, looking at the men laying on the ground, as though I could somehow have been responsible for defending myself against these two men.

He didn't answer; he looked at them and just shrugged his shoulders; they deserved it.'

Looking up at him, the question must have been written on my face.

'Army training, it comes in handy sometimes,' he smiled.

'I need to get away from here. Will you walk me back to my car?'

'Yes, of course, I will, but what about these two?'

'I'm sure they'll think twice before attacking another woman and besides, if I was to press charges the police will expect me to stand up in court and tell everyone what has happened. Apart from being made to look like a fool and a slut for going into a pub on my own. I don't think advertising to the world that I was incapable of looking after myself will do my reputation as a private detective any good, do you?'

'If you insist, but before we go, I have one last thing to do.' Rex lifted the man with the broken nose to his feet.

'Listen, old chap, I know the both of you now. I trust you are both going to go home and reflect on how lucky you both are that my lady friend here is not pressing charges against you. But remember this, if you see her walking towards you, you will cross the street to avoid meeting her. If you find yourselves in the same room with her, you will leave it. Remember, I know your faces. I know how to find you, and I promise you'll never, ever, want that to happen. Now go!' Rex released the man he held against the wall and let him slump to the pavement, again.

I was still trembling as Rex took my arm and led me back down West Gate towards my car. We walked in silence until we found it. I knew I had to say something to him even if it was only thank you, but I was a mess, completely unprepared for what had happened. It had frightened me more than my midnight caller at the hotel. I fumbled in my handbag for my car keys, nearly dropping them as I inserted the key in the door lock.

'Here, let me.' Rex took the keys and opened the passenger door. 'I'll drive you home.'

‘Thank you, but not yet, I need to visit a friend, first.’ He looked at me as though I was mad. But, five minutes later we arrived at Jennifer’s house.

‘Do you mind waiting in the car?’ I asked.

‘If you insist.’ I left Rex sitting in the car and went to knock on Jennifer’s front door. She opened it almost immediately.

‘I saw your car pull up. What have you found out?

‘David is not having an affair.’

‘Oh, thank God for that. Where is he; what is he doing; why isn’t he with you? Sorry, come in. What about your friend in the car?’

‘That’s Rex. No, Jennifer, wait!’ It was too late. Leaving me on the doorstep, she pushed past me to get to the car.

‘Hi Rex, I’m Jennifer, don’t sit there, come in. I’ll make us some tea.’ She returned without waiting for Rex and led me to her living room, stopping in the middle of the room to turn towards me.

‘What is David doing?’

‘Well, he’s not having an affair; I can reassure you of that.’ As I sat down, I forced myself to focus on Jennifer. ‘He has a second job earning some extra cash so that he can surprise you. He asked me not to spoil it for him. He said he’d explain everything to you when he gets home. So don’t spoil his surprise.’

‘That stupid boy, doesn’t he know how much worry he’s given me? I’d better make that tea. Who’s your friend?’ I looked at Rex and could feel my face burning. He smiled back at me, making me feel worse. Jennifer picked up on my embarrassment, ‘No, wait until I come back, she said’

Tea in hand, I explained how David was helping his brother in the pub, and how later, I was confronted by the two workmen outside. She looked shocked until I mentioned how Rex had saved me from who knows what.'

'You were lucky he was passing.'

'Yes, I know. I don't know what I would have done without him.'

'Wait till I tell, Annabelle and Patsy, about it.'

'No, don't, please. Tonight's been embarrassing enough.'

'I'm sorry. If I hadn't been such a fool, this would never have happened to you,' said Jennifer.

'No, I'm the fool. I should have realised how dangerous my job is. I need to think about what to do next. I have to decide if I should carry on as a detective.'

Rex, who had been sitting patiently and silently in an armchair, spoke for the first time since we sat down.

'What you need is a partner, someone to watch your back, someone who can look after himself, and you, when there's trouble about. Can you think of anyone like that?'

'Oh, yes, April, Rex is just the person you are looking for,' squealed Jennifer with delight.

'What, no, I don't know. I need to think about it.' Standing up, I picked up my coat. 'It's time I was going; it's getting late and your David will be home soon.'

'I couldn't do it anyway, not that I wouldn't, it's just that I already have a job. I couldn't be there when you needed me,' said Rex. 'But, I can drive you home.'

'No, I'll drive you home, I owe you that. But first,' 'Jennifer may I use your bathroom. I need to straighten myself up before I go home. Mummy would be shocked if she found out what had happened tonight and Daddy would put a stop to me working.'

As I drove Rex home to Wetwang, I didn't know what to say to him. I didn't want to talk about what had happened, and Rex didn't bring it up. As I pulled to a stop outside Rex's home, I placed my hand on top of his.

'Thank you, Rex.' He didn't answer me, not with words, it was with a look. He already knew what I was trying to say. All he did say was, 'be careful, April. I might not be there for you next time.'

His words of warning carried a chilling edge. I snatched my hand away from his.

When I arrived home Mummy was in the kitchen making cocoa to take up to bed. 'Would you like some, dear?'

'Yes, please. I'm sorry, I missed dinner. Are there any biscuits?'

'What have you been doing?'

'Solving a case for a friend.' I told her about Jennifer and her worries about her husband staying out late on Friday's. It was good to tell her about a case that ended well, but before we knew it, it was getting late. Just before we parted to go to bed, Mummy kissed me on the cheek.

'You need to tell me when you are working late, I worry about you. You get strange men coming out when it gets dark. You know, I sometimes wonder if you should be out at all when it is dark.'

I nearly spilt my cocoa. Had word about tonight reached home already?

‘I made a meat pie for tonight’s dinner and you didn’t come home. You are going to have to eat it for dinner tomorrow, I’m not wasting it.’

‘Yes, Mummy, I’m sorry, it was selfish of me to forget to tell you I would be late. It won’t happen again, I promise.’

‘Good girl.’

I kissed her on the cheek. ‘Good night. I’m taking my cocoa to my room.’

Sighing with relief as I closed my bedroom door, I stripped off my clothes, put on my nightie and climbed into bed. As I sat with my mug of hot chocolate in my hands, I cried until my head hurt as I gave in to the fear and realisation of what could have happened to me.

Chapter Eight

I spent that entire weekend at home, helping mummy clean the house and Daddy deadhead flowers in the garden. The sun shone and in the afternoons we sat in the garden drinking homemade lemonade. It was like being a child again. The hedges and fences around our house, keeping the world at bay and the three of us safe and snug inside. But all too soon the weekend was over.

Monday.

I awoke with a headache, not sure that I wanted to go to work.

When I opened up the office on Exchange Street there was already a pile of post on the floor. I picked it up but the enthusiasm to rummage through it quickly and filter out anything addressed to me was gone. I opened my office door and looked around the room, 'Aunty Violet was right,' I said to the empty room. 'This room is dull and lifeless; it needs a makeover, some colour, something to make it more welcoming. But, who am I trying to kid?' Are my days as a private detective, are coming to an end? I should never have taken this case. I'm only playing at being a private detective.'

Self-doubt was firmly in control. I had to face up to it; Aunty Violet was a horrible person who cared for no one but herself. The claim that someone wanted to kill her was the ramblings of a paranoid old woman with a guilty conscience. And, the person who attacked me in the hotel was probably just some escaped lunatic looking to steal money from an easy target. Why did I ever think I could become a Private Detective based on solving one murder case and embarrassing the local police in doing so? I'd had the arrogance to think I could solve any case that fell into my lap. I dropped the post on my desk and took off my coat, hanging it on the back of the door.

How was I going to explain to Patsy, Annabelle and Jennifer that I was giving up? I closed my office door ensuring the sliding notice showed 'In Conference,' so no one would come barging in. I didn't want to get caught in the kitchen making tea and have to talk about what had happened on Friday or over the weekend. I wanted to be left alone.

A gaggle of voices in the hall warned me that the others had arrived. I heard them go into the kitchen. They were laughing, 'well at least someone has had a good time over the weekend. Before I had time to wallow in my own self-doubt and self-loathing any further the door opened and the three of them bundled in.

'We've brought you some tea and a plate full of biscuits,' said Patsy.

'The sign on my door shows I'm in conference!'

'What, at twenty to nine in the morning. When did you last have anyone call on you at this hour? Anyway we are celebrating how you saved Jennifer's happy marriage,' said Annabelle.

'Thank you, April. I owe you big time for helping me,' said Jennifer. 'How's Rex?'

'What, you've told them about Rex?'

'Yes. I told them that you met him in town and how, as it was getting dark, he walked you to my house.'

'Who is Rex?' asked Patsy plonking her bottom securely in my interviewee's chair. Three pairs of eyes fixed on me like searchlights hunting down an escaped prisoner.

'Have you had a falling out?' asked Jennifer.

'Is that why you've tried to hide away?' asked Annabelle.

'He didn't try to, you know, try it on did he?' pressed Patsy, leaning in closer.

'No, no and no. Rex is just a family friend who I met by accident on Friday. There is nothing between us at all,' I looked at Jennifer as I finished the sentence. She responded with raised eyebrows and with a look that said, 'We'll see.'

'Come on, we haven't got time for this. Sort your post out and let's get ready to start work.' I pushed the post into the centre of my desk.

'We'll continue the interrogation at eleven when we stop for refreshments,' said Patsy as she headed for the door. I was left with three brown envelopes. The first one was a gas bill, the second an electric bill. The third one was larger and thicker with a Harrogate postmark.

It was from Inspector Allswell informing me that the blood toxicology report had come back from York. Aunty's blood contained traces of poison, in a high enough amount to have brought on her heart failure. There was a copy of the toxicology report included with the letter but, the report did not specify which poison had been used. Regrettably, the Inspector was not going to tell me everything. Inspector Allswell's letter also informed me that Aunty Violet's death had been upgraded to a murder investigation and that the attack on me had been changed to attempted murder and was no longer classed as a robbery. I read the letter twice to make sure I hadn't missed anything. For some strange reason, I felt jubilant. I lay the letter on my desk and leaned back in my chair, questions racing through my mind.

'Which poison had been used? Why wasn't it listed in the report? Was the Inspector holding that information back from me for a reason or didn't he know what it was?'

The old April Showers was back and as determined as ever to continue the investigation.

'Who should I interview next?' With my renewed confidence I flipped open my notes and scanned the list, The Reverend Warlock and his wife were at the top of my list, their address was The Vicarage, Easington. I didn't know the area well, though I knew where it was. The village is located at the top of a narrow spit of land called Spurn Point, which runs out into the River Humber estuary. I estimated the drive to be about forty miles each way, mostly along narrow, twisting country roads. I looked at my clock. It would be over an hour's drive in each direction, plus the time I spent with the Reverend; but I could be back in Driffield by two o'clock at the latest, which meant I wouldn't need to inform Mummy that I would be home late for dinner. I placed

Inspector Allswell's letter and the toxicology report in my file and then tucked put the file away in my drawer. Picking up my handbag, I was on my way to the door when I was stopped dead in my tracks.

'Good morning, I thought I'd come and see how you are. I'm sorry, are you going somewhere.' Rex blocked my exit.

'Yes. I'm well, thank you. As you can see I'm going out.'

'Mind if I tag along.'

I took a step back from the door, now I was confused. I had become so focused on the case again and getting to Easington, that the sudden appearance of Rex had ruined my train of thought. I couldn't dismiss him, not after Friday night, but I didn't want him to come along either.

'I'm going to visit a suspect. It's a long drive and I may be gone a few hours. You can come if you like, but I don't know when I'll get back.' I smiled at him warmly and stepped to the side to get around him, not believing he would want to go with me.

'Great, I haven't anything to do today. I know, I'll treat you to lunch while we are out if you wish, that is? Where are we going?'

I gave in, 'Easington!'

'Oh, very nice; I don't think I've ever been there.'

As we drove out of Driffield I couldn't help but feel irritated by the way Rex had invited himself along. He was using Friday night as a lever, knowing I couldn't refuse him. Though, secretly, I felt it reassuring to have him with me. I glanced at him and smiled.

Why are you really here? What are you after? I wondered.

‘I thought you had a job at the BBC. Why aren’t you at work?’

‘I will be, soon.’

‘What is that supposed to mean?’ I took my eyes off the road for a second to glance at him. He was smiling at me, with an irritating expression on his face that said, ‘I know something you don’t,’ look.

‘Well, they’ve given me a couple of weeks to sort a few things out. You know settle in at home after leaving the army. That sort of thing’

‘That sounds unusually generous of them.’

‘Yes, I suppose it is. I expect it is because I’m still an army reservist.’

‘You mean you are still in the army?’

‘No. Well, yes. I can’t tell you. I just work for the BBC. I suppose I’m a Civil Servant.’

‘I thought they all worked in London, wore bowler hats and carried umbrellas?’

He smiled that smile at me again, ‘Only when there is an R in the month.’

‘Stop it, now you are making fun of me!’

‘I’m sorry. It’s true, I’m a civil servant who works for the BBC and as such, I cannot talk about what I do.’

I felt as though I was being treated like a child. But for what he did for me last Friday evening, I would have stopped the car and thrown him out.

Not concentrating on my driving because I was so angry with him, I had a near-miss with a car coming in the opposite direction. It happened on a tight bend. I braked hard and turned the car in towards the kerb at the last minute, narrowly missing the other car. I pulled over and stopped to get my breath back.

'Now, look what you made me do.' I screamed at him.

He didn't answer me. He just kept staring forward out of the windscreen. That irked me even more than if he'd come straight out and blamed me for the near-miss.

We made the rest of the journey in cold, tense, silence until I pulled up outside the vicarage in Easington which was down a lane opposite the village church. All Saints Church stood proudly on a mound in the centre of the village. The vicarage seemed to be a rather large house and garden for the vicar of such a small village, but after giving it some thought it was probably because the church and village were miles from any sizable town and had to service a large rural parish. The vicar would need the extra land to grow his own vegetables and probably run a few chickens and a pig or two.

I ordered Rex to wait in the car to which he saluted and responded with 'Yes, Ma'am. So I slammed the car door as loudly as I could. As I opened the garden gate I entered a well-tended garden with more varieties of Dianthus than I had ever seen before. The scent was heady and intoxicating. After knocking on the vicarage door, it was Mrs Warlock who answered, 'May I help you?' she asked.

'I'm sorry to disturb you and arrive unannounced. My name is April Showers. We met briefly in Harrogate; at the hotel.' Mrs Warlock looked surprised as she remembered me.

'What is it you want?' she asked.

I handed over my business card, 'I would like to speak to you and the Reverend Warlock about what happened that day.' Mrs Warlock looked back over her shoulder for a moment as though looking for help or seeking advice from someone on what to do. Then she looked at my card again and then at me.

'You had better come in.' I followed her to the front sitting room.

'The Reverend is in his study, I will see if he has time to speak to you.' She left me to go find her husband.

The sitting room showed signs of age and neglect. It was clean, there were no signs of dust anywhere, but, it was just that the carpets and furniture had seen better days. A large slate mantle clock ticked rhythmically above the fireplace. Mrs Warlock returned. 'The Reverend is just finishing his sermon for Sunday, he will come through shortly. Would you like some tea?'

'Yes please.' I continued to study the room. A large wireless sat on an occasional table near the window. Books lined the alcoves on either side of the fireplace and a brass coal scuttle sat in the cold hearth. A vase of fresh garden flowers adorned a long, heavy, dark wood sideboard that must have been in the house since the old queen passed away. Mrs Warlock returned with a tray laden with tea and fruit cake. She set them down on a low table in front of the fireplace, 'milk and sugar?'

'Just milk, please.' She handed me the cup and saucer. 'Help yourself to the cake. I made it myself.'

'Thank you. I was just admiring your flowers.' I looked up at the Victorian sideboard.

'Yes, they are nice, aren't they? We have a lovely large garden here. Christian likes to grow vegetables, whereas I prefer traditional English flowers.

‘Don’t you find it lonely here in such a small village?’ The question seemed to catch Mrs Warlock off guard.

‘Not really, the church attracts people from all the surrounding villages on Sunday and the Reverend is constantly trying to help those in need. You are right though, this is a very rural community and a bit isolated. The young people today all head off to Hull, Leeds and York to find work. They can earn more money in the towns, these days. So we are left to do what we can for the poor and the elderly.’

‘It must have come as a nice surprise to get the invite to Harrogate?’ I asked, changing the topic.

‘A surprise, certainly. Though for the life of me, I can’t understand why we agreed to go when we knew that woman was to be there, but Christian insisted even though it would mean him missing a Sunday service. He said it was our duty to forgive the sins of others and that if we didn’t go it would look like we had let her win. And that we had to show her that we had risen above what she did to us and had forgiven her.’

‘You know, I was there as her companion, but she was also my Aunty. I gather you didn’t like her, so may I ask what happened between you both. Only, after interviewing other guests from the hotel, I have learned that there was history between and Aunty Violet as well.’

‘Yes, of course. I will never forget that day. It started like any other, except it was the day of the village fete. Every year the Parish Councillors organised a fete on the school football field, not here, of course, we lived in Hutton Cranswick back then. All was going well until Christian was asked to judge the flower competition. There were a lot of entries and standards were high. He studied the exhibits for some time, they were all very good but he had to pick a winner. He chose Fred Murray's carnations in the end. They are his favourites you see. Well, when the winner was announced at the end of the fete, there was uproar. Some people accused Fred of stealing the flowers from Jack Pringles allotment. Some people accused him of buying them from a gardener who worked at Bishop Burton house. But your Aunty Violet was the worst of all. She had spent a lot of time and money growing some rare orchids and under normal circumstances, they may well have won the competition, but Christian found a withered petal on one of the flower heads. She accused Christian of deliberately sabotaging her blooms because Fred Murray was his friend. But, the thing is; it was a blind competition, none of the entries was visibly labelled, everyone had to leave their names under the plant they had entered. She accused Christian and Fred of fixing the competition and demanded Fred be disqualified for cheating and a new judge be appointed. The Parish Councillors disagreed and said Christian's decision should stand. It took a few weeks for the fuss to die down and life got back to normal. Or so we thought. It turned out that Fred Murray, the winner had received so much publicity in the press about his carnations that the local ITV television news reporter heard about them. He went to see Fred and the flowers he grew. He told Fred that he would arrange for him to appear on the television in The Gardening Club with Percy Thrower. Fred was thrilled and told everyone about it. And then, come the day of his television recording, he and Percy Thrower hit it off right from the start. Percy kept asking Fred to come back on his show. Fred became so popular with the viewers that he attained national notoriety and acclaim, winning a prestigious television award. After that, he wrote a book which made him so much money that he was able to set up his own garden centre in Ferndown in Dorset. It made him a fortune almost overnight.

Well, a narcissistic woman like Violet Birch was never going to forgive or forget Christian for missing out on a chance of something like that when she should have won the competition and got all that fame. So, she started a rumour about Christian, saying that he was using the money from the church collection to go out at night and entertain young men in private clubs around Hull. There was never any proof, but you know what people are like. The Bishop heard about the rumours and thought it prudent to move Christian to a small, out of the way, village parish where no one knew him, and so his promising career within the church ground to a halt, and he never made bishop. He's never got over the disappointment. He's tried several times to explain to the Bishop that it was all a tissue of lies, but the Bishop is old school and won't have the church's name brought into disrepute, so we upped-sticks and moved to this backwater.'

It was just as Mrs Warlock was finishing her story that the Reverend entered the room.

'I'm sorry to be late; I just had to finish writing my sermon. One has to do these things when the spirit moves within one. I hope Faith has been keeping you entertained. Now then Young Lady how may I help you?'

'This is Miss Showers, she's a private detective. It turns out that Violet Birch was her aunt. Do you remember her, dear? Miss Showers was at the hotel in Harrogate with us all.'

I had accessed Mrs Warlock to be about the same age as my mother. But, the reverend looked younger than his wife. Her lined face gave me the impression of someone older. It was only when I looked closer that I saw the signs of someone younger and more in keeping with the vicar's age.

'Welcome, my dear. I thought you looked a little familiar. The trouble is I see so many people I get a bit confused as to where I have met them before. Violet Birch, eh, well that's a name I didn't think I would ever hear again. Don't tell me she's come back from the dead to haunt some poor unsuspecting soul. I sorry my dear, I shouldn't be so flippant about a member of your family.'

'Mrs Warlock has been telling me about how Aunty Violet ruined your career in the church. I'm sorry. I am learning a lot about my aunt, all of it bad. I always knew she was a difficult person. She has upset plenty of people in our family, but it seems we only knew half the story. The main reason why I'm here is to inform you that my aunt died of heart failure. I just thought it was the right thing to do. To come and let you know, that is.' He didn't react to what I said his expression stayed the same, so I stood up to leave.

'That is very kind of you,' said Faith.

I noted that Mrs Warlock looked a little relieved now that I was leaving. 'Not at all, and please, let me apologise for the trouble my aunt has caused you both.'

'You know what they say,' said the vicar, holding out his hand, 'you can choose your friends, but not your relatives.' I shook his hand before Mrs Warlock led me to the door.

'Thank you for talking to me, I understand my aunt a little better now.' As she closed the front door behind me I walked slowly down the garden path thinking over what Faith had told me. It was only as I reached the front gate that I remembered that I'd left Rex sitting in the car. For a second I didn't care, I hadn't wanted him tagging along, then, guilt pricked my conscience. As soon as Rex saw me he got out of the car, 'I promised you lunch; would you like me to drive?'

I owed him this treat, 'very well, thank you.'

'There is a hotel in Beverley; its restaurant has a good reputation. We'll go there for lunch.' Rex brought my car to life and set off back the way we had come, before asking. 'How did you get on with the Reverend?'

'It was his wife I spoke to for the most part. It seems like the Reverend had a promising career within the church until he fell afoul of Aunty's interference. I got the impression that Reverend Warlock has accepted his loss. It's his wife who seems to be suffering the most in that rundown vicarage. At first, I miss-took her for a much older woman. It was only when I looked harder, that I realised her older hard warn looks had probably been brought on by stress.'

'Do you think the Reverend was involved in your Aunty's death in some way?'

'No, not really; he didn't seem the type.'

'Who do you plan to interview next?' asked Rex as we left the village.

'I don't know yet. I'll have to go back to my office, make some notes, and then decide. I just have to be patient. One of my suspects will do or say something that will make me suspicious or give me a clue to work on.'

'Is there anything I can do to help?'

'No, thank you, I can manage. Friday night was the first time anything like that has happened. I'll be more careful next time. Anyway, what help can a civil servant possibly be to a private detective, unless you want a job as my secretary?'

'Ooh, that was a bit below the belt.' Rex put on a pained expression.

'Sorry, that was rather unkind considering how you saved me from those men.'

'Apology accepted. Look; all I can tell you about my job is that I'm a Civil Servant because I work for the BBC.'

'Yes, so you have said. But you've never said what you do at the BBC.' There was a pause before Rex spoke again.

'Look, you must promise not to breathe a word to anyone; promise, on pain of death?'

'Now you are being melodramatic?'

'No, I'm serious, not a word, promise?' I nodded my agreement.

'Whilst I was doing my national service out in Kenya. You know about the troubles out there?'

'Yes.'

'Well, I was part of a signals company collating messages and passing on information to our army patrols and local police. I was good at it, so my Commanding Officer sent me for some further electronics training in England. I came out top of my group, so, instead of sending me back to Kenya, my C.O. asked me if I wanted to volunteer for more advanced communications training. Well, of course, I said yes. I didn't want to go back to Africa. Yet again, I came top of my class. That's when everything changed. I was called into the C.Os. office again. There were two men in suits with him. They said they were looking for men with an aptitude for radio communications, electronics and cryptography. They asked me if I would be interested in joining them and doing something important for my country. I didn't know what they were referring to and they wouldn't elaborate, except to say, it would entitle me to early release from my National Service if I joined them. So I said yes. They sent me for even more training at a big house near London where I learnt what my new job was all about. After I finished my training they sent me to the radio station outside Scarborough.'

'The one with all the big masts?'

'Yes, that's the one.'

'I thought that was a BBC radio station?'

'Good, that's what I hoped you would say.'

'But, you mean it's not a BBC radio station?'

'Let's just say it is, and leave it at that?'

'You are saying it's not a BBC radio station. So what is it?'

'It's the place where I work.'

'Huh, you are infuriating.'

Rex brought the car to a halt in Beverley outside the hotel/restaurant on North Bar Within. I wasn't sure if I was doing the right thing by accepting Rex's invitation to lunch, I didn't want him to get the idea I was interested in him but, a debt of honour had to be repaid. Anyway, what harm could it do? By this evening I would be able to put Rex out of my mind. I was impressed with his location for lunch, he'd chosen the best hotel and restaurant in Beverley. I'd been here before with my parents but rarely and only on special occasions. Inside, the restaurant had wood-panelled walls on which hung oil paints of country scenes. Gleaming silver cutlery, cut glass crystal and crisp white napkins adorned every table. An immaculately dressed waiter showed us to a table for two by the window.

'When you said you would take me to lunch, I wasn't expecting you to bring me here.' A waiter arrived with a bottle of wine and showed it to Rex. He nodded and the waiter took the wine away to open it.

'You had this planned. The table, the wine, you never said a word when we arrived, they just knew what you wanted?'

'Yes, I wanted to impress you.'

'Well, I'm impressed.' I conceded, conscience-stricken at the way I had been avoiding him since he came home from the army.

I started with mushroom soup, followed by a chicken salad. Rex ordered the Brussels Pâté with lamb cutlets, sauté potatoes and asparagus to follow.

Over lunch, Rex enquired after my parents and then more directly about the case I was working on. He didn't offer me advice but simply listened to my enthusiasm for investigating the crime. With just a few minor questions from Rex, I explained everything that had happened from the time Aunty

Violet and I arrived in Harrogate, to me leaving the following day. He sat quietly, though Rex did raise his eyebrows a little when I told him about my night-time intruder. Over coffee, Rex removed a notebook from the inside pocket of his jacket and wrote down a telephone number, and then handed it to me.

'If you ever need my help, you can call me.'

'Thank you, Rex, that is very kind of you. You can be reassured that I have learnt my lesson now and I will be more cautious about visiting pubs on my own in the future. That was a very nice lunch. However, I still need to return to the office and write up today's notes. Is there somewhere I can drop you?'

'No, thank you, I shall walk into town before getting the bus home. My leave finishes at the end of the week then it is back to work. Come, I will see you to your car. As I settled into the driver's seat Rex said, 'Farewell.' I drove out into the road, heading towards North Bar before stopping and doing a U-turn in the road. Driving back towards the town centre, I saw Rex up ahead. I drove past him and then parked my car in the market square before walking back in the direction that I had seen him. We met just as he was about to enter the bank on the corner of the square.

'April! You said you were going back to Driffield.'

'I changed my mind. It's a nice day and I fancied a wander around Beverley. I just happened to see you and thought I'd join you. You don't mind do you?'

'No, not at all, I'll just be a minute or two in here then I'm going to see my tailor to get measured for a suit. Do you fancy giving me some advice on the type of material I should choose?' asked Rex.

'I'd love to.'

The tailor's shop was just across from the bank and faced onto Saturday Market. While Rex was being measured, I leafed through samples of fabric, setting aside examples for Rex to see.

'Is your suit for a special occasion or just casual?' I asked.

'Work.'

'Umm, then it needs to be smart, not so loud that you stand out, but distinctive enough to show taste and professionalism.'

'You see, I knew you would know what I needed.'

'How about one of these then?' I suggested, showing him my choices.

'You decide,' said Rex.

'Well, I think the Navy Blue with the very fine grey pinstripe is your colour.'

'A very fine choice, Miss,' interjected the tailor.

'I agree,' said Rex.

'That's me done,' said Rex as we left the tailor's shop. 'I'll have to get the bus home, now or I'll get caught up with everyone as they leave work.'

'Why don't you have a car of your own?' I asked.

'I will by the end of the week; that is the next thing on my shopping list; care to help me choose one of those as well?'

'Maybe, if I'm not too busy. I do have this case to solve, you know? I may be out of town when it's time for you to choose it.'

'I shall call you at your office on Wednesday morning, that's when I've arranged a test drive with the garage.'

'I shall have to check my diary when I get back to the office.'

'Fine, do that, I will call for you on Wednesday.' Rex turned towards the bus terminal in Saturday Market, but before he'd taken more than half a dozen steps I called after him.

'If you like, I could drive you home.'

'No it's fine, I'll get the bus.'

'Rex!' He stopped and turned around.

'I owe you for lunch, I insist.'

'Oh well, if you insist, that's a different matter,' he responded, secretly pleased.

As I drove Rex home to Wetwang, he told me more about his time in Kenya. How the people had revolted and formed the Kenya Land and Freedom Army turning against the white settlers.

'The official version of what is going on out there is that the communists are stirring up the local people and turning them against the settlers. In truth, it's more complicated than that. But that is for the politicians to sort out. My job was to send coded messages to our forces after the intelligence people had learnt where the KLFA were going to strike next. After a while, I suggested that I should be working directly with the intelligence guys. That way I could get their messages out quicker. The colonel arranged it, saying he would give me a chance to show what I could do. I not only sent messages to our own military units, updating them on where trouble was brewing, I also sent false messages to the different factions of the KLFA to cause confusion between their groups. It worked so well and I had them so confused at times, that they even started fighting amongst themselves. Divide and rule as the colonel used to say. It was shortly after that that the colonel sent me for further training in intelligence and signalling. You know the rest.'

'How exciting.'

'Not really; it's lots of listening and writing down of gibberish before someone else decodes it.' As we pulled up outside Rex's house he asked me in for coffee.

'No thanks, I really do need to get back to the office. I have to plan my next interview.'

'Don't forget to leave Wednesday free,' said Rex as he closed the car door.

As I drove back to Driffield I went over what I had learnt about the case so far. It wasn't a great deal, but having related it all to Rex over lunch, it somehow seemed clearer in my mind. Also, unexpectedly, I had enjoyed my day with Rex.

When I arrived home that evening, Mother was waiting for me.

'What's wrong?' I asked her as she walked towards me from the front door.

'Nothing dear, I'm just pleased to see you.' She kissed me and looped her arm through mine.

'Mummy, You don't normally stand on the doorstep waiting for me to get home, what has happened?'

'Nothing, everything is fine. I just thought you might have something to tell me before your father got home.'

'Tell you? About what?'

'I received a telephone call from Margery Offshot, she saw you in Beverley, with a man.'

'Oh, I see. What are we having for dinner?' I asked, hoping to change the subject.

'Well, who is he?' she persisted.

'No one special, just Rex, he took me to lunch.'

'I thought you said you didn't like Rex.'

'I don't.' It was only a half-lie, I just didn't like the idea of us being thrust together by my mother.

'Then why did he buy you lunch?'

'I don't know; you'll have to ask him.'

'April, stop it, I'm your mother. I need to know these things.'

'If you must know he starts his new job next week and he had a bit of free time on his hands. So he popped into my office this morning for a chat. We went to interview a suspect together, and on the way home he bought me lunch.'

'Oh, that is nice. I always did like that boy. When will you be seeing him again? You must invite him over.'

'No mother. I'm too busy and so is he.'

Chapter Nine

Tuesday.

On the day after my lunch with Rex, I sat at my desk, list of suspects in hand, trying to decide on whom to visit next, but kept getting distracted by thoughts of Rex, our lunch and mother's matchmaking attempts, finally forcing myself to concentrate on the task at hand.

Let's see, what about the Ramsbottoms? I asked myself. 'They had kept a low profile after the dinner. I wonder if they are hiding, something? When everyone else in the room had been as keen as mustard to leave the dining room, they had stayed calm and awaited their turn to give their statements. Had they planned and rehearsed what to do after killing Aunty?

Looking up their address told me they lived near Richmond in North Yorkshire. It would be a long drive. A glance out of my office window confirmed that the sun was shining and it was a lovely day out there.

It's as good a day as any and I've never been to Richmond. I hear it's a very beautiful part of the country. I needed no further convincing. The day was perfect for a trip out into the countryside. The final decider was the sound of a tortured violin penetrating my room from above as one of Patsy's pupils started their music lesson.

Unfamiliar with the route, I consulted my Michelin route map of the north of England. Richmond was further away than I had imagined. The most favourable route seemed to be from Driffield across to York and then on towards Harrogate to pick up the A1 and then head north to Richmond. Having only recently passed my driving test, the idea of driving on a busy road like the A1, with lots of lorry traffic travelling at speed, gave me goosebumps up and down my arms. However, as the noise from the room above grew worse, the fear of driving on the A1, dissipated.

With just one stop to fill up with petrol, I arrived in Richmond in one piece and parked in the marketplace. After such a long drive, I thought I'd treat myself to a cup of tea, a sandwich and a cream cake. Maggie's tearoom, just across the empty marketplace, looked inviting. So, before asking around for directions to the Ramsbottom farm, I treated myself to a little refreshment.

It turned out that Maggie had never heard of the Ramsbottom's, but pointed me toward Arkwright's the ironmongers.

'If they are farmers, Arkwright will know them,' she informed me. I thanked her and strolled across the marketplace, enjoying the sunshine. Arkwright's was part of an island of shops that sat in the centre of the marketplace and Arkwright's was the centre shop of three. Outside the green and white painted shop stood an animal feed trough, rolls of chicken wire and a galvanised dustbin. In the shop window, amidst a myriad of strange tools and other items, hung bicycle wheels, tyres and a sign advertising BP Motor Spirit. When I opened the shop door a tiny bell rang to announce my arrival. Inside I was met with the smell of oil, dust and ageing wood. As I looked around, every inch of wall space was covered with goods hanging from nails. The floor was littered with wooden boxes and sacks with just a narrow maze of walkways between them. All the boxes had been left with their lids off and their contents on display. There seemed no order to the boxes and sacks. One filled with taps was next to one filled with door hinges, sacks of seed potatoes sat side by side with bags of chicken feed. Suddenly, I got the urge to tidy up and put the clutter into some sort of order. But the sound of a cough took my attention away from the chaos of the shop and towards the direction of the sound. A short, hairless man stood behind the counter wearing a tan coloured shop coat and tiny wire-rimmed glasses.

'Mr Arkwright?' I asked.

'Aye. That's right.'

'My name is Miss Showers. I'm looking for the Ramsbottom farm. Maggie in the tearoom said you would know where it is.'

'Aye.'

I waited for him to continue, but he just kept staring at me. 'Could you give me directions, please?'

'Aye.'

I continued to wait for a more helpful response until I gave in, 'Well?'

'Do you need to buy a notebook and pencil?' he asked me.

'No, why?'

'You'll need one.'

'Why?'

'To write down directions of course.' I was getting a little vexed now, but went along with his suggestion and retrieved my notebook from my handbag, in the hope it would speed things along. Poised with notebook and pencil I said, 'ready when you are, Mr Arkwright.'

'Don't you want to buy owt?' I signed and looked around the shop. Remembering my father's birthday was coming up soon, I bought a hand trowel with a matching fork. He laid them reverently on the counter and asked for five shillings and sixpence.

'Now, Mr Arkwright, if you please. It is very important that I speak to Mr and Mrs Ramsbottom.'

'Are you getting the bus or walking?'

'I have a car, Mr Arkwright.'

'Ah, yes. You'll be one of them city girls then. I thought you looked a bit posh for a farm girl.'

'Mr Arkwright! The directions, if you please.'

'Oh aye, well let me see. You go out of the shop and turn right, though you could go left if you prefer. Look for the castle. It's that big place with the surrounding wall.'

I gave him an incredulous look.

'Well,' he continued. 'You go past there on to Bar Castle Hill. No, no, wait a minute that will bring you back to the market. You want New Road and then onto Bridge Street. Not Bargate, don't get the two confused or you'll be going in the wrong direction. Bridge Street will take you over the river. If you cross the river you know you are going the right way. Slee Gill. That's what you want next, but don't go too fast there a bit of a bend in't road. Then you go past the Holly Hill Inn, a nice drop of ale in there, but the landlord charges top prices and he waters down his beer that he sells to the tourists. I don't know how he's got the nerve. Mind you, his dad were just the same, money-mad, do owt to make an extra penny, them two would. Now, where was I?'

'I drive past the Holly Hill Inn,' I reminded him.

'Aye, that's right. You been up this way afore?'

'No, Mr Arkwright. The Ramsbottom farm, if you please?'

'Aye, right you are. Hudswell Lane, you want Hudswell Lane. You go down there a bit and't farm is ont' right. You can't miss it. You'll see beasts in't field.'

'Thank you, Mr Arkwright,' and with my father's birthday present in hand I left the shop.

With my directions to the farm propped up against my windscreen, I set off for the Ramsbottom farm; luckily it was only a few minute's drive out of Richmond and easy to find with Mr Arkwright's directions. Pulling up at the farm gate which displayed the family name, I could see that there was a long lane to traverse before reaching the farmhouse. After a series of bone-rattling jolts, I questioned my wisdom of driving along the lane and not walking, as the floor of my car scraped over the uneven ground. I was relieved when my car made it to the farmyard without falling apart. Unfortunately, it was only after I opened the car door that I noticed the car was standing in a sea of sloppy mud.

The sound of my arrival had brought Mrs Ramsbottom to the farmhouse door and there she stood, arms folded beneath an ample bosom, watching me as I tried to decide if I was going to get out of the car or not. She was wearing a flower-patterned apron over a cotton dress and had pink, fleece trimmed slippers on her feet. She didn't wait at the door for long before returning inside. However, at least she left the door open for me. Having come too far to be put off by mud now, it was time to take the plunge. Stepping out of the car, my sensible town shoes were no match for the black, cold, smelly ooze. As the dampness penetrated through to my toes, I tried tip-toeing through the filth, but after slipping twice; I gave in to the inevitable and squelched my way to the kitchen door. I knocked on the door and looked down at my feet before entering. Mud clung to my shoes, making them feel twice as heavy as they should have been; they were ruined. Mrs Ramsbottom's voice floated out to me.

'Take your shoes off and come in, Lass.' Just inside the door, I noted sets of wellingtons, boots and slippers laid in a neat row against the wall. I made a mental note to buy myself a pair of wellingtons and keep them in the car for any future visits to farms. Crossing the small boot-room to the kitchen door opposite, I found Mrs Ramsbottom pouring tea into three cups on the kitchen table. Feeling a little self-conscience I looked down at my feet; I could see the tidemark left by the muddy water which had penetrated my shoes, drying around the feet of my stockings. As I crossed to the table I spotted a Border Collie laying in its basket. Its tail wagging as crossed the kitchen.

'That's Bess; soppy old girl is getting old now, but she's more part of the family than a working dog now. Sit yourself down; Ewan will be here in a minute. Help yourself to milk and sugar. I've got a nice bit of fruit cake left from yesterday, Ewan likes a bit of cake with his tea.'

'Thank you. My name is April...'

'Aye, Lass. I remember you from Harrogate. What brings you out this way?' She cut me a wedge of cake big enough to use as a doorstop. Mrs Ramsbottom had only just sat down when the master of the house entered the kitchen.

'Oh, I wondered who the car belonged to. I saw you drive up the old lane. I'm surprised you made it, what with it being full of all them there big holes. Why didn't you use the main farm entrance further down't road?'

I took a bite out of the cake and didn't answer, but I could feel myself blushing. I washed the cake down with a mouthful of tea before speaking.

'I'm here to ask you some questions, if I may. You see, the lady that died at the hotel in Harrogate was my Aunty Violet and I have since found out that everyone who was at the hotel that weekend knew her, but not necessarily each other. I'm trying to find what the connection is between us all.'

'Why?' asked Mrs Ramsbottom. The question threw me for a moment.

'Well, as you know she died and I know very little of her past, so I'm trying to find out if there were any other family members at the hotel that I didn't know about.' It was the best reason I could come up with on the spur of the moment.

The fact that Mrs Ramsbottom had recognised me so soon had ruffled me a little.

'No, we are not related to her or you, as far as I know, Lass. We hated the old woman. Good riddance to her; no offence meant to yourself,' said Ewan. 'I'm sure your now't like your Aunty.'

'What was it that made you dislike her so much?' I asked.

Mr and Mrs Ramsbottom looked at each other before Ewan answered.

'It were a good few years back now. We had a different farm then, a small sheep farm on the Wolds near Thixendale. We may have been small, but we produced award-winning sheep's cheeses, which we sold throughout Yorkshire. We didn't know it at the time, but your Aunty was a regular customer.'

The first we knew of anything being wrong was when health Inspectors came round snooping and asking questions, in't that right Corrie?' She nodded in response. 'Your Aunty had put in a complained against us,' he continued. 'It even got reported in the local papers. Your Aunty liked her cheeses and always bought a large wedge from us when she passed the farm shop. We got to hear that every month she held a port, cheese and biscuits gathering for the ladies of the Women's Institute. Seems like, she fancied herself as a leader of the local branch when they next voted for their officials. Well, after one such get together her lady pals all became very ill with a stomach upset and your Aunty blamed our cheese. She was so incensed over the humiliation of them all being made ill, that she wrote to the newspapers and the council complaining that the hygiene at the farm was below standard. It caused us no end of trouble before the Ministry of Health got around to declaring that the illness had not come from us. But, word had got out about our lack of hygiene and we lost all our biggest customers. Our business went sour, finally collapsing not long after. Later on, we heard from an old customer that your Aunty had got ill again, but from eating cheese bought in a shop. That's when she called in the pest controllers because she'd found mice in her pantry and they had been helping themselves to the cheese. It was the mice that had caused the cheese to become tainted and make all her friends ill. But it was too late for our business by then, the papers weren't interested in putting the story right. We had to give up on sheep farming and making cheese and we moved away from Thixendale. We came here and started again but with cattle this time.'

'I'm sorry, Lass. But, we won't lose any sleep over the death of your Aunty. She caused us a lot of trouble and the loss of a great deal of money. If you must know, we are still paying off the loan we got to buy this place,' added Mrs Ramsbottom. 'I'm sure I can speak for Ewan when I say, we are both sorry for your loss, but the world is a better place with that woman not in it.'

Their bluntness hurt me, even though I too held no great affection for my Aunty. Mr Ramsbottom continued before I could formulate a suitable rebuke.

'The only good thing that has come out of this is that we now have a prize herd of beef. We breed them to sell to other farmers. Financially, touch wood, we'll be back on our feet again soon, but it was touch and go for a while.'

I thanked the Ramsbottoms for their time and left still feeling slighted at their attack on a member of my family. I couldn't understand why I should feel so hurt, but I did.

At the backdoor, I cringed as I slipped my feet into my cold, damp, muddy shoes and crossed the yard to my car with another story to add to my collection of people destroyed by my Aunty, but who had fought back against adversity to restart their lives afresh somewhere else. Sitting in my car with cold, damp feet, I swore revenge on the person who had murdered Aunty Violet and in doing had so caused me to ruin my favourite pair of shoes. I had no alternative but to drive back to Richmond and buy a new pair of shoes to drive home in. As I looked at myself in the review mirror, I apologised to Aunty.

'You are far more important to me than my shoes or the Ramsbottoms, even if you were not a very nice person.'

I arrived home still smelling like a farmyard to find Rex waiting for me. Mummy seemed very pleased to have him there.

'I've asked Rex to stay for dinner dear.' Her eyes sparkled as she told me. I couldn't believe it. I was standing there with mud splattered stockings, smelling like a dung heap, and Mummy had invited Rex to dinner. All I wanted to do was have a bath, eat and go to bed with a good book.

'Been for a walk in the countryside?' asked Rex with a smile, as he looked at my legs. I slammed the sitting-room door as I ran upstairs.

I was enjoying a good soak with lots of bubble bath in the water when there was a gentle tap on the bathroom door followed by, 'dinner will be ready in five minutes, dear.'

At dinner, Rex reminded me about going with him to choose his new car. Mummy looked at me and smiled.

'I'm just returning a favour, Mummy. Don't read anything into it,' I said, rather sharper than I should have. Rex stayed for an hour before declaring he ought to catch the bus home.

'Oh, don't worry about that, April will run you home in her car.'

'Mummy!'

'No, don't bother; I'll be fine on the bus,' said Rex.

'I insist. It looks like rain and April has nothing else to do this evening. April, take our guest home. I'm sure he would have done the same for you if the situation were reversed.'

When I opened the car door, I was greeted with the stink of wet mud mixed with cow manure.

'It's an interesting aroma your car has acquired. I'll have to ask the garage if it's available with the model I'm buying.'

Slamming the car door, I wound down the window, started the car and heard gravel hitting the bottom of the car's wheel arches as I exited the drive. I drove him home without speaking to him and as soon as he was out of the car, I drove off without saying goodbye.

Wednesday.

The postman tapped on my open office door before coming in and dropping the day's delivery on my desk.

'You working on any good murder cases, Miss Showers?' he asked.

'Yes, George, as it happens.'

'What really; who are you after?'

'A real nasty murderer of the most hideous crimes – it's a woman who strangles her victims and then dumps their bodies in a dustbin so they can be carted away with the rest of the rubbish.'

'Wow, any idea on who it might be?' George leaned in a little closer.

I lowered my voice. 'The crucial clue comes from the choice of her victims. They are all postmen who ask too many questions.' George stood back and straightened his jacket.

'Good one, April, you had me going for a minute. I thought I was going to have a bit of tasty gossip to take back to the sorting office, then.'

'Maybe next time George, bye!' I shuffled through the post, one for Patsy, one for Jennifer, a large one for Annabelle, probably a manuscript for editing; and an official-looking one for me.

Um, this is no gas bill. The envelope was made from good quality paper, so I opened it carefully. Reading the letterhead I noted it was from a solicitor's practice in Pocklington, Messrs Blackthorn, Cherry and Maple. The letter stated that they had learned of Aunty Violet's death, and in accordance with her will, to whom I was the only beneficiary, they would hold her estate in trust for me until the murderer of Miss Violet Rose Birch had been arrested and found guilty. Then there was a bit that seemed very unfair. It specified that I had to have taken no part in the murder or the planning of it. I was stunned. Aunty had left everything to me, but I might not see a penny of it if I didn't find her murderer or the police thought I'd been involved in her death in some way. The solicitors or Aunty were implying that I could have been involved in her death. I couldn't believe it, and to make matters worse, there was a clause in her will which stated that should I fail to fulfil the conditions of the will, her entire estate was to be dissolved, and the proceeds donated to a cats charity.

When the police find out about Aunty's will they'll jump to conclusions and include me as a suspect, I may even get arrested. My initial thoughts were to telephone Inspector Allswell, be upfront with him and tell him about the contents of the letter and ask for his advice, but then changed my mind. It could be two or three days before the police got to hear about my connection to Aunty Violet's will. I needed to get a move on. It was time to interview the last two suspects on my list and as soon as possible find the murderer and prove my innocence.

Roofus Stone and his wife lived in York. Thankfully, their address was a shop off Hull Road, which was on the main route into the city. When I arrived, I found an end terrace house with a lane to the side. A sign directing me to Stone's Builders Merchants pointed to the rear of the property. I drove into the yard to find Mr Stone had a very large garage-type structure with a board above the entrance advertising building materials at low prices. At the back of the yard stood stacks of bricks, with sand piled high in the corner. I entered the building.

'Is there something I can help you with, Miss?' I turned to find a tall, muscular man in overalls coming out of a side door.

'Mr Stone, you may not remember me; my name is April Showers. We met at the hotel in Harrogate a couple of weeks back.'

'Ah, yes. That was a weekend I'd like to forget. What brings you here?'

'I'm looking for everyone who was at the hotel when Aunty died, to apologise for her outburst at the dinner table. She was ill and not herself. I hope you understand?'

'Ill, you call it. She can't have been a close relative then, because you clearly didn't know her very well,' said Mr Stone.

I continued with my deception in the hope of getting Mr Stone to open up further about his relationship with Aunty Violet.

'No, I'm afraid I didn't, I hadn't seen her for many years before that weekend in Harrogate. My memories of her are as a warm, friendly person.'

'That's very strange because the person I met was completely different.'

'Mr Stone, I'm sure there must be some mistake.'

'I don't wish to speak ill of the dead, Miss Showers, but the person you describe is not the person I knew. Come to my office, I will explain.' He led me to a corner of the warehouse he'd kept as a makeshift office. It had a large window that allowed him to see anyone entering the yard and DIY part of the warehouse. A kitchen table served as a desk, on which lay scattered papers and a pint-sized mug for tea. A battered filing cabinet was wedged in the corner against the back wall and on top of it sat a kettle, a teapot and a half-empty bottle of milk. Propped against the cabinet sat off-cuts of copper pipe and battens of wood.

'Tea?' he asked me.

I took another look at the stained mug and declined his offer. He continued to make one for himself whilst speaking to me at the same time.

'I met Miss Birch when she asked me to do some renovations to her cottage. The usual stuff, it was nothing I couldn't handle, though it was a big job. It meant continuous work for a couple of months, that's why I was keen to take it on. I spent a few weeks at her house, taking down an inner wall, building an extension, laying a new path to the front door. The profit I was going to make on the job was going to pay for a new car for my wife. Well, I finished the job, but she refused to pay the full amount we had agreed, claiming I had taken longer to finish the work than I should have and that I'd broken a valuable antique vase when I was doing the inside work. It wasn't true, I promise. So I started writing demanding letters to her for none payment of debts, stating that I was contacting my solicitor and would take her to court. She still refused to pay, which started a legal battle. She got another builder to declare my work unsafe, which it wasn't. Anyway, somehow the press got to hear about me harassing an old lady and they took her side of the story. Legal costs got out of hand; the bad publicity caused my work to dry up; I went bust. So in the end, she didn't pay me anything. And, just to rub salt into the wound, she received donations from well-wishers to cover her legal costs. I ended up having to sell my house and had to start again. I bought this little house and the run-down motor garage which I turned into a warehouse. I found selling building supplies to other builders and homeowners who wanted to do a bit of DIY work for themselves more profitable than doing the building work myself. If things keep going as they are, I plan to open another builder's merchants on the other side of town, next year.'

'Roofus!' The call came from the yard.

'That's my wife calling. She calls me Roofus because we met when I was fixing her neighbour's roof. My actual name is Ralf, but the Roofus name kind of stuck.' 'I'm in here, love,' he called out of the office door. A few seconds later a blonde lady entered the office.

'This is Miss Showers; she is a relative of the woman who died at the hotel.'

'What, the woman that ruined us?' 'What are you doing here? No, don't tell me I don't want to know. Get out; get out now before I throw you out.' 'And, what are you doing entertaining her kind? You stupid man, have you learnt nothing after the last time you had dealings with her family?'

Her sudden aggression took me by surprise. Frightened Mrs Stone would attack me, I backed away from her. However, Roofus stayed calm and got between us.

'It's alright, Love. She's not asking for work to be done. This is a different matter. She's come to apologise for that woman. I was just telling her all about what she did to us. It's alright, we've finished talking now. Look at the time, is dinner ready yet? I'm starving.' Mr Stone took his wife by the arm and escorted her from the office. As she left the office she gave me one last withering look of warning. I was about to leave when Roofus returned without his wife.

'I'm sorry about that. Because of the trouble caused by your aunt, she lost the baby she was carrying when our house and my business were repossessed by the bank. I thought she was over it now or I would never have gone to the hotel, but it brought it all up again. I wanted to give your aunt a piece of my mind, but all that happened was that Bonnie got depressed again.'

'I'm so sorry, had I known, I wouldn't have bothered you. I hope your wife will be alright.' I felt terrible and couldn't get out of there quick enough.

Back in my car, I could feel my body trembling. I wondered how I would feel if I lost a baby under those circumstances.

I took a deep breath, 'That was an ordeal I could have done without.' Driving to the end of the street, I turned the car towards home. Though I felt sorry for Mrs Stone, I now had my first real suspect, one mentally unstable enough and with a motive strong enough to make her a killer. Buoyed up by my discovery, I headed back to the office.

On my desk was a note.

'I called to collect you, but I was told you had gone out. I'll come round to show you my new car after I collect it and I know you will be at home. Call me. Rex.'

I picked up the telephone to call him and apologise for not going with him as agreed but changed my mind. I'd call him from home, later. After writing up today's interview and making a special note to look into Mrs Stone's past, I went home with conflicting feelings over what I'd discovered.

We had all finished dinner and were settling down to listen to the news on the wireless. I had selected a book to read for later. It was just as Mummy was bringing a tray of tea through to the sitting room when we heard the headline news item. It was the announcement of the sudden death of a Hollywood film producer. He'd been found dead in his hotel room in London and a woman was helping the police with their enquires. I sat up straight to listen for more details, but the newsreader went onto another topic.

'Did you hear that? I said to my parents.

'What's that, dear?' asked Mummy, setting the tea tray down on the coffee table.

'You mean that Hollywood chappie, who's died?' said Daddy.

'Yes. It has to be Mr Boysack; it's too much of a coincidence for it to be anyone else. He was one of the people at the Harrogate hotel when Aunty died. I interviewed him just the other day when I went to London.'

'Oh dear, what does that mean?' asked Mummy.

'I don't know. I shall telephone Inspector Allswell in the morning and ask him what he knows about Mr Boysack's death.' I had no choice, now. I'd have to tell the Inspector everything I had discovered or risk being included as a suspect in Aunty's death if he found out that I'd been to see Miss Starbrightly. He may even think I had something to do with Mr Boysack's death. My telephone call to Rex had been totally forgotten.

Chapter Ten

Thursday.

The following morning's telephone conversation with Inspector Allswell was not very productive, apart from confirming that the person found dead in London was Mr Boysack. All he would tell me was that he'd made enquiries into the hotel death and been told by the Metropolitan Police that because it had occurred in London, they would be investigating it, and as far as they were concerned, there was no evidence to show a link to the death of Miss Birch.

To me, it was clear and disappointing. Scotland Yard was not interested in what happened up in deepest, darkest, Yorkshire. So, I was left with sharing a rundown of my investigation with Inspector Allswell, hoping he would reciprocate. However, he seemed unimpressed with what I had discovered and volunteered no additional evidence.

'We have our suspects in this case.' He told me, 'but we are unable to disclose who they are to members of the public.'

'Please, Inspector Allswell. If we share information, we will find the murderer much faster.'

'You mean, you think you can. I'm sorry, Miss Showers, I cannot do that. Though you have done the right thing by telling me everything you have learnt, and I thank you for that. You can leave the rest of the investigation to us, now. Goodbye!' He hung up on me.

I slammed the phone down. I was furious; fobbed off by the police after I had cooperated and shared everything I had learned with them. How dare he do that to me? I'd show him! I had to get to London as soon as possible. I was certain that a courtesy call on Miss Starbrightly whilst she was vulnerable and shocked could get her to reveal something new. So, the sooner I got to London the better, especially, as she may be inclined to return to America to take advantage of all the publicity and sympathy which would come from the death of her husband. I dashed home to pack an overnight bag for a stay in our capital city then, caught the next train to London.

When I arrived at Miss Starbrightly's hotel, the lobby was full of newspaper reporters waiting for the widowed film star to put in an appearance. Mummy had telephoned ahead to arrange a room for me. So, after checking in, I had a discrete word with a hotel porter as he carried my overnight bag to my room. I told him I was Holly's friend and had come to comfort her in her hour of need. With a flutter of a tearful handkerchief and a ten-shilling note, I got him to remind me of Holly's room number.

I rapped gently on the actress's door. 'Holly, it's okay, it's me, April Showers. Are you alright?' I waited, just before I was about to try again. The door opened a crack.

'Oh, it is you,' she said in a fearful voice.

'May I come in? I thought you might like to talk to a friendly face. I didn't know if you had anyone else to turn to for support. You must be devastated. Please accept my sincere condolences. Is there anything I can do for you?' I smiled at her reassuringly.

'Thank you, no. That is unless you can make that lot downstairs go away.'

'Have you eaten?' I asked, 'because I'm starving. I've just arrived in London.'

'No, I'm broke. I would have left the hotel by now, but I've no money to pay the bill. As my manager, Hector took care of all that kind of thing. Our American bank has frozen his account until his death has been investigated. I need our American lawyers to turn his accounts over to me before I can access any of our money, but until I can prove I didn't kill Hector, they are refusing to do anything. And then there's well, er, other people involved.'

'What do you mean, who?'

'No one you can help me with. They're people Hector borrowed money from. I need to get home to sort this mess out, but I can't leave because I've got no money. I don't know what to do? All I can do is stay here until the lawyers sort everything out.'

'Oh, dear.' I looked Holly up and down. 'I have an idea; come to my room.'

Once in my room, I began to tell her my plan. First, we're going out to get something to eat, I'll pay. It won't be anything fancy; I don't have a lot of money. Take your clothes and make-up off, I have a spare dress you can put on. We can't have you walking the streets of London looking like a million dollars and hope to stay incognito. When you are ready, we'll go out the back way and then find some small cafe where we can eat and talk.'

'Why are you helping me like this?' she asked as she undressed.

I had to think fast; I couldn't tell her the whole truth about why I was there, so I gave her a different truth.

'A friend helped me recently when I was in a desperate situation. Later, when I heard on the wireless about what had happened to your husband, I figured you may need someone too. Was, I wrong?'

'No, April. I'm grateful to you.'

'Alright then, just for this evening, we are sisters. We will go out and get something to eat and together we will plan what we will do next.'

Wearing my spare dress and with most of her make-up removed, Holly allowed me to lead her downstairs. Arm in arm we walked towards the hotel dining room, with only a cursory glance from the reporters waiting at reception. In the dining room, Holly pointed to the door that the waiters used to get to the kitchen. Going through into the kitchen, one of the cooks asked what we were doing in the kitchen, but I explained that we were new and that we were looking for the staff entrance. We exited the kitchen through the staff entrance at the back of the hotel. Once on the street, it didn't take us very long to find a cafe. With coffee, sandwiches and cake in front of us, Holly relaxed and giggled.

'It's like a plot from a Hollywood movie; sneaking out of the hotel to escape the police or the bad guys and then going on the run.' I shared in the amusement, pleased that Holly was more at ease with me.

'But, this is for real, isn't it?' she continued, as the smile left her face.

'No, it's more like sneaking out without paying. It's wrong, but lots of people do it. Only, you will return, later to pay the bill.'

'I suppose so, but I don't want to go back.'

'What do you mean?'

'The press is the least of my worries. I was very fond of Hector, but we married in haste, not genuine love.'

'I am sorry to hear that. Apart from having to wait for the lawyers to release Mr Boysack's bank account to you, is there anything else troubling you?'

'You mean, like, confessing to murdering Hector? No, Hector died of a heart attack. I think the stress was getting too much for him.'

'I'm sorry. I didn't mean to insinuate that you killed him.' I was rapidly growing to like Holly. She was vulnerable and easy to get along with as well as being close to my own age.

'Why Are you questioning me like this? I thought you were here to help me and that we were supposed to be sisters for the day,' said Holly.

'Yes, that's true and, as my one and only sister, I do plan to help you, but you must understand, sisters, tell each other everything.' I kind of liked the idea of having a sister.

'Well, you had better let me get used to the idea of having a new best friend and sister, first, before I confess all. You may not want to hear about my other troubles.'

'You mean you are having a baby?'

'No! Thank God. That would be the end of everything. This is not the place to talk. I need somewhere private; somewhere safe, but with no money, I can't even pay for this coffee and sandwich; what can I do?'

'Well, I've been thinking about that. You are going to come home with me tomorrow.'

'What? How?'

'Listen, this is what we do. When we leave here, we'll go back to the hotel and stay the night. Tomorrow morning order an early breakfast in bed. The hotel staff will not be expecting you to come down with all the press waiting to pounce as soon as you show yourself. Ensure your room is in a bit of a mess, so the waiter gets the idea that you are staying for a few more days. Then, as soon as you have finished eating, put my dress back on and leave the hotel the same way we did this afternoon. Leave all your film star clothes behind, only bring what you can stuff in your handbag. There is a train to Hull leaving Kings Cross at nine o'clock in the morning. I will buy you a ticket. Meet me under the station clock at eight-thirty.'

'What happens if I get caught?'

'You won't. You said it yourself; your life is in a mess. You can't pay your hotel bill; you have nowhere to go and no money to get there. How can it get worse? You'll be far better off coming with me and letting me help you. Just give yourself plenty of time and be careful.'

'You don't understand, it can get a whole lot worse, and probably will do.'

'What do you mean?'

'Not now, later. I'll tell you when we are on the train tomorrow.'

Friday.

The chill morning air nipped at my neck and face as I stood below the clock in Kings Cross Station. I was early, but after a night of tossing and turning, waiting for the morning to arrive, and then being unable to face breakfast; I was standing below the station clock sooner than I had expected. I shivered for what felt like the thousandth time. What is it about a railway station concourse that always makes it cold, regardless of the time of year? Minutes felt like hours, I checked the clock to see that only a minute had gone by, only to scan the entrances of the station once again looking for Holly. I scrutinised every face hidden behind an upturned coat collar, hoping to find her. Eight-thirty came and went. Was there another clock in the station? Was she standing there thinking that I had deserted her? Should I go to look for her? Had she been caught trying to sneak out of the hotel? I looked at the extra ticket in my hand, wishing her to appear. The more I thought about it, the more panicky I became. I picked up my suitcase and put it down again. I had to stay where I was; it was far better that she found me than both of us go wandering around the station looking for one another. By ten-to-nine, it was decision time. I didn't have enough money to stay in London another night. I'd have to go home alone and hope that Holly could find a way out of her mess without my help. Picking up my suitcase for the last time, I reluctantly walked towards the platform where my train was waiting. I saw a man running down the platform towards the front of the train, his urgency, infectious. I too felt the need to rush and not miss the train. My pace increased, then slowed as I worried about Holly.

'April! April!'

Holly's voice echoed in the station hall. Dropping my case, I turned to see her running across the station concourse, waving at me. I felt so relieved; I wanted to cheer.

We found an empty compartment and sat opposite each other next to the window.

'You had me worried for a moment. I didn't think you were coming.'

'I'm sorry, April, I got held up. I made it down to the kitchen when I got stopped by a waiter. He asked me what I was doing. The only thing I could think of was to say I was a new member of staff. He took me to the head housekeeper's office and told me to wait there for her to arrive. After he left me, I waited for a minute, then ran for it. A hotel is a very busy place first thing in the morning; it took me longer than I thought to get out without being seen again.'

'Well, thank goodness you made it.'

'Do your family know you are taking me home with you?'

'No, but Mummy won't mind. I just don't know what she will do when I tell her that you are a famous film star.'

'Won't they notice on their own when they see me?'

'Probably not. They don't go to the cinema very much.'

As the train pulled away from the platform, I asked the one question that Holly had refused to answer until we were safe.

'Okay, now it's time to tell me the entire story. Yesterday in the cafe you inferred that you and Hector were in more trouble than just a few money worries with the hotel.'

'Yes, oh, where do I start? As I said earlier, I went to America because I couldn't get work in England. When I got there, I joined an agency and they sent me for various auditions on and around Broadway, but I only got small parts in off-Broadway shows. I barely earned enough money to scrape by. Then, I met Hector at one of the theatres where I had done an audition. He liked me and said I had talent. He seemed like a nice man. He told me that if he became my manager, he would get me better jobs in the theatre, so I said yes. I was still an unknown actress, but Hector worked hard at getting me bigger parts in some off-Broadway shows. Then, through a friend, he got to hear of a low budget film being shot in California. He made a few phone calls and got me an audition for the leading role. Unbeknown to me, that's when the trouble started. Hector said I needed to show up to the audition in style, so he bought me lots of new clothes and we travelled first class on the train from New York to Los Angeles. Hector wired ahead to the press to say that the latest sensation from England was arriving in town. Well, we spent five days on the train and one thing led to another so that by the time we had arrived in L.A. Hector had proposed to me and I had accepted.'

'What Hector didn't tell me was that he had borrowed all the money to buy my new clothes, first-class train ticket and publicity from some very shady people in New York. Well, to cut a long story short, I got the part in the film. The film became an unexpected success, and I suddenly became famous. Everything seemed great, but I'd left all the film contract details for Hector to arrange. I got a small fee for doing the film which covered our immediate expenses, but the rest of the money was tied up with the film profits scheme. I was to be paid quarter yearly from the film's profits. The shady people in New York wanted their money back and started adding interest to the amount that Hector owed them, lots of interest. It seemed the more publicity I and the film got the more interest was applied to the loan. We came to London not only to promote the film, but we also hoped we could escape the men in New York until we could raise more money to pay them back. But, unfortunately, it didn't happen. The film isn't making as much money here as the promoters hoped. Then, just after some poor press releases, the invite to Harrogate arrived. Hector said it would allow us to take advantage of the newspapers in the north of the country, so we should go. Only your Aunty died and we didn't get the kind of publicity we wanted. When we got back to London, Hector received a phone call to say the men in New York knew where we were and wanted their next payment. It was the phone call that brought on Hector's heart attack. Before you arrived, I was at my wit's end.'

'Don't worry, so long as we are careful, I can't imagine anyone will find you in Driffield. It's just a busy little market town in East Yorkshire. The highlight of the week is when a new film comes to the cinema.'

We spent the rest of the train journey talking about our childhood, our likes and dislikes and our hopes for the future. Holly explained to me that at the time of her christening her parents had been very poor and hadn't been familiar with the term Hollywood and its association with the film industry. It was simply that Mr and Mrs Wood had liked the name Holly when they named her. They'd only heard of the similar name associated with the film studios in America later when Holly was growing up. Holly, on the other hand, had loved the name association and had been drawn to the stage from an early age, taking part in school and village amateur dramatics. With her pretty looks, she was soon getting small parts with provincial theatre groups. Her parents are tenant farmers just outside Norwich. Holly hasn't seen her parents for a couple of years, and she's worried about how they will take the news that she has gone missing. I listened as she recounted her entire life story through the train journey. I suggested to her that she should write to them and reassure them she was safe and well. But not say where she was staying, for now.

By the time we arrived in Hull and changed to the Driffield train, I had worked out what I would tell everyone about Holly. She was a distant cousin, come to stay with us for a while. Only Mummy and Daddy would know the truth.

As we pulled onto the drive, Mummy came to the door to greet me. She looked a little surprised when she spotted Holly, but it was clear from her relaxed demeanour that she hadn't recognised the film star.

'Hello, Mummy. I hope you don't mind, but I have asked a friend to stay for a few days. I'm sorry I couldn't give you more notice of Holly's arrival, but I will explain over a cup of tea.'

I kissed her on the cheek and encouraged her inside the house with Holly on our heels. Depositing Holly in the sitting room, I went through to the kitchen to help Mummy make tea and to break the news to her about Holly's stage name. As I expected, Mummy got flustered. She dropped the cup she was taking from the cupboard shelf. The sound of it shattering on the tiled floor caused her to throw up her arms in surprise.

'Sit down Mummy, I will clear this up and make the tea.'

'Oh, dear, what will I do, what will I say to her. I've never met anyone famous before. What will the neighbours say?'

'The neighbours won't say anything, because you will not tell them who she is. Not unless you want every newspaper reporter in the entire country camped on your doorstep. Now that really would give the neighbours something to gossip about. Just treat her like you would any of my friends who have come to stay.'

'But why is she here? Why isn't she staying in some posh hotel?'

'I will explain everything when Daddy comes home, then I will only have to say it once. In the meantime, relax, she will not bite you. She is just as frightened of being here as you are of having her stay. She is only a couple of years older than me. If it helps, try to think of her as one of the cousins.'

'But the neighbours will recognise her.'

'No, they won't; you didn't. Without her fancy clothes and make-up, she looks just like me, ordinary. No one is going to give her a second look.'

'Wait until your father gets home, I don't know what he will make of it all. Oh, by the way, that nice boy, Rex called. He was driving a very nice new car.'

'Who's Rex?' asked Holly from the kitchen door.

'Oh, no one special, just a friend of the family. I was supposed to help him choose a new car the other day, but I forgot he was coming to collect me.' It was only then that I also remembered the telephone call I should have made to him to apologise for missing our date.

'I'll call him tomorrow and apologise.'

After tea I took Holly upstairs and settled her in the spare room, providing her with a few of my clothes to be going on with.

'It's Saturday tomorrow, I'll be able to show you around and then we can go shopping in Driffield and Beverley to get you some new clothes.'

'This is very kind of you, I don't know what would have become of me had you not come to my rescue. What about your mother, she seems to be a bit resentful at having me thrust upon her?'

'No, Mummy is fine; she loves the fuss. When all this is sorted out, she'll be able to tell her friends all about it. She'll be the toast of the Women's Institute for months when they learn you have been to stay with us.

On Monday, if you don't want to stay here with Mummy, you can come to work with me, if you like. I still have one more set of interviews to do.'

Saturday and Sunday.

I spent the weekend driving Holly to the seaside and local beauty spots as well as clothes shopping. The weekend passed by far too quickly.

Chapter Eleven

Monday.

Introducing Holly to my work colleagues as a cousin from Norfolk, who had come to stay for a few days and wanted to see what being a detective was all about, seemed like the simplest way to explain her sudden appearance. Holly played her part well, and it wasn't long before we were all on our second cup of tea and the biscuit tin was suffering some real damage. Patsy produced a copy of the morning newspaper and pointed out a photograph of Holly Starbrightly on the front page.

'Have you seen this? A film star has gone missing in London after the death of her husband. Just walked out of her hotel without paying her bill, she did. Would you believe it? These film stars think they can do what they like.'

'It's probably the shock of losing her husband,' suggested Jennifer.

'It says here the police are worried about her state of mind and are searching the river for her,' continued Patsy.

Holly was looking distinctly uncomfortable. 'Have any of you been to Norwich?' she asked, hoping to change the subject.

Holly's saviour arrived in the form of a young, smartly dressed lad, carrying a box file when he interrupted our tea party.

'Excuse me, Miss Clark. Mr Kibitzer from our solicitor's office has asked if you have the time to type six copies of each of these documents; they're for a case he is working on?'

'Right you are, Johnny. I will bring them over as soon as they are ready.' Jennifer gave the lad a sweet smile and ruffled his hair. The lad jumped back from her touch and red-faced ran out the door. Jennifer laughed.

'Work calls, Lady's,' announced Jennifer as she tucked the box file under her arm and headed off to her office.

'She's right, come on, I have a suspect to interview.' I led Holly to my office to look up Mr Steel's address.

'Do you still consider me a suspect?' asked Holly.

'No, of course not; you are far too nice a person to be a murderer, besides you've got enough on your plate without trying to plan the death of Aunty Violet. Whoever did murder her is carrying a real grudge.' I flicked through my list of addresses.

'Ah, here it is. Helmsley, North Yorkshire, let's hope the weather stays fine, and the address is not a farm.'

'What's wrong with living on a farm? I did.'

'It all depends on whether you remember to take your Wellington boots with you or not. But, we should be alright;

Mr and Mrs Steel didn't give me the impression that they were the farming type.'

Shortly after setting off for Helmsley, Holly fell silent. I assumed that she was just looking out of the window and enjoying the countryside of East Yorkshire. But as we approached Malton, Holly confessed.

'I could get used to this; it feels like I'm on holiday. It's only the horror of being discovered that spoils it.'

'Don't worry, leave it to Daddy. He said he would look into your financial problems for you and he will. He just needs a few days to talk to your bankers in America, and with the telephone call I made to Inspector Allswell this morning, explaining your situation and telling him you were with me, he has given you a reprieve from being arrested. Especially, as the Metropolitan Police gave him the brush off about there being no connection between you and what happened in Harrogate. The Inspector said he finds it quite amusing to know that they are searching high and low for you in completely the wrong location.'

'April, I've been thinking. I may give up being an actress once this is all sorted out. Go back to be just being an ordinary person. It has advantages, you know. I could come and go as I please without being hounded by the press. I wouldn't have to dress in my finest clothes all the time. I could take my time when I'm out shopping. It would be freedom. I'd almost forgotten what it was like to just do things I wanted to do when I wanted to do them.'

'Don't be fooled by this lifestyle, Holly. You have more money than I ever will. That buys you an awful lot of freedom and your fans must adore you. Apart from my family, I don't have anyone who loves me.'

'What, not even a boyfriend?'

'No, I don't have time for one. I'm a career girl. I love Mummy to bits, but all I have to do is look at her for her to remind me that I want more from life than just a husband, house, children and the Women's Institute.'

'Well, I hope you find what you are looking for. It's a big wicked world out there,' said Holly.

'I will. I'm sure of it.'

We drove into the large, ancient, market square of Helmsley where I stopped the car. The square was surrounded by mostly Georgian sandstone buildings, but one or two were much older, their timber-framed structures hinting at their age. It a place I'd been to many times before, but never tired of.

'We're here,' I said to Holly.

'I won't come in with you unless you want me to. We passed the sign for a castle back there and it's such a nice day, I think I'll have a look around it. I'll meet you here after your interview with Mr Steel.'

Before I could answer, Holly was out of the car and on her way. Castle Street, where Mr & Mrs Steel lived, wasn't far away, so I drove around the corner and parked up. Checking my notes to remind myself of the house number, I found an engraved brass plate with Doctor Robin Steel, Psychologist, engraved into it. Just before ringing the doorbell of the traditionally built workman's cottage, a thought suddenly crossed my mind; who would be interviewing who when I went inside?

The person who answered the door was wearing a deep blue dress with short sleeves and white buttons up the front. The white trim around the neck and cuffs contrasted nicely with the dress's colour and matched the buttons. Her hair had been permed and her make-up was tasteful and discrete.

'Hello, my name is April Showers; may I speak to Dr Steel, please?'

'Do you have an appointment?'

'No, I called on the off chance Dr Steel would see me, you see...'

'We have met before, haven't we?' the woman interjected.

'Err, yes. That is what I am calling about. I am a private investigator. I'm looking into the death of Miss Birch at the Harrogate hotel.'

'I'm sorry; Dr Steel is far too busy to see you. Come back when you have made an appointment.' The door began to close.

'Please wait,' I put my foot in the gap before the door closed.

'If Dr Steel won't speak to me, then I'll be forced to return with the police and you wouldn't want that now, would you?' The door flew open.

'And what do you mean by that remark?'

'Only, that I am aware of Dr Steel's past life and wondered how many of his clients are privy to the same information?' It was a bluff, but I hoped it would rattle her enough to get me through the door.

'That was a long time ago, he was innocent of the crime; he'd been framed.'

'Then give me a chance to clear his name regarding my Aunty's death.' We glared at each other over the doorstep. Finally, Mrs Steel relented.

'Come through.' She stepped back from the door.

Inside, the cottage was as small as it appeared to be from the exterior, but it was decorated to a high standard.

'Dr Steel must be doing well in his new career.' I said, appreciatively.

'Yes, and everything you see has all been bought and paid for. I have the receipts if you would like to see them?'

'I'm sorry, that is not what I was implying.'

'If you really want to know what has paid for all this you need to look no further than the last war. A lot of men came home suffering from stress and shell-shock. The men that were showing symptoms at the time of their return received some treatment, but for many men, the symptoms didn't appear until much later. It may be over ten years since the war ended, but there are still many ex-soldiers suffering behind closed doors, too ashamed to seek help. It was when Robin was in prison that he saw the after-effects of war on the other inmates and the suffering they still went through. They'd not received any proper treatment for their condition after leaving the forces and in their inability to readapt to civilian life they'd turned to crime. That's when Robin got the idea to study the mental effects of war on soldiers. Now, he makes his living helping those who can afford to pay him for his therapy. It may sound like a mercenary attitude but, we all have to make a living these days.'

'I understand. Is he with a patient now?' Mrs Steel checked the clock on the mantelpiece, 'Yes, but he'll be finished in a few minutes. It's his last patient of the day.'

Shortly after the clock struck noon, I heard a door open on the other side of the house and two men speak, 'thank you, Doctor, goodbye.' 'See you next week, Derek.'

Dr Steel came into the sitting room, 'Robin, this is Miss Showers; she is a private investigator and would like to ask you some questions. She's already threatened you with the police.'

'Thank you, Heidi, I think I will be safe enough with Miss Showers; would you make some tea, please? I could do with a cup and I expect Miss Showers would like one too.' Heidi glared at me once again before leaving. After Mrs Steel had left the room, I let out a sigh of relief.

'Your wife was telling me how you help ex-servicemen suffering from shell-shock.'

'Yes, but it is not just ex-soldiers. Many civilians suffer from it too, Heidi for one. She lived in Germany during the war. She had been trapped in the rubble of a bombed house for three days before she was found. Her parents, brother and sisters died.'

'I'm sorry, she didn't say. I hope I wasn't rude to her?'

'Why are you here, Miss Showers?'

'I'm conducting an investigation into how Miss Birch died and speaking to everyone who was at the Harrogate hotel. The police know she was poisoned, but are not acting quickly enough on the information for my liking.'

'And, you suspect me is that it; because I have a criminal record?'

‘No. I didn’t know that you had been in prison until your wife mentioned it. I got lucky when I tricked her into telling me that was where you had seen the after-effects of the war and how it led to you studying psychology.’

‘Ah, I see. Yes, I was in prison thanks to Violet Birch. We knew each other once, or I thought we did. We were friends until a disagreement occurred. Then she turned on me. It was as though she had become a different person. We argued and then separated.’ I took out my notebook. ‘What was the argument about?’ I asked.

‘Money. We met and became friends, or so I thought. I was an architect for the local council. Violet asked me to design some improvements to her house. We talked, liked each other and so I suggested we see more of each other. Then, out of the blue, she asked me to help her pay for the building work even though we lived separately. I refused; after all, we had only known each other a few months. We argued. She said the money would just be a loan, but I wasn’t prepared to take the risk. All seemed well for a week or two then, she brought it up again. We argued again. That’s when I told her I’d had enough and ended the relationship. She came round a day or so later to patch things up, but I said no. That’s when I think she planted her jewellery in my house. The next day I got a visit from the police. They searched my house and found your Aunty’s jewellery hidden in a drawer. It was that planted evidence and her damming testimony, all of which was made up, that persuaded the jury I was guilty. However, I was pardoned five years later.’

Why?’

'It was whilst your Aunty was taking tea in a respectable teashop in York that a magistrate overheard her confessing to a friend, that she had lied at the trial to get revenge on me for not helping her financially and then leaving her. Your Aunty had got the idea when she saw the photo of another convicted thief in the newspaper and read his story. After I was free, I could have pressed charges against her for lying about me, but my experience in jail had changed me. Instead, I agreed to an out of court financial settlement. It was that settlement that helped set me up here and start my new business. As you know, it was whilst I was in prison that I read about the new ideas in psychology coming from America. I studied the subject and took some exams, and now I help people with mental disorders. It's just a pity it is too late for Violet to be helped. That weekend in Harrogate was the first time I had seen her since my trial and going to prison. I went to try and convince her to get psychiatric help'

My opinion of Aunty Violet had reached rock bottom after listening to his story.

'Thank you, Dr Steel, for being so honest with me.' The smile suddenly dropped from his face.

'It's a pity you could not do the same with me, Miss Showers. You see, I learned of your relationship with Violet and, of your occupation as a private detective whilst we were at the hotel. After Violet's death, I wondered if you would come to see me. I also didn't like the way you threatened my wife with the police when you arrived.' Surprised and unmasked, I was speechless and flustered.

'It seems dishonesty still runs deep in your family, Miss Showers. Don't worry, I won't tell anyone. Doctor, patient confidentiality, you might say. Would you like to become a patient of mine, Miss Showers? I'm sure you find your job very stressful.'

In that instant, I stopped feeling sorry for him. Instead, I just wanted to slap his face and get out of his house. I turned towards the door to see Heidi with a smirk of pleasure riding her lips. Shoving past her, I slammed the front door behind me.

Fumbling in my handbag, I retrieved my car keys, opened the door and climbed in. I glanced back at the house and spotted Heidi looking at me through the window. Red-faced, I started the car and with a screech of rubber pulled away. It was only when I reached the end of the street that I remembered I had left Holly behind. I returned to the market square and parked.

Dr Steel had thoroughly humiliated and embarrassed me. Impatiently, I seethed in my seat whilst waiting for Holly, wishing her to get a move on so we could go home.

By the time I caught sight of Holly coming towards my car, the worst of my embarrassment and rage had subsided.

'How was the castle?' I asked before she'd even got seated.

'There's not much of it left. Something to do with Oliver Cromwell blowing it up but, I found a seat near what remains of one tower. It was in a bit of a suntrap, so I took advantage of it. Just when I was about to fall asleep, I heard a speeding car which reminded me that you may be waiting for me, so I came back.'

I flushed a little knowing I was the driver of the over accelerated car and looked out of the door window to hide my embarrassment.

'How did your interview go?' she asked.

'He's the guilty one! I'm sure of it. I just have to prove it.' I knew I was making assumptions about Robin Steel, but I'd really taken a dislike to the Steel's. I wanted then to be involved so I could send him back to prison.

'Wow. What makes you think that?'

'Instinct, knowing the criminal mind and, he was acting very cagy when he answered my questions.'

'What happens next?'

'When I get back to my office, I'll go through the evidence again. Robin Steel is the murderer; I just have to prove it.' In my eagerness to be on our way, I let the clutch out a little too fast and poor Holly was jolted back in her seat. The car stalled.

'Steady on!' complained Holly.

'Sorry, my foot slipped off the pedal.' I took a deep breath and started the engine again. This time, I carefully eased the car away from the kerbside. As we drove home Holly pestered me for more details of the interview, but I put her off by saying I needed to think about what he had told me in case he had let slip a piece of evidence that I hadn't noted in my book, but in reality, I didn't want to talk about what had happened.

When we arrived home, my anger had abated, but the sight of Mummy on the doorstep as the car came to a halt made me feel very defensive. She was bound to ask how the interview had gone and she would spot a lie a million miles away. I got out of the car and hurried to the front door.

'Did you have a nice day, dear?'

'Later Mummy, must dash.' I headed for the bathroom and locked the door. Below the bathroom, in the kitchen, I could hear female voices. Holly was helping Mummy finish preparing dinner and telling her of her day in Helmsley Castle. I would have to tell them the truth about my day, just not the bit about Dr Steel being aware of my deception about why I was interviewing him. I flushed the toilet, washed my hands, put on a brave face and went downstairs. By telling an enthusiastic version of the interview, with Dr Steel being very helpful, I managed to make it until bedtime without Mummy twigging the interview hadn't gone my way.

Chapter Twelve

Tuesday.

Holly came with me to the office and whilst I sorted through the post, she made the tea. That was when I found the note on my desk from Rex. He'd called in to see me the day before and was asking me to give him a telephone call. I stared at the note for a moment, wondering if I wanted to see him or not. Unable to decide for the moment, I laid it aside and continued sorting out the post. I'd just put the post into four piles and begun reading my own when Holly returned with the tea.

'What are we doing today?' she asked.

'Nothing exciting, I'm afraid. I going to do some research into Dr Steel's background, so I'll be spending a lot of time on the telephone.'

'What should I do,' asked Holly, looking somewhat deflated at the prospect of being on her own all day.

'Um, I see what you mean, you have nothing to do and you don't know anyone around here. Well, as you could be staying with me for some time. Have you thought about getting a job, even a part-time one?'

'Not really, all I've ever known is acting.'

'What did you do between acting jobs?'

'It depends on where I was at the time and how much money I had. If I was hard-up and there was no work on the horizon, I would go home, other times I would stay in town and get a job as a waitress for a few weeks and look for a part in a play.'

'There you are, then. I will get you a job at the hotel in Driffield. The manager knows me, I'm sure he will help you. After all, it won't be for very long. Just until your husband's finances are all sorted, and you go back to Hollywood.'

It didn't take long to walk up to the hotel and with Holly's good looks and previous experience; the manager hired her immediately. To stay incognito, she gave her birth name, Holly Wood, to the hotel manager.

Back in my office, Inspector Allswell seemed like the best person to ask for some background history on the arrogant Dr Steel, so I telephoned him straight away.

'Good morning, Inspector, it's April Showers; how are you?'

'Fine, and yourself? How is your investigation going?'

'Very well, I would just like to ask you about Dr Robin Steel – he was one of the people who were at the hotel when Aunty died. What can you tell me about him? I already know he has served time in prison.'

'You are doing well. From whom did you learn that?'

'You know I cannot divulge that kind of information, Inspector.'

'And I cannot give out personal information about a suspect to a member of the public.'

'Yes. I know that, but I went to interview him yesterday, and he was very uncooperative and aggressive. I'm sure he's hiding something.'

'You know he was the victim of a miscarriage of justice?'

'Yes, Inspector, I know he served time for a crime he did not commit, but that does not mean he didn't harbour a grudge and want revenge on Aunty Violet.'

'True, but you have any proof he killed Miss Birch?'

'But, Inspector, that is what I am doing; I'm trying to find the evidence that links him to the murder.'

'I'm sorry, Miss Showers, I have nothing to add to what you know already.'

'Inspector, please, there must be something you can tell me about him. Which prison was he in?'

There was a long pause before the Inspector spoke again, 'Leeds,' he said in a hushed voice

'Thank you, Inspector.'

I put the phone down. 'Armley', I said to myself.

Hello, Governor, my name is April Showers. I'm a reporter for the Morning Tribune, a local newspaper in East Yorkshire. I am writing a feature on a prisoner once held in Armley Jail, a Dr Robin Steel. I spoke to him the other day. He told me he'd been sent to Armley a few years ago, but that with your help and encouragement; he studied hard and earned a Doctorate in Psychology. That's a fantastic achievement; you must be very proud of him.

'Well, er...'

I quickly continued. 'My editor and I think this is very forward-thinking of you, Governor, and we are sure our readers would find the story of your innovative and inspiring rehabilitation methods very illuminating. As governor of a famous jail for dangerous criminals, I would like to get your impression of Dr Steel, and some further background on him. Something like; how even though he had been wrongly imprisoned; he remained a model inmate; helping fellow prisoners with their psychological problems: that kind of thing.

The Governor tried to interrupt me. 'But, but...'

Not allowing him to stop me, I continued. 'Some details of his life before he came into prison would also be useful. I promise I won't print a word without his permission, after all, I want to show him in the most positive light possible. How do you spell your name? I must get it right for my readers?'

'So, he was married before going into prison: her name was Georgina, I'll just make a note of that.'

'They had a child that died whilst he was in prison, I didn't realise. That's terrible.'

'The girl's name was Elizabeth; that is interesting. He must have been devastated.'

'On hearing the news he went into a deep depression. I'm not surprised.'

'But later, after he recovered, he began to study psychology. That's good; I suppose it helped him get over her death.'

'Yes, I will change the names of those not directly involved with Dr Steel, Governor. Thank you, goodbye.'

I put the phone down before he could ask me any awkward questions about when the article was going to be published or the address of the newspaper office and editor.

Pleased with what I had discovered about Dr Steel, I felt better prepared for when we had our next encounter. Just when I was feeling very pleased with myself for deceiving the governor so easily, I heard the front door slam and then feet on the stairs. Someone for Patsy or Annabelle, I assumed. Partway through writing up my telephone conversation notes, I heard a horrible sound coming from the room above mine. Evidently, the footsteps on the stair had been some little monster who had come for a music lesson. The strangulated cries of pain from a tortured violin were too much to cope with after such a successful morning, so I grabbed my coat and handbag and headed out for a coffee and a piece of cake at a local cafe.

'Morning April. Patsy got a new pupil, has she? I bet she'll be in later for a cup of tea and a couple of aspirin. What can I get you?' asked the woman behind the counter.

'Morning Dot. Yes, she has. I need a quiet place to think things through. I'll have a cup of tea and a slice of Victoria sponge, please,' I placed a two-shilling piece on the counter.

'Sit down, love. I'll bring it over,' offered Dot.

I selected a small round table close to the window, away from two other couples in the cafe. Moments later Dot brought over the tea and cake.

'On a case are we? I was sorry to hear about the death of your Aunty. I suppose you're feeling a bit low, are you? It can get you like that. I remember when my uncle Bert died. I hardly knew him, but it hit me like a ton of bricks. You know what I mean. Suddenly, I realised, I would never get the chance to know him.'

'Thank you, Dot. Yes, something like that.' Two more customers entered the cafe, so Dot left me to go and serve them. As I stared out of the cafe window, a travel agent's shop caught my eye. '*I'd love to go abroad and see the world; maybe go to America like Holly.'* Raindrops splattered against the window. *'Somewhere warm and sunny; I'd drink cocktails on the beach or by the swimming pool, just like they do in films. Huh, there's a fat chance of that happening; I don't even have a passport, never mind being able to afford the holiday. But, I could save up, and if I asked Mummy for my birth certificate, there is nothing to stop me from getting a passport. One never knows; as a private detective, one may need to go abroad urgently on a case. I fantasised over the idea of a client sending me abroad on a case. I'll ask Mummy for it tonight.'* My thoughts returned to my tea and cake when the two new customers sat at the table next to mine, distracting me from my daydream.

After wiping the last of the icing sugar that had dusted the cake and the cream filling from my lips with the paper napkin, I said goodbye to Dot and returned to the office via a stop at the travel agents to collect a travel brochure.

Back in the office, I refreshed my lipstick at my desk before laying out my file of suspects. I had interviewed them all, but still had no conclusive evidence to point me to the murderer. What was I missing? I didn't expect any of them to confess during my interviews, but I had expected to find something that made one of them stand out as having more of a motive than the others. I read down my list, weighing up each person or couple in turn.

Reverend Warlock and his wife Faith
The reverend doesn't seem like the kind of man to get involved in murder, no matter what someone had done to him. His wife, Faith is very devoted to him. However, she is very bitter about the damage Aunty has done to his reputation and his loss of career progression.

Ewan Ramsbottom and his wife Corriedale
Farmers who had suffered badly at the hands of Aunty Violet, due to the loss of their first business. They may be good farmers, but they didn't give me the impression of people who knew a lot about poisons and how to administer them. They didn't seem wealthy enough or intelligent enough to set up an elaborate murder like this one.

Rocky Punch and his wife, Judy
Mr Punch is making a mint from his new business protecting the showbiz world and could well afford to set up an expensive murder. As an ex-boxer who is used to hurting people, I expect he would find it relatively easy to kill someone.

Ada Betterman
Has the medical knowledge of how to administer poison. Her retirement home looks like it is doing very well. So she probably has the finances to pay for a weekend break at a hotel in Harrogate for all these people.

Holly and Hector Boysack
No, it couldn't be either of these two. Hector is dead and had never known Aunty and Holly is my new best friend, come honorary sister. Besides, she doesn't have any money, unless she used it all to pay for the hotel in Harrogate.

Roofus Stone and his wife, Bonnie
These two have suffered at the hands of Aunty Violet. They lost their house, business and an unborn child to Aunty's vindictive actions. Though Roofus gives me the impression of being philosophical about what had happened. Bonnie Stone is still boiling with anger. I don't know if she'll ever come to terms with what has happened to them.

Mr and Mrs Steel
He's been wrongly imprisoned.
Heidi is suffering from mental health issues after being trapped in a bombed building during the war.
As a Doctor, he has access to the drugs needed to kill.
Dr Steel married someone called Georgina.
His daughter, Elizabeth, died whilst he was in prison.
He suffered from depression after he heard the news of his daughter's death
I added the notes I'd made after my telephone conversation with the Armley Jail Prison Governor, to the one's I had already put in my file.

Natalie West

She hasn't bounced back from her encounter with Aunty Violet like most of the others. But unless she'd stolen more money, she could never have set up such an elaborate end for Aunty. Not unless, she'd been stealing from the bank's other customers as well. Maybe taking a bit from this account and that account, and Aunty Violet had been right about her and the missing money. But that would mean the bank manager would have to have been in on the theft as well. After all, it was he who had done the audit on her till that day. I only have Natalie's word that Aunty had found the money and returned it to the bank. She told me Aunty had confessed to the bank manager that she had made a mistake. That doesn't sound like the Aunty I know. She would have deposited the missing money in the bank and not said a word to anyone about her mistake. I think I need to go back to Bridlington and do some more investigating on Natalie West and see if the bank manager turns up at her flat or in the cafe.

I gathered up the papers from my desk and called it a day.

'Tomorrow, I'll go to Bridlington to watch the cafe waitress. I want to see who she meets.' I checked my notebook was in my handbag and went home.

When I arrived home, Mummy was in the kitchen preparing tonight's dinner.

'Mummy, do you know where my birth certificate is?'

'What on earth do you want that for?' she asked confused by my unexpected request.

‘I was thinking of saving up to have a foreign holiday and I need the birth certificate to get a passport.’

Mummy put down the spoon she was using to stir a pot to give me her full attention. ‘Where would you go?’

‘I don’t know. I picked up this brochure in town to get some ideas of places and prices. Spain seems very reasonably priced.’

‘Who would you go with?’

‘No one; I’m a big girl now!’

‘I’m not sure, April. Do you think you would like all that oily food?’

‘Well, I’d like to try it, Mummy.’

She went through to the living room before continuing. ‘I keep all our special papers in a box in the sideboard.’ I followed on her heels. Reverently, she lifted an old shoebox onto the top of the sideboard and removed the lid. Inside, on the top, were old part used ration cards. The war had been over for more than ten years, but rationing hadn’t ended until 1954. Next came my parent’s war-time identity cards, and below them was my birth certificate. My mother lifted it out and unfolded it. She read it without saying a word, but I could read her face, the memories transporting her back in time.

‘You were such a tiny, fragile thing,’ she said as she handed it over. I read the details of my birth in the neatly handwritten, black pen, scribed on the document, When and where born, name if any, sex, name and surname of father, name, surname and maiden name of mother, occupation of father, fathers name and address, date when registered and last of all the registrar's name. I refolded the birth certificate and propped it up on the sideboard against a photograph of my parents on their wedding day.

'I'll go to the post office and get a passport application form tomorrow.'

'Alright dear, I'd better get on with dinner; your father will be home soon.' She kissed me on the cheek and looked into my eyes before going back to the kitchen. I got the feeling she wanted to say something more but didn't know how to broach the subject, so I followed her.

'What is it, Mummy?'

'What do you mean, dear?'

'There is something you are not telling me, but you don't know how to say it. I've learnt a little about reading peoples' faces, doing my job and I've known you rather a long time.'

'Oh, it's nothing, just old memories.'

'Yes, I can see that. It was when you took my birth certificate out of the box. There is more, isn't there? I've often wondered why I was an only child; is it something to do with that?' Mummy looked at the clock and let out a sigh.

'Make a cup of tea. I'll be back in a minute.' I heard her go upstairs. When she returned, she was holding another piece of paper. I placed our cups of tea on the kitchen table where we both sat down. She slipped the folded paper across the table without opening it.

'I suppose now is as good a time to tell you as any other,' she said almost in a whisper. I unfolded the paper to see a second birth certificate, dated two years after my birth. The name of the child was Michael. I looked up at her; she had tears on her cheeks. Rising from my seat, I went around the table and kneeling on the floor next to her, I put my arms around her shoulders. She hugged me tightly for a moment before releasing me.

'You had a brother, but he didn't survive more than a few months; there was something wrong with him. His had been such a difficult birth, we both nearly died. After I recovered, I was unable to have any more children.'

I returned the birth certificate to her. She slipped it into her apron pocket, resting her hand on it for a moment. Then, in an instant, her mood changed.

'Gosh, look at the time. Set the table for me whilst I put the lamb chops on. Your father will be home in a few minutes. Holly is working late at the hotel and won't be home until after ten o'clock.' She wiped the last of the tears away and continued preparing our evening meal as though nothing had been said.

She surprised me with her sudden suppression of sadness and the return of the woman I had always known. I watched her when Daddy came home and over dinner, there was no hint of the hurt and sadness she had revealed to me earlier that afternoon. I couldn't help but wonder how she coped with such sad memories and manage to keep cheerful for those around her. My thoughts returned to my birth certificate and how much information it held about me. That's when it gave me an idea. After dinner, I helped Mummy with the washing-up.

With just the two of us in the kitchen, I popped the question. 'Where are records for things like birth certificates kept?' Mummy looked surprised for a moment.

'Why, what do you want?' she asked.

'Oh, nothing to do with our family, it's to do with my investigation into Aunty Violet's death and my list of suspects. If I could get some background details on them, it may help me solve the case.'

'Well, if they were local people their records would be kept at the registration office in Hull, but there is a central records office at Summerset House in London; everyone's records are kept there; births, marriages and deaths.'

'Thank you, Mummy. What would I do without you?'

Wednesday.

At work the following morning I opened my file on Aunty's case and wrote a list of all the names I was taking to Summerset House and then telephoned Inspector Allswell in Harrogate.

'Inspector, how are you? I have a question you may be able to help me with. Please may I have the dates of birth of all the suspects in our murder case? I'm trying to establish a link between them.'

I had expected some resistance to my request, but the Inspector was very forthcoming with the details I requested, unlike my previous request for background details on Dr Steel. I didn't ask the Inspector why he'd had a change of heart. I just accepted my good fortune, assuming the Inspector was happy for my help with the case. Armed with the dates of birth of my suspects and with the information gained during their interviews, I booked a train ticket to London for the next day. In the meantime, I returned to Bridlington to keep watch on Natalie West.

After parking the car along the promenade, I made my way to the cafe where Natalie worked and went in to speak to her.

'What time does your shift finish?'

A glare from the cafe owner who was behind the counter preparing ice cream sundaes prompted her to answer quickly.

'Two o'clock.'

'Is everything Okay, Natalie?' The Cafe owner asked in a strong Italian accent.

'Yes, Mr Visconti. It's just a friend asking when I finish work.' 'Go away and leave me alone!' she hissed.

'I must speak to you,' were my parting words as I headed for the door.

After smelling the warm doughnuts and freshly brewed coffee, I'd left the cafe feeling hungry. I couldn't stand on the doorstep for an hour, so I crossed the road to a seafood restaurant from where I could keep watch on the American style cafe. I ordered a crab salad and a glass of Chablis. I'd never eaten a meal in a restaurant decked out to look like a fisherman's wharf before. Just as I was finishing, I spotted Natalie leaving the cafe opposite with her coat on. Glancing at my watch, it read ten minutes to two.

Voicing my thoughts and smiling to myself, 'she's leaving work early.' It was what I had expected her to do. I waved a pound note at the waitress, then stuffed it under my plate, grabbed my handbag and made for the door.

'Sorry, must dash. Keep the change!' I called to the waitress.

As I ran from the restaurant, I saw Natalie rushing up Prince Street, so I set off after her. A loud beep on a car horn and a screech of brakes caused my heart to miss a beat as I raced across the road. The sound of the car horn made Natalie look around, too. She must have spotted me because she continued at a half-run. I saw her turn into Woolworth's before I could catch up to her and hoped I hadn't lost her for good. When I entered the shop, I saw her down the centre aisle. She stopped for a second, looked back and spotted me. She fled, barging past shoppers browsing the myriad of bargains on the open counters. She exited the store through the doors that led onto Cliff Street. I tried to follow her but was frustrated by the crowds in the store, forcing me to give up the chase. I continued to the exit she had used, but once outside she was nowhere in sight. I considered going to her home address to find her but changed my mind. If she did return home, it wouldn't be anytime soon and I didn't want to spend hours waiting for her. I had a trip to London tomorrow which I hoped would yield more productive and reliable information than Natalie West would have volunteered.

*****

Unseen by me, whilst I was chasing Natalie West

From inside the pub on the corner of Prince Street, opposite the American style cafe in Bridlington, Rex Barker was keeping an eye on the cafe and its waitress. When he saw April enter the cafe, he put down his glass of beer and paid closer attention to what was going to happen in the cafe. Jotting down the time of April's arrival in his notebook, as he looked up again, he saw April leave the cafe and then cross the street to a seafood restaurant on the opposite side of the three-way road junction. From his observation spot in the pub, he could now see the entrances to the cafe and seafood restaurant.

'What are you doing, April? You shouldn't be here.' He whispered. Rex's mind worked overtime wondering why his private detective friend should be meeting with one of his suspects. Rex followed April as she chased after Natalie West. But he hung back not wanting to be seen and hoped April wouldn't frighten off the man who Natalie was going to meet. Instead of following April into Woolworth's Rex took a shortcut through an alley, coming out in time to follow Natalie to her rendezvous.

Chapter Thirteen

Thursday.

'May I go with you?' asked Holly, when I announced over the breakfast table that I was going to Somerset House in London. 'It's my day off today; I could help you search through the archive?'

'Yes, if you like. I don't have any plans to go shopping, but don't let that stop you if you want to come.'

'Thank you. I'd like to help if I can.'

'Great, I'll enjoy the company.'

Throughout the train journey, Holly chatted about her job at the hotel in Driffield, sharing some hotel gossip with me about the Head Chef and the Head Housekeeper who were believed to be having a secret affair. Only, all the hotel staff knew about it, but haven't let on. It seems that on Saturday nights, the Head Chef stays overnight in the hotel. He volunteers to cook breakfast for the hotel guests on his own. This means that on Sunday mornings, the rest of the kitchen staff get a lie-in. The Head Housekeeper stays overnight Saturday night, so she can make an early start the next day. There is always a lot to do in the hotel over weekends, they are the days when most guests leave or arrive. It was the night porter who had spilt the beans on their affair after he spotted the Head Chef leaving the Head Housekeeper's room early one morning. No one cares. The people who work in the hotel trade live in their own little world. With most hotel staff working unsociable hours, it's only natural that relationships flourish between work colleagues. As Holly chatted about her experiences at the hotel, my thoughts visualised the hotel in Harrogate and what had happened the night Aunty had been murdered. What was happening between the staff in Driffield's hotel was probably true of many other hotels all over the country, especially one as large as the one Aunty and I stayed at in Harrogate. I made a note in my little book to pay another visit to the Yorkshire Dales Spa Hotel and speak to the staff. There had to be staff gossip about what is going on in the Spa.

Standing outside Temple Tube Station in London, I consulted my street map, it showed Somerset House to be on Lancaster Place, just a short walk from the underground station. As Holly and I walked along Victoria Embankment we enjoyed the views of the River Thames until we turned onto Lancaster Place and found Summerset House.

Inside the grand building, the dark wood-panelled archive room was filled with large, heavy-looking, red books. It felt very intimidating. Row upon row of books, all stored in order, by year and then alphabetically. They stood on shelves, three high from the floor up. Long, solid-looking, polished tables ran the length of the room. But, apart from one other person, we had the room to ourselves.

‘Where do we start?’ asked Holly.

‘I’m not sure. Find the record of your birth. You know the date and place where you were born. If you can find the record of your own birth in one of these books, we will know we are using them correctly. I’ll do the same with my birth date.’

It didn’t take long before we both dropped large red books on the table and were thumbing through the pages to find our names.

‘Got it,’ I said excitedly to Holly.

‘Me too, look,’ she pointed to the spot in her book where her name was printed.

‘The letters and numbers at the end of each row must be the references we need to order a copy of the certificates.’

‘Right, let’s get started. If we work together, we should get through my list pretty quickly. I’ll retrieve the books that I’m looking for one at a time; you put them back after I’ve made a note of the relevant reference number. Once we’re all done, I’ll go to the office and order copies of the certificates that I’ve been looking for. With a bit of luck, we may have time for some sightseeing before we have to get the train home.’

By one o’clock we were finished, but although I’d found a number of people with the name Elizabeth Milbank, with no birth dates to work from and guessing at possible birth towns, I could only guess at which birth certificates to order. After leaving Summerset House, I took Holly for lunch at a little restaurant off the Strand. It was a little more expensive than I’d budgeted for, but I was enjoying Holly’s company and I didn’t know where else in London to get something to eat.

After leaving the restaurant, we only had time for a quick visit to St Paul's Cathedral. All was going well until we visited the Whispering Dome. We started by whispering to each other from opposite sides of the dome and ended up in fits of the giggles like two errant schoolgirls. After some disapproving looks from other visitors and an 'Shh' from one which echoed around the dome making us giggle even more, so we escaped before we got thrown out.

We arrived home just as Mummy was putting the finishing touches to dinner.

'Ah, you're home, I was just about to put the kettle on. I suppose you are both ready for a cup of tea?'

'Oh, yes, please.' Holly and I said in unison. It was strange, over this past week, it really felt as though Holly had become the sister I never had and had never missed, until now.

Daddy arrived home, but unusually he was carrying a bottle of wine.

'Get the glasses out; I think we will want to celebrate this evening,' said Daddy.

'Why, whatever has happened; have you robbed the bank?' asked Mummy.

'Metaphorically speaking, you are not far off the mark. Let me open this bottle and I will explain whilst we eat.'

I hastily placed dinner on the table and Daddy made a long-drawn-out affair of opening the bottle of wine and then pouring each of us a glass of the dark red grape. We waited eagerly for his announcement as he built up suspense around what he was going to say. Daddy had us all so wound up it was like sitting down to Christmas dinner instead of lamb cutlets with mashed potatoes, peas and carrots.

'Well, get on with it!' demanded Mummy. 'Dinner is getting cold.'

'A toast; to Holly!' He raised his glass into the air. 'The police are no longer looking for you in connection with the death of your husband. I have received a telegram from your bank in America. I have received confirmation that they have released some, not all, of the money owed to Holly. I've asked your bank to pay your hotel bill, adding a little extra for the inconvenience of you leaving without paying your bill and, I have arranged for the hotel to forward your luggage to us here, in Driffield. I have also asked your bank to transfer some money to my bank, in your name, so you now have an independent income to use, instead of having to rely on your husband's accountants. I also telephoned the London police. They too have confirmed the news that your husband's death was natural causes. They are still interested in your whereabouts for leaving the hotel without paying your bill and it won't take them long to figure out that you are in our neck of the woods, so I suggest you speak to them before they come knocking on our door.'

'Will I be arrested?' asked Holly looking frightened.

'No, I shouldn't think so. That's not the impression I got from speaking to them, though I do expect they'll give you a severe telling off. But, given that you are a famous film star and no real crime has been committed now that your hotel bill has been settled, I suspect they will let you go,' said Mr Showers.

Friday.

Rex turned up unexpectedly at my office shortly after I had arrived.

'Good morning, April. How is your case progressing?'

I gathered up the file I was reading and slipped it into the top drawer of my desk.

'Very well, thank you. I expect to have some new leads within the next few days. Holly and I had an interesting day in London yesterday. I'm just waiting for the fruits of our endeavours to blossom.'

'Who is Holly?'

'Just a friend who is staying with me for a few days.'

'So, I take it you are not busy today, whilst you're waiting for your new leads to arrive, I mean?'

'Why, what do you want?'

'I picked up my new car yesterday, it took the garage mechanic a couple of days to get it ready for me, but it's outside and I was wondering if you would like to come for a drive? It's a nice day and I have some free time. I thought we could spend it together.'

I'd forgotten about his car and that I should have returned his call to explain why I hadn't gone with him to help choose it. So I agreed to be taken for a drive. Anyway, I couldn't progress my Aunty's murder case any further until the certificates arrived from Summerset House.

As we stepped out into the street, he marched up to the flashiest car I had ever seen. It was open-topped, dark blue and only had two seats.

'This is yours? I am impressed.'

‘Yes, it’s a Jaguar XK120. But, don’t be too impressed. It’s second hand and my father had to help me arrange a bank loan to get it. I’ll be in debt to the bank for a long time before I pay this off.’

‘It looks lovely.’ I pulled a headscarf from my handbag and put it on. ‘Where are we going?’

‘We’ll go down to Beverley, then up the coast road. There are some long straight stretches near Beeford, where I can get a bit of speed up and see how she runs.’

As we drove along the High Street in Driffield, the guttural rumble of the car’s powerful engine turned a few heads in our direction. Leaving town, I gripped hold of the car seat as the car’s acceleration forced me deep into its soft leather upholstery. With the noise of the wind rushing over the car and the roar of the engine, conversation was impossible as Rex took every open bit of road as an opportunity to push the car harder. The sporty car responded instantly to Rex’s touch, taking the twists and turns in the road with ease.

Once we’d left the built-up area around Beverley and were heading towards Bridlington, the road between Leven and Beeford straightened out with only long, gentle bends which allowed Rex the opportunity he’d been waiting for. A motorcyclist kept up with us for a while. His body bending low over the bike’s petrol tank to make him more streamlined, but he gave up the chase after a couple of miles and we had the road to ourselves. As we entered Beeford, Rex slowed the car to a more acceptable speed.

‘We’ll stop for coffee in Bridlington,’ he shouted. But before I could reply we were through Beeford and Rex was speeding up once again, the roar from the car engine making any answer I wanted to give inaudible. Ten minutes later we were entering the seaside town.

'Wow, she's fast,' I said, as Rex slowed down to the speed limit.

He parked the car close to the seafront in time for us to see a large steamer full of day-trippers rise and fall on the choppy waves as it left the calm waters of the harbour on a sightseeing trip around the bay.

'Ready for that coffee?' asked Rex.

We walked along Prince Street, towards the centre of the town however, as we walked past Woolworths it suddenly occurred to me where we might be going. Instinctively I stopped, fearful of meeting Natalie in the cafe.

'Wait! If you don't mind I would rather walk along the seafront, that drive has made my head spin a little. I think the fresh air will make me feel better.'

'Are you sure? A good strong coffee and doughnut would be more stimulating. You could be suffering from low blood sugar. It's one of the things I learnt in the army. Caffeine and sugar make a good pick-me-up. There is a great cafe just down the road here.'

'No, no, I couldn't. The fresh air on the seafront will do me more good. If you like, you can buy me a candyfloss, there's lots of sugar in that.' I turned and started towards the beach, forcing Rex to either abandon me or catch up. As we turned away from Prince Street and walked along the seafront, he bought me a pink candyfloss from outside an amusement arcade and then we crossed the road to the seawall. Leaning against the blue painted rail that topped the seawall, we watched families on the beach making sandcastles. I picked clumps of candyfloss off the stick; it was how I'd always eaten it as a child. I stared out to sea thankful for my narrow escape I'd just had. What would Natalie have done if she'd seen me with Rex? She'd have thought we were both spying on her.

Rex had gone quiet, and I wondered if I'd hurt his feelings by not letting him buy me a coffee, so after finishing the candyfloss, I suggested we go for a coffee, but at a different cafe to the one where Natalie West worked. I chose one on the seafront.

'Thank you, Rex. I'm feeling much better now.'

'Good.'

'Shall we continue our walk? It's still a nice day?' I suggested.

Rex looked at his watch. 'Well, if you don't mind I'll take you back to Driffield. I have something to do this afternoon.'

Rex drove me back to the office at a much-reduced pace to that at which we had left it. Our conversation during the drive was infrequent and short. Rex's mood had changed, and I didn't understand why.

Back at work, my office partners were in to see me before I'd settled in my seat. They wanted to know where we had been and what we'd been up to. What was it like in the car and when would I be seeing Rex again, were their first questions. Unfortunately for them, I didn't feel as excited as they thought I should at having such a good-looking boyfriend with a fabulous car.

'He is not my boyfriend. He is just a friend of the family, that's all. We just went for a drive together in his new car.'

I put up with the boyfriend chitchat for a little while; after all, it was Friday afternoon.

'Right lady's, now that you have mapped out my life for me, I'm going to call it a day. I am going home. I will see you all on Monday morning.

'Have a pleasant weekend with Rex, we'll want to know what you get up to over the weekend,' said Jennifer suggestively, as I left the building.

'I'm sorry, Jennifer, I have no plans to see Rex over the weekend, he's not my type.'

Chapter Fourteen

Saturday and Sunday.

The weekend turned out to be a complete bore, Holly was working on both days, Rex didn't call me and it rained on both days, so I couldn't go out, which left me with helping Mummy do the housework. I made myself a promise, that, if I ever became rich enough, I would hire a housekeeper to do this kind of work for me. I toyed with the idea of calling in at the office to do some work, but put it off; Saturday and Sunday were Patsy's busiest days. The office walls would be reverberating to the sounds of groups of children doing their very best to destroy the instruments their parents wanted them to learn how to play.

Having spent all Saturday helping mother, after dinner I wanted to get out of the house, so I went to the cinema to watch an Errol Flynn film set in the days of King Edward III. It was full of chivalry and romance; a bit of real escapism. The film that preceded it was a crime drama in a modern-day setting and was about jewellery smuggling across the English Channel.

In the Errol Flynn film, he saved the helpless princess from the evil French knight. It brought back memories of how Rex had saved me from those two men outside the pub a few weeks earlier, and Rex's chilling words when I dropped him off at his house, 'Be careful, April. I may not be around for you next time.' Rex was right, I was no better than a damsel in distress waiting for her knight in shining armour to rescue her in her time of need. However, it was a scene from the B movie which surprised me the most. The hero was temporarily defeated in a fight on the smuggler's boat. The bad guy escaped by using a Judo move to throw the hero overboard. The good guys win in the end, but the scene stayed with me. Maybe I didn't need to be the damsel in distress; maybe, I could learn how to do Judo.

By the time I arrived home, Holly was home from work. Mummy and Daddy had gone to bed and Holly was watching a comedy show on the television.

'Fancy some cocoa, Holly? I'll watch the show with you.'

'Yes, please. Your mother said you had gone to the pictures, anything good?'

'Not bad. I went to see an Errol Flynn film. Holly, can I ask you something about actors and filmmaking?' Minutes later we were sitting together on the settee with our cocoa and I was ready to ask my question.

'In films, when there is a fight scene, how real is it?'

'Not very. They rehearse the fight scenes over and over. Most of what makes it look realistic are the camera angles and the skill of the stuntmen. Sometimes an actor can get hurt if he or she doesn't duck at the right moment, but most of the time everything is fine.'

‘So none of the actors know how to fight properly then?’

‘Ah, well. I didn’t say that. In westerns, they learn how to ride and fall off horses and how to handle a gun. Actors like Burt Lancaster and Audie Murphy do a lot of their own stunt work. Errol Flynn is very good at sword fencing and doesn’t need a stunt man for those scenes. There are probably lots more actors who have skills that help them in films: it’s just that I haven’t had the chance to make many films and get to meet them before we came back to England. Why are you asking?’

‘Don’t laugh, but I’ve had an idea. I’m going to start taking Judo lessons, so I can learn to defend myself.’ Holly gave me a long stare of disbelief.

‘April, it takes years of practice to become any good and Judo. What has happened to you to make you want to do that?’

‘Nothing, I’m just being careful.’

‘Liar! I can see it in your eyes. What’s happened?’

‘Promise you won’t tell anyone?’ I recounted the events outside the pub and how Rex had saved me.

‘Well, as an actress I have learnt three things about getting unwanted attention from men. One, don’t get yourself into those situations in the first place. If you are visiting a man for the first time, it doesn't matter if it is at work or home; have someone with you who you can trust. Two and three; if a man does try it on, stick your fingernails in his face, and give him a good, hard knee to the groin. That will slow any man down and give you time to run away. Leave the fancy stuff like Judo for the movies.’

It wasn't the answer I had wanted, so I finished my cocoa and said, 'goodnight.'

The following morning I slept late, however, when I got up, I spent the rest of the morning helping Mummy in the kitchen by making an apple pie to have as dessert after our Sunday roast. Holly's words from the previous evening wouldn't leave me alone. The decision as to whether I should take Judo lessons plagued me for the rest of the day. So much so, that when Holly returned from work that evening, I found it a struggle to speak to her. However, by the time I went to bed, I'd made up my mind.

Monday.

I started the day by working my way through the usual pile of post. From the amount, I could only surmise that anyone who wanted to send out a bill waited until Friday before posting it, just so it would land at the recipient's destination first thing Monday morning and spoil the rest of their week. However, it wasn't all bad news. One letter turned out to be a request for a meeting with a possible new client, and the last letter was postmarked, Harrogate. On the front of the letter, written in a bold hand, was Private. Inside was a single sheet of paper, with nothing to identify who the sender might be. On it was one sentence.

Large amounts of Aconitum found in the victim.

I sat back in my chair, confused by what I'd read. I knew the letter had come from Inspector Allswell; no one else in Harrogate would be privy to this kind of information other than the murderer and I was sure it wasn't the murderer giving me a clue. So, why was Inspector Allswell sending this to me anonymously, and what is Aconitum? The answer to one of my questions was easy to resolve with a visit to the local library.

The lady at the reception desk peered over her spectacles at me and sniffed. Are you a member of the library?

'I'm a private detective; I'm researching a case.' I smiled at her reassuringly. Her expression didn't change.

'You are supposed to be a member of the library before you use it.'

'My mother is. Does that help?'

'No, it does not. In that case, you will not be allowed to remove books from the library.'

'Thank you, I'll remember that.' I was about to walk away to look for the book I needed when she added in her superior, hushed, nasally tone. 'You could become a member if you wish?'

'Later, if that's alright. I'm in a bit of a rush. I've got a case to solve.' I smiled politely.

'You could try looking in the science section under chemistry or the gardening section under poisonous plants.'

I followed her suggestion and went through to the shelves marked Sciences. After browsing the shelves for a minute or two, I found a book called the Chemical make-up of Poisons. Flicking through the pages, I soon discovered it was too technical for what I wanted. So, I went over to the gardening section of the library. I found a book on natural poisons in plants found in your garden. This was more in line with what I was looking for. It listed, in alphabetical order, various common plants grown in the garden that contained dangerous poisons. I didn't realise there were so many; some I recognised instantly, Mummy was growing them in her garden. Taking the book to a nearby table, I made a list of all the plants I recognised and a few I did not, along with the name of the poison they contained.

Half an hour later I was on my way home to speak to Mummy. I felt an urgent need to warn her about the dangerous garden plants she was growing. When I told her what I had discovered at the library about some of the plants in our garden, I was somewhat taken aback by her response.

'I know that,' she told me as though it should be obvious to anyone. 'Come with me.'

She gave me a tour of our garden pointing out plants that were toxic and had to be handled carefully, others that had medicinal properties, and some which were supposed to be edible. I listened intently.

'Plants like the Artemisia help keep pests away; Mirabilis or Four O'clocks, to give them their common name; they keep beetles away from your flowers. Foxgloves contain digitalin, which can be of help to people with heart problems, but too much brings on heart failure, whereas lavender helps you sleep. Plants are wonderful things if you know how to use them.'

'What about *Aconitum?'*

'Oh, Monkshood, some people call it Wolfsbane; it has a pretty blue flower. That one is very dangerous. I don't have any of those in the garden.'

'Thank you, Mummy, I didn't realise there were so many uses for garden plants and flowers. I thought they just made the garden look pretty and were good for the bees.'

'I can see I've neglected your education; didn't they teach you these things at school?'

'Not the school I went to.' I smiled at her reassuringly. 'We had to do Maths, English and History and on Friday afternoons, dress-making.'

'You know what I mean. I'm not the clot you think I am, you'll understand that one day. Come on, it's nearly twelve o'clock, are you staying for lunch?' she asked.

'Yes, I think I will.'

I never got back to work. I spent the afternoon listening to Mummy tell me what she had learnt about garden plants and how in the olden days people used them for all sorts of things.

Tuesday.

After spending the previous day with Mummy learning about plants and their uses, I was full of enthusiasm to restart my investigations armed with my new knowledge. With Aconitum so easily available to a would-be murderer, all I had to do was find the suspect who was growing the plant with the poison and I would have my murderer. However, as I drove to the office, I couldn't help but look into peoples' beautifully front gardens with renewed insight, noting the varied flowers they all contained. I began a game of eye-spy but quickly gave up as garden after garden was full of similar plants. I hadn't realised that growing Foxgloves, Lilly-of-the-valley, Sea Squill and Oleander, which all contained poison, were so popular. My rush of enthusiasm to seek out the deadly plant in my suspect's garden waned as I spotted more and more dangerous plants growing in every garden I drove past. By the time I got to work, I'd realised this line of enquiry would be fruitless. But, there again, my suspect would need to be someone who knew how to extract a plant's poison and turn it into a drug. They would also need to know how to administer it; someone with scientific knowledge of drugs? A person such as an ex-nurse called Ada Betterman.

At the nursing Home in Scarborough, I quickly scanned the front garden for poisonous flowers before ringing the doorbell. I entered to be greeted once again by Mrs Chaperon, the secretary.

'May I be of assistance?' she asked automatically, before remembering my face. 'Oh, it's you. I'm sorry, Miss Betterman is too busy to see you without an appointment. You should have telephoned before coming.' She pushed her spectacles back up her nose and stood her ground as though defending the entrance to the house.

'That's a pity. I was hoping she would be able to spare me five minutes. I'm close to finding my Aunty's murderer and Miss Betterman's expertise as a nurse could resolve the last clue for me.' It was only half a lie.

'Oh, well, in that case, I will speak to her and see if she can spare you a moment or two.'

'I smiled, politely, 'thank you, that's very kind of you. I do so hate to be a bother when you as so busy.'

Miss Betterman was standing behind her desk when I entered her office.

'Good morning, I'm sorry to bother you at such short notice, but I desperately need your help.' The nursing home owner's shoulders dropped as she relaxed.

'How may I help, you,' she asked, still on her guard?

'Miss Betterman, it has come to my knowledge that my Aunty died of an overdose of Aconitum. I hoped that you, with your medical background, could advise me on how a person might get an overdose of this drug and where it might have come from?'

'I thought I was one of your suspects for the crime, Miss Showers.'

'Not Really. You were just one of seventeen people sat around that table, my Aunty and myself, included. I wouldn't be doing my job if I didn't interview everyone who was there at the time. There is nothing personal in it, I assure you. That is why I am here asking your advice.' I lied as sweetly as I could.

'I see, well in that case. Unfortunately, I may not be able to help you very much. My career was cut short. I had only been qualified for less than a year before your Aunty caused the trouble that made me leave nursing. The ward was very busy that night. I should have asked for help, but I thought I could cope. They gave me a choice, resign or restart my training from the beginning. I couldn't redo my training, it would have made me look like a fool in front of the other nurses and everyone would talk about me, so I resigned. Unfortunately for you, Miss Showers, I didn't take an advanced pharmacology qualification course. What I learned in my Pharmacological classes was the basics; an understanding of how drugs work in the body to achieve the desired effect. How to anticipate and recognise the potential side effects they may have on a patient, but not the preparation of such drugs.'

'That's a pity. I had hoped you could point me in the direction of who the killer might be.'

'I'm sorry, Miss Showers, I cannot. Is there anything else I can help you with?'

'No, not for the moment, thank you for your time,' I got up to leave, but before I reached the office door, I stopped and turned to ask one more question.

'Where would one get hold of Aconitum, if I wanted some?'

'It is not a drug I'm familiar with. In any case, you couldn't; most drugs can only be obtained by prescription from a doctor or hospital.'

'Thank you.' Sitting in my car, I cursed under my breath. The trap I'd hoped to set for her had failed. She had not given herself away. She was either being very clever or she wasn't the person I was looking for. I needed to find a suspect who knew about apothecary.

After my failure with Ada Betterman, I wanted a positive result to end the day on. So I went for a walk along the cliff-top to think.

'I was left with Natalie West. She may not know about drugs, but working in a bank gave her access to lots of personal details on its customers. Some of whom may also have had run-ins with Aunty that I don't know about. She may even have found one willing to help her arrange the murder.'

I convinced myself that Natalie West made a better suspect than Ada Betterman, and therefore, was worth re-investigating.

Arriving at the cafe in Bridlington where Natalie West worked, I looked through the window rather than going inside as I did last time. A different waitress was serving at the tables.

'Where are you, Miss West? Is this one of your days off or do you work the late shift today? Hopefully, I'll find you at home.'

As I peered inside, a customer seated at a table close to the window looked up at me and smiled. Seeing his face made me jump away, suddenly embarrassed by what I must look like to onlookers. I backed away from the window.

'Bother, I'll have to try her home address.'

The walk to her address didn't take long. However, as I walked down the street, I spotted a large black car parked at the kerb in front of her gate. 'Did she have visitors?' I stopped. There was no point in going to see her now. If she had someone with her, she would never let me in to speak to her. On the other hand, if she did have someone with her, I wanted to know who it was. If it was her old bank manager, it would explain where she had got the money from to set up Aunty's murder. I looked around for somewhere to hide and wait to see who came out to the car. The trouble was it was a terraced street and all the houses had tiny front gardens. If I went back to the car park to fetch my car, I risked missing who Natalie's visitor was. While I dithered on the pavement trying to make up my mind on what to do next, the decision was made for me. Natalie's front door opened and two people stepped out. I turned to the closest house and knocked on the door, keeping my back towards Natalie's visitors. I took a notebook out of my handbag as the door opened.

'Good morning, sir. I'm doing a survey on soap powder. Would you mind telling me which brand you use?' It was only then that I noticed how the man was dressed. All he had on was a pair of trousers and a vest. His vest was covered in the stains of what looked like a week of meals eaten whilst sat in front of the television.

'Get lost!' He slammed the door. A second later, I heard a car starting. Spinning around, I was in time to see the big black car drive past me, with Robin and Heidi Steel in it.

*****

Unnoticed by me.

On the same street, Rex, dressed in old overalls and wearing a flat cap, pushed his little dustcart a little further along the street and then swept up a pile of litter onto his shovel before depositing it into his cart.

Chapter Fifteen

Wednesday.

George, the postman, arrived with a large bundle of letters. 'You're suddenly very popular, April. What is this lot; fan mail?'

'No, but I've got a good idea what it is and where it has come from.'

'Oh, yes. Somewhere important, is it? To help you solve the case you're on, I take it?'

'I won't know that until I've studied it all and I know you don't have the time to hang around and wait that long. Shouldn't you be on your way?'

'You're a spoilsport April, you never let me in on any of your cases. We postmen get to see and hear all sorts of interesting tittle-tattle that could be useful in solving a crime.'

'Right you are, George. I'll remember that next time I have a murder that happens on your rounds? You'll be my prime suspect.'

'Okay April, I'll keep my eyes and ears open; hey, what do you mean, I'll be your prime suspect?'

'Bye, George.'

Eagerly, I opened the molehill of mail on my desk. Most of it, as I suspected, was from Somerset House and contained the birth certificates I'd requested, but why they had all arrived in separate envelopes, baffled me. Unfortunately, there were no marriage certificates included with this batch. So, assuming they'd arrive tomorrow or the day after I got on with reading each birth certificate, then placing it in its allotted suspect's file. Holly's birth certificate confirmed everything she had told me about where she had come from, and so did all the men's birth certificates. The only female birth certificates that had arrived had been those for the unmarried women, Natalie West, Octavia Tone, Ada Betterman and Robin Steels daughter, Elizabeth. They were still using their birth names. Glancing through the certificates I didn't see anything that would help me a great deal, but I reckoned once the marriage certificates arrived, I would have the maiden names of all my other female suspects and be able to request copies of their birth certificates from Somerset House. The only other thing that arrived from Somerset House was a note saying that there was no birth certificate for an Elizabeth Milbank, matching the locations and dates that I had provided. This was disappointing, though not unexpected. I had suspected that the name would turn out to be a fictitious one. However, I'd still needed to check it out.

Glancing through the birth certificates once again, I checked for any places that might show a link between my suspects. Most of my suspects came from Yorkshire, except Holly, who had been born near Norwich in Norfolk, Octavia

Tone, who was from Edinburgh and Natalie West came from Sterling in Scotland. I wrote down the name of each town that each suspect had been born in and looked for alternative matches.

The first match that came to mind was that Natalie West and Octavia Tone were both single women and both came from Scotland. I wondered if there was a chance they had known each other before they moved to Yorkshire? Ada Betterman had been born in Driffield, as had Aunty Violet. Everyone else came from a scattering of places. I needed the marriage certificates to make further progress with this line of enquiry. Though there was one line of enquiry that I hadn't looked into yet, Aunty Violet. She had lived in various places in Yorkshire and had, to my knowledge, never had a job or husband to support her. So, from where had she got the money to support herself? Mummy would know.

'Your Aunty Violet was a very shrewd woman. Our father, your grandfather, owned an antique shop and Violet worked for him after leaving school. It seemed a bit old-fashioned and dull to me, so I never bothered with it, but your Aunty Violet loved it and continued to run the shop after your grandfather died. It was during those early years that she grew to appreciate paintings, landscapes mostly, and collected a few for herself, not that they were worth much. Anyway, during the war and just after, times were hard. Your Aunty Violet soon discovered that soldiers who had brought stuff back to England that they had found or bought cheap during the war, would sooner have some money in their pockets than keep their souvenirs. Most, if not all of them, didn't know the true value of the items they were selling; they just wanted a couple of pounds for something they couldn't use. Your Aunty Violet got a reputation for buying this junk. She would pay two pounds for it, no questions asked. After the war, more and more ex-soldiers turned up to get rid of their finds. Only, not all of it was junk. Now and then something rare was brought in. Violet still only gave them two pounds, but she would then sell the rare, valuable items at a London auction for hundreds and sometimes thousands of pounds. She quickly amassed a small fortune. It didn't take her long to realise that buying and selling antiques from the shop was slow and unpredictable work, so she sold the antique shop and bought an auctioneer's saleroom in York. That business provided her with a steady income and she could afford to pay for someone to run it for her. She hired accountants to keep an eye on the finances and she became a lady of leisure, able to do as she pleased.'

'Well, some people have all the luck,' I said enviously.

'Yes, there was a bit of luck involved, but Violet worked hard in those early days. She earned her money. Unfortunately, it turned her into a selfish, bitter woman as well. I suppose you could say; it was her ambition that became the death of her. If only she had married and settled down, things may have turned out differently.'

'I know she moved about a lot and didn't settle in any one town, why was that?' I asked, now that I'd got Mummy talking about Aunty Violet.

'Yes, she did. I suppose it was due to all the people she kept upsetting.'

‘Do you still have her old addresses and when she lived at them?’

‘Yes, I have an address book. Each time she changed her address, I had to make a fresh note in it, along with the date she moved in. It was the only way I keep track of her. Why?’

‘I know there’s only a remote chance but, I would like to check the places and dates where she lived, against the addresses and dates on my list of suspects to look for more clues.’

Thursday.

I started the day by making a chart that included the birth addresses of each of my suspects. In the next column, I put their current address. In the third column, I put a tick if the town corresponded with a place where Aunty Violet had lived at the same time. There were only a few suspects that had an address, with dates that coincided with Aunty Violet living in the same town. They were the Rev Warlock and his wife, Natalie West and Mr and Mrs Stone. Bonnie Stone certainly had enough of a motive to want to kill Aunty. Inconveniently, Robin Steel didn’t have any address that matched one of Aunty Violet’s previous addresses. I couldn’t help but feel disappointed at my lack of progress. Mrs Stone had been very hostile during my interview with her husband, and though he seemed to be an upstanding member of the community now, he had a past, and I couldn’t shake the feeling that they were both hiding something. I was sure I was missing something. So I started examining my evidence once again. However, looking at my lists told me nothing I didn’t know already. I couldn’t see a connection between my suspects, no one person stood out more than any other; all I had was hunches and feelings. In a fit of frustration, I screwed up my chart and tossed it in the bin; I needed those marriage certificates to arrive, soon.

Maybe I was tackling the problem from the wrong direction. What if I took out from my list of suspects all the people I believed didn't kill Aunty Violet. Who would that leave me with?

If I took out Holly because she'd spent the last couple of years in America, Octavia Tone because she lived in Scotland for even longer, the Ramsbottoms because they were wrapped up in their cattle farm and Ada Betterman; No, I'd better keep her in for now. That left me with:-

Ada Betterman
Reverend Warlock
Natalie West
Rocky Punch
Roofus Stone
Robin Steel

The murderer, whoever it was, needed to be well organised and wealthy enough to pay for the hotel rooms, the museum trip and the dinner. They also had to be angry enough, possibly deranged, to hold a grudge for years and to plan and commit this murder. Working my way down my list, picking out the ones who had the skills to organise a murder of this type was one thing, but not all of them had the money to pay for it and those that did have the money didn't give me the impression that they would want to risk everything they had by organising it. However; what if it wasn't one person who murdered Aunty Violet? What if two or more of these people were working together? If I could find a link between them, other than simply being a victim of Aunty Violet, it may lead me to the evidence I needed to make a case against them. Oh, when would the marriage certificates arrive?

A knock on the door broke my train of thought.

'Fancy a cuppa?' asked Jennifer.

'I could murder a cup of tea right now, thanks.' I was in the middle of getting up to go through to the kitchen when it hit me. TEA, Mrs Downy. I'd put it to the back of my mind. Who had attacked me during the night, and why? It had to be linked with the death of Aunty because no one except Aunty Violet and the hotel receptionist knew I would be there until I arrived, so with me turning up, it meant my attack was not part of the original murder plot. There may be more to find at the hotel. It was time to go back to Harrogate and talk to the hotel staff.

'Sorry, Jennifer, I've got something to do; I must dash.'

Resolutely standing in front of the hotel reception desk, I asked to speak to Mr Bunkhouse.

'Is there a problem, Miss? May I be of assistance?' asked a smartly dressed man behind the counter.

'Would you be kind enough to inform Mr Bunkhouse that Miss April Showers, private detective, would like a word with him?' I handed the receptionist my business card. He looked at it and then back at me.

'I will find out if he is available; one moment, Miss.'

He quickly returned with the hotel manager hot on his heels.

'Miss Showers, how nice to see you again; please come through to my office.' 'Mr Usher, coffee for two in my office, if you wouldn't mind.'

'Yes, Sir.'

'Miss Showers, what brings you back to our hotel? Are you planning on staying with us, my offer still stands?'

'No, Mr Bunkhouse. I've come to question your hotel staff in connection with my Aunty's death.'

'You mean you think one of them did it?'

'No, but they may know something that the police have overlooked. Hotel staff see and hear a great many things that guests do not appreciate. I would like to speak to the waiters who served us that evening, the night porter and the chambermaid who cleaned my room after I left.'

'Miss Showers, what you are asking is quite impossible, think of all the disruption it would cause; never mind upsetting the hotel staff.'

'Mr Bunkhouse, someone killed my Aunty that night and came close to killing me. The Harrogate police have assured me that they are investigating this as a murder and attempted murder, so unless you want me to fetch them here and get them to interview your staff; I suggest you let me do it a little more discreetly!'

'But, but.' A knock on the door was followed by Mr Usher, the receptionist, bringing in a tray of coffee.

'Will there be anything else, sir?'

'No, get out!' snapped the hotel manager.

The receptionist, looking shocked, placed the tray on the corner of the hotel manager's desk and quickly left the room.

‘Miss Showers, please be reasonable. What could you possibly learn from the staff that you don’t already know?’

‘That is just the point, Mr Bunkhouse. Until I question them, I will not know what I don’t already know. Will I? We can start with the receptionist who took the booking for my room from Aunty Violet.’

‘I insist on being present during the interviews with my staff.’

‘No, Mr Bunkhouse, I cannot allow that. I need your staff to feel that they can speak freely. If you are in the room, they will feel intimidated and refuse to talk openly.’

‘That’s ridiculous; I get on very well with all the staff.’

‘Nonetheless, that is what I want; unless you’d rather have the police trampling through your front door.’

Reluctantly, Mr Bunkhouse gave in, knowing he had no choice but to do things my way.

I started with Mr Usher.

‘Mr Usher, your manager tells me you were the receptionist who took the telephone booking from Miss Birch, to reserve a room for me. How does the booking system work?’

‘I was on the early shift that day. I wasn’t in the hotel when your Aunty died.’

‘I understand, but that is not what I asked. Please explain the room booking system.’

‘I’m sorry I don’t remember the exact telephone call I received from Mrs Birch, but all room bookings follow the same pattern. A person calls to make a reservation and the receptionist checks the availability of a room and gives a price for the length of stay. If the client is happy to book the room, we pencil a reservation into the reservations book for the date requested. Then, if there's time for it to arrive, we ask for a letter of confirmation and a deposit. If not, we hope for the best that the client turns up when they say they will.'

'Did Miss Birch send a letter?'

'Yes, I believe she did.'

'What happens to the letter after they have made the booking?'

'It's kept on file by the head receptionist until the guest has left the hotel, after which it is thrown away.'

'What time does the night porter come on duty?'

'Old Mr Scops, he starts work at eight o'clock, but he's usually here just after seven. He likes to get a bit of supper from the kitchen before he starts work.'

'Thank you, Mr Usher, that will be all for now. I will return later to speak to Mr Scops.'

Interviewing the waiters who had been on duty over the weekend in question proved fruitless. There was nothing more I could learn from them, for now. As I would have to wait a few hours for Mr Scops to come on duty and even longer before I could speak to the chambermaid, I took advantage of the manager's telephone and called Mother to let her know I would be staying in Harrogate overnight. However, after what happened last time, I would not be staying in this hotel again, so I booked a room in a smaller hotel around the corner.

After dinner at my hotel, I returned to the Harrogate Spa to speak to Mr Scops. The night porter was in the hotel staffroom, an undecorated room with a large kitchen table at its heart and a variety of mismatched chairs set around it. As I entered the room, Mr Scops looked up from his supper and froze, his hand halfway to his mouth with a fork full of food.

'I'm sorry to disturb you, please finish your meal.'

'You can't come in here; this is staff only.'

'It's alright; I have permission from the manager, Mr Bunkhouse. It is you I would like to speak to.'

'What about?'

'Finish your dinner. I can wait. I wouldn't want it to get cold.'

He continued to eat, eying me suspiciously over his plate. Wiping his mouth on the back of his hand, he pushed his plate away, his eyes searching my face.

'I've seen you before somewhere. What do you want?'

I could tell from his expression that he hadn't remembered where he had seen me. So I reminded him.

'Yes, Mr Scops. I stayed here a couple of weeks ago. You came to my room after I had been attacked during the night. It was the same night that Miss Birch died in the dining room.'

'Weren't nowt to do with me! Takes me all my time to get up and down all those bleeding stairs, never mind killing old ladies and attacking young lasses in their beds.'

'I'm not accusing you of anything, Mr Scops. In fact, I'm grateful for the help you gave me that night. I would just like to ask you a couple of questions about that night.'

'O, aye, like what?'

'Did you see anyone running away from my room after you came to see what all the fuss was about?'

'No. I told the police that at the time. There was no one, just me until I got to your room.'

'You saw no one at all, please try to remember; anyone at all?'

'No one passed me on the stairs. Shortly after you screamed Mr Bunkhouse came into reception, that's all. It was Mr Bunkhouse who sent me up to your room.'

'What was he doing up so late?'

'I don't know. Checking everything was locked up out the back, I suppose. That's usually his last job before going to bed.'

'I heard a scream and people moving about. Normally, I wouldn't have bothered to come up, but Mr Bunkhouse insisted, so I thought I'd better go and see what was happening. Sometimes guests get a little drunk and have wild get-togethers in their rooms late at night. They don't like to be disturbed if you know what I mean. But sometimes, I have to, because other guests complain about the noise.'

'Why didn't Mr Bunkhouse come up with you?'

'I don't know. Suspect he thought it was my job to sort it out.'

'When you went back downstairs to fetch him, where did you find him?'

'He'd left reception so I went up to his flat on the top floor of the hotel.'

'That's strange. If he had to come up the stairs to get to his flat, why didn't he stop off at my room to see what was wrong? You may have needed help?'

'There are stairs on the other side of the hotel which lead up to the staff quarters.'

‘So, there are no stairs to the staff quarters on this side of the hotel.’

‘O, yes. But, we’re not allowed to use them. There’s a door at the end of each corridor, marked private and fire escape. You don’t have to use the main stairs if you know your way around.’

‘Thank you, Mr Scops. How very interesting. That will be all for now.’

After leaving the staffroom I made my way up the main stairs to find the room I had stayed in that night. Sure enough, the door at the end of the corridor led to the fire escape and a second staff staircase. When I opened the door, I found the stairs were narrow and not well lit, but I could see that I would be able to get to all floors of the hotel without being seen by other guests. I returned to my hotel and settled in for the night, satisfied with my bit of detective work.

Friday.

After checking out of my hotel, I was about to drive around to the Harrogate Spa when I noticed how low on petrol I’d let my car get. So leaving my luggage in the car and the car in the hotel car park, I walked around to the Harrogate Spa.

‘Would you kindly inform Mr Bunkhouse that Miss Showers has arrived and would like to interview the hotel chambermaid that cleaned my room? He is expecting me.’

The receptionist at the Harrogate Spa scurried away and left me under the scrutinising eye of his colleague, only to return moments later on his own.

‘I’m sorry the Manager is busy at the moment. He has asked me to assist you, Miss Showers. Your room I believe was on the second floor so you will need to speak to Mable and Nancy; they prepare the guest rooms on that floor.'

We found them stripping a bed of used linen. My receptionist guide entered first.

'Miss Showers is a private detective; Mr Bunkhouse has said you are to answer her questions.' The women looked shocked.

'It's perfectly all right, you are not in any kind of trouble,' I reassured them. The receptionist stood in the doorway, watching us all. 'Thank you, you may return to the reception desk, now.' After a peeved look from the man, he spun on his heel and marched off.

'Now ladies, please be seated, I won't keep you long.' Both of them sat on the edge of the bed they'd been making.

'Do you always work together?'

'Yes, Miss. Except when one of us has a day off, then we work on our own,' answered Nancy, but that's only on Mondays and Tuesdays.'

As I kept them talking, I looked over their uniforms for any missing buttons that matched the one found in my ripped pillow, but I couldn't spot any. However, that didn't mean a lost button hadn't already been replaced.

'When you finish here, what do you do?' They looked at each other as though surprised by the question.

'We go home. We've got families to see to,' they answered in unison.

'So you don't live on the premises like some other staff?'

'No, not us; we live local; on Station Road.'

'After I left, and you were cleaning my room; did you find anything?'

‘Like what, Miss?’ asked Mable.

‘I haven’t lost anything. It’s just that a button was found and the police think my attacker lost it. I was wondering if anything else had been found in the room that shouldn’t have been there?’

‘No, Miss. All property that guests leave behind, we hand into reception and we didn’t find anything, did we, Mable?’

‘Thank you, Ladies, I won’t keep you any longer. You have been very helpful.’

I made my way back downstairs. I had learnt little except that the hotel was larger than it appeared and had a hidden staircase, which explained why no one had seen my attacker fleeing the scene. Stopping off at reception, I asked the receptionist to thank Mr Bunkhouse for his and his staff’s help in my investigation. The man who had shown me up to the second floor smiled and said he would pass on my thanks.

‘Oh, by the way,’ do you know where I can get some petrol for my car. I have a long drive home and I seem to be getting low?’

‘Yes, Miss. The closest petrol station is down by the shops on Swan Road near the pub.’

‘Where is that?’

‘Here Miss, I’ll draw you a map. The receptionist quickly drew a pencil sketch of the Harrogate road system showing the way I should go to get to the petrol station.’

‘Thank you, you are very kind. I slipped the paper into my handbag and left.’

Back in my car, I propped the map up on the dashboard and started the engine. The sun was shining, and I was looking forward to a pleasant drive home. With glances at the map, I soon found the petrol station. Whilst the petrol station attendant filled my car and with the sun beaming through the windscreen, I was just about to put my little map away when something caught my eye. An image captured within the paper. Opening up the paper and holding it to the windscreen, I saw, highlighted by the sun, a watermark in the shape of a lion. It looked familiar, yet I couldn't remember where I had seen it before. As I was trying to remember where I'd seen the lion before, the petrol station attendant tapped on the car window.

'That'll be seven shillings and nine-pence, Miss.'

I put the paper in my handbag to study later, got out my purse to pay the man and then whilst he was giving me change from a ten-shilling note another car pulled in behind me. Not wanting to hold the driver up, I dropped the change into my handbag and drove off.

Saturday.

Mummy woke me at nine o'clock with a cup of tea and two slices of toast.

'What's this? Breakfast in bed; is it my birthday?'

'No dear, though I do have a favour to ask of you. My friend, Mrs Jones from down the avenue is worried about her daughter. I know you like to keep your weekends free but Mrs Jones didn't want anyone to see her going into your office, so I said that she could speak to you here at ten o'clock.'

'Mummy, did you have to?'

'I'm sorry, April, but she is a good friend and she is worried stiff about Andrea.'

'Alright, let me drink my tea. I'll come downstairs as soon as I'm ready.'

Whilst talking to Mrs Jones I learnt that Andrea was staying out late at night and spending most of the weekend away from home, but not saying where she was going or who she was with. Mrs Jones wanted me to find out what her fifteen-year-old daughter was up to.

'Andrea will be out of the house by eleven o'clock in the morning and not come home until nearly midnight.' I looked at the clock. If I was quick I could follow her.

As I reached the garden gate Andrea was passing by on the opposite side of the avenue. Taking my time I followed her keeping to my side of the road until we reached the street at the top. She turned left and headed towards the main road at the top of the street. Casually I followed behind her. She reached the main road and went directly to the bus stop to catch the bus into town. Unfortunately, I'd rushed out without my handbag and purse so I was unable to follow her. However, tomorrow, if she did the same thing again, I would be at the bus stop before her to catch the same bus.

Sunday.

As Andrea went to the top deck of the bus, I stayed on the lower deck taking a seat on one of the side benches so I could watch for her getting off. She didn't get off until the bus reached the bus station, where she met a much older man who was waiting for her. She kissed him and then, arm in arm, Andrea was led towards a parked car. I ran after her.

'Hello, Andrea, would you like to introduce me to your friend. I'm a private detective hired by your parents.'

The man looked at me in horror, unlinked his arm from Andrea and fled towards the car. Andrea turned to me and screamed at me.

'What have you done that for? I love him and he loves me.' I grabbed her by both arms and gave her a shake.

'If he loved you, why did he run off and abandon you?' I spent the next two hours walking around town with Andrea, talking about older men taking advantage of young girls and how it always ended with the man going to prison and the girl's life is ruined forever.

'If you love him, Andrea, you wouldn't want him to go to prison, would you? When I take you home tell your parents that you had been seeing a boyfriend, but he dumped you today and that you will never see him again and that you will never stay out late again without telling them where you are going or I will tell them the truth.

Chapter Sixteen

Monday.

The postman delivered the long-awaited certificates, so as soon as he was gone, I separated the certificates and spread them over my desk, matching them up with the birth certificates to my suspects. Holly's was missing because she was married in America and there were none for Natalie West or Octavia Tone, they were still single. I already knew Aunty Violet had never married. That detail had been confirmed by Mummy and had not come as a surprise.

The Rev Warlock and his wife Faith had been married in Leeds, and so had Rocky and Judy Punch. However the marriage certificates didn't tell me where Faith and Judy had been born, but they did give me their maiden names.

Roofus Stone and his wife Bonnie had been married in York. That linked up with Octavia Tone, but the Stone's had no musical or Scottish link.

Now that I had the maiden names for Bonnie Stone, Faith Warlock and Judy Punch, I had to get their birth certificates to complete a full background on them. I was too busy to go back to London to find them.

The three remaining unmarried women on my list of suspects were Octavia Tone, the music teacher, she's living in Edinburgh; Ada Betterman the nurse, running a nursing home in Scarborough and Natalie West the waitress in Bridlington. Of the three, it was Natalie West who troubled me the most; there was something not quite right about her. She had every reason to still hold a grudge against Aunty.

The information on all the married couples' marriage certificates was what I had expected to see, except the one for Robin Steel and Heidi. Their marriage certificate showed they had married in Leeds and that Heidi's maiden name was Katin, an unusual name that I hadn't come across before. Thinking about it, I also realised that Heidi isn't a common British female name and with the surname of Katin, it was possible, that she'd not been born in Britain. I remembered Robin Steel telling me about her being in Germany. Her father's name was Peter Katin, shoemaker (deceased). But what came as an even bigger surprise was that one of the witnesses on the wedding certificate had signed her name, Faith Warlock. I stared at the certificate for a moment, unable to believe what I was reading. Why was Faith Warlock listed as a witness on the Steel's wedding certificate? What was the Warlocks' connection to Robin Steel? So, with no birth certificate for Heidi, as I hadn't known her maiden name before now, she too joined Natalie West as needing further investigation, and with her went Faith Warlock.

I knew, from what the prison governor in Leeds had told me, that Robin Steel had been married before, and that his daughter had died whilst he was in prison, but I hadn't thought to order the marriage certificate from his first marriage. I knew his first wife was called Georgina, I should have looked it up whilst I was there, so now, it meant a return trip to Summerset House. I looked at the clock, it was too late to get to London and back today, so it would have to be a job for tomorrow. Today, I'll pay another visit to the vicarage in Easington.

I parked my car around the corner from the church, on Beck Lane and made my way back to the church. It was the first time I'd taken any notice of it, even though its prominent place on the raised ground in the centre of the village gave it a domineering presence over the buildings surrounding it. The green island of the churchyard was filled with old tombstones from a time when the village had seen more prosperous times. Walking up the path from the village square, under the shade of the churchyard trees, on a warm summer's day was like being in a large garden. It felt peaceful, a place of tranquillity until I drew closer to the church. As I caught sight of a fresh grave with flowers covering it a chill ran up my spine. My mind became fuzzy and I became unsteady on my feet. Sitting on the footpath wall, I put my head in my hands. A sense of foreboding crowded in on me. Flashing images of people dressed in black, my mother in tears and a tiny coffin being lowered into the ground came to mind and repeated over and over. Just before I passed out, I felt a hand on my shoulder and I heard a voice asking, 'are you all right, my dear?'

My head cleared, and I looked up into the face of Reverend Warlock.

'Yes, thank you. It must be the heat,' I blurted, feeling embarrassed.

'Come inside and sit down until you feel better.' I let the reverend take me by the hand and lead me to the church door, but the feeling returned.

'I'm sorry, I can't. I'll sit here if that is alright.' I took a seat on a bench close to the church wall.

'Should I fetch a doctor?'

'No, no. I'll be fine in a minute or two. Thank you.' The reverend looked at me for a moment before asking.

'What brings you here, my dear, visiting someone in the village?'

I was just about to respond and say, 'Yes, you and your wife,' when I realised he hadn't remembered me from my first visit when I had spoken mostly to his wife because he'd been busy.

'No. I live in Leeds. I'm just taking a short holiday in the area. I was passing the church and thought I would stop to look at it, but I became a little shaky and sat down.'

The reverend sat on the bench next to me. 'That's a coincidence; I used to have a parish in Leeds. It included Armley Jail, you know.'

'Really, isn't that where they put the most dangerous criminals?'

The reverend smiled a little, 'some, not all of them. Some are just lost souls in need of being shown the right path. My wife used to visit the jail every week to talk to the prisoners. She became friends with some and they would confide in her.

She helped them keep in touch with loved ones at home, that sort of thing. We even got invited to the wedding of one ex-prisoner. They asked me to bless their joyful union.'

With my heart racing, I stood up. 'Thank you, Reverend, I'm feeling much better now. I think I'll be on my way.' I shook his hand and headed back down the church path with my new evidence to find my car. Faith must have known Robin Steel for years. So why didn't she and Robin Steel speak to each other when we were all together in Harrogate?

That evening I helped Mummy with the washing up after dinner as usual.

'I went to interview a suspect today, a reverend at Easington,' I told her.

She stopped what she was doing, 'A vicar, surely not.'

'Yes, it's true. He and his wife were at the hotel in Harrogate when Aunty died.'

'And, you think he had something to do with it?'

'I'm not sure, yet. But he and his wife knew another couple who were there, a Mr and Mrs Steel. He'd been a prisoner in Armley Jail where the Reverend was chaplain and his wife a prison visitor. But, whilst I was walking through the churchyard a strange thing happened to me. I became dizzy and nervous. It got worse the closer I got to the church. It got so bad, I had to sit down. It's silly, I know. It's just that I can't understand why it happened, I felt fine before I reached the churchyard. I kept getting flashes of a coffin and people dressed in black. The Reverend Warlock found me just before I passed out. Talking to him for a few minutes helped clear my head. That's how I learned about his connection to one of the other suspects. Do you think I need to see a doctor about the dizziness?

'Maybe, but I've just been reading in a novel about a woman who suffered from similar symptoms. Her problem was repressed memories from her childhood. You may be suffering from something similar now you know about your brother and that he died soon after birth. He is buried in the local churchyard. You found it very upsetting to see his coffin lowered into the ground.'

'Do you think that is what I was remembering; my brother's funeral and I have blocked it out for all these years?'

'It's possible. The mind can play funny tricks on us. Sometimes, during the night, I think I can hear Michael crying.'

Tuesday.

Waking early, still feeling tired after a night of strange dreams, I wasn't looking forward to a long train journey.

When I arrived in Hull, I turned into the car park at Paragon Station. The smell of steam, smoke and burning coal wafted across the platforms and stuck in my throat making me cough. I needed my morning tea and biscuits, but they would have to wait until I was on the train. I bought a couple of magazines from the WHSmith kiosk and headed for my train.

Finding an empty compartment, I sat by the window and dropped the magazines on the seat at my side. It was only as I was jolted awake when the train left the station that I realised I had dozed off as soon as I lay my head against the wall of the carriage. I discovered that a middle-aged couple and a young boy had joined me. The boy was sitting opposite me, looking out of the window. I blinked at the light as the sun shone in my eyes.

'Going far?' asked the woman.

'London.'

'We get off at Doncaster. I've never been to London,' she replied. I smiled at her but didn't reply. Getting up I went to buy the tea and biscuits I'd promised myself before getting on the train. Staying in the buffet car until I'd finished my refreshment allowed me the time to wake up properly. Returning to my seat, I passed the time reading. By the time I'd finished reading my magazine, we'd arrived at Doncaster and the family left, leaving me on my own for the last leg of the journey.

Before the train reached London, I'd had another nap and was now feeling ready to tackle Summerset House.

I knew the dates Robin Steel had been in jail and that his daughter had been ten years old when she had died. I didn't need a death certificate for Robin Steel's daughter, as I had been told when and why she had died. Knowing her first name was Elizabeth meant all I had to do was find a girl of the correct age, born in Leeds, to parents called Robin and Georgina Steel ten years back from the dates her father had been in jail. This gave me a limited date range and reduced the number of books I had to look through to find her birth certificate. The birth record would also give me the maiden name of the daughter's mother enabling me to find Robin Steels first marriage certificate.

After a few hours of searching and with aching arms from lifting the heavy reference books, I ordered the certificates from the reception desk. This time, I paid extra to have them prepared the same day, that way I could take them home with me and wouldn't have to wait for the post. I still had to wait until five o'clock for them, but at least I wouldn't have to come back again. Unfortunately, it meant catching a later train home than I'd hoped to.

It was too late for lunch so I took a stroll along Victoria Embankment, found a cafe and enjoyed an Italian-style coffee with a large slice of Ricotta Cassata Cake. It had been a long day, I could only hope it had been worth the effort.

Just before five o'clock, I made my way back to Summerset Hose and collected the certificates. Without stopping to look at them, I rushed outside and hailed a taxi to take me to Kings Cross Station; with a bit of luck, I'd catch the five-thirty train, home.

Finding an empty seat in a crowded compartment, I squeezed between two large ladies. I was dying to open my envelope to read the certificates, but the idea of the ladies on each side of me staring over my shoulder to see what I was reading put me off. It was a stop at Peterborough which allowed enough passengers to leave the train to gave me space to slide along the seat to the window before opening my envelope.

First out was the marriage certificate for Georgina Milbank and Robin Steel, married in Leeds at the registry office. Then I took out the birth certificate, Elizabeth Steel, born to Georgina and Robin Steel; mother's maiden name, Milbank.

Of course, Milbank; Elizabeth Milbank was the name on Aunty Violet's invitation to the hotel weekend. These certificates gave me a positive link between Robin Steel and the hotel invitations. Something troubled me about the name Elizabeth Milbank, something someone else had said. I scratched my head and then started going through my interview notes. It took me a few minutes to find. During her interview, Octavia Tone had told that her invitation had come from Aunty Violet. So why would Aunty have done that? It could only mean she didn't and someone else had planned the hotel gathering very deliberately and carefully. Also, Nr Bunkhouse, the hotel manager never did contact me with the name of the person who had paid for all our hotel reservations. Wait until Inspector Allswell gets to hear what I've discovered.

The rest of the train journey back to Hull seemed to take far too long. When we arrived, I ran to the ticket barrier, throwing my ticket at the ticket collector on the gate as I rushed through to get to my car. It was getting late, I couldn't go back to my office, so I went straight home. I'd telephone Inspector Allswell with my news from there.

'Sorry, Mummy must dash. I need to telephone someone urgently.'

'Hello, may I speak to Inspector Allswell, please? My name is April Showers; we are working on a case together. I have some very urgent information for him.'

'Well, when will he be in?'

'He no longer works on the case or works in Harrogate. What do you mean? Where is he?'

'Who is in charge of Miss Birch's murder case?'

'Sergeant Duffy. Thank you. Yes, I will telephone him on Monday morning.' I slammed down the receiver.

'Now, now, dear. What's happened to get you so upset?'

'I'm sorry Mummy. It's just that I've discovered a major clue to who killed Aunty Violet, and the police don't seem interested at all. I don't understand.'

'Never mind, dear. It will all become clear when you speak to that sergeant on Monday morning. Have you had something to eat? Come and tell me about your day over a cup of tea.'

Holly's film star clothes had arrived from the hotel in London a few days ago and had been sat in her bedroom ready for when she went back to Hollywood.

She'd just finished telling us they did not need her at the hotel in Driffield until that evening when I got my flash of inspiration.

'Holly, would you like to help me with Auntys murder investigation? It would mean leaving your job at the hotel and moving to Harrogate, but if you could get a job there, you could act as an undercover agent.'

'What would I have to do and where would I live?'

'Hopefully, you'll get a job as a waitress or chambermaid and live in at the hotel, some of the other staff do.'

'Well, I was thinking of giving up my job here in Driffield now that I have an independent income; however, if you think I can help you, of course, I will. But, I should go as Holly Starbrightly, the film star.'

‘You’re right. Very well then, go as Holly Starbrightly and promote your film. You are no longer wanted by the police. So Holly the film star is free to hit the big time once again. I will telephone the press and let them know you are coming. I’m sure they will want to know where you have been hiding all this time; but please don’t tell them about us. Just say you took a job at the hotel in a small town, keeping a low profile until the mess with your husband was sorted out. I can’t see the manager turning you away from the Hotel with all the publicity you will bring it. Then, whilst you are there, you simply ask the staff about Aunty’s death. They’ll know you were there at the time it happened. So, I bet they’ll tell you everything they know for the price of an autograph.’

‘Very well, it’s the least I can do to make up for all the help you and your family have given me.’

‘Thank you, Holly. I will telephone you in a day or two to find out how you are getting on.’

Chapter Seventeen

Wednesday.

As soon as I arrived in the office, I was on the telephone to the Harrogate police asking to speak to Sergeant Duffy.

'Good morning, Sergeant, my name is Miss Showers. I'm investigating the death of Violet Birch at the Yorkshire Dales Spa Hotel in Harrogate. I believe you have taken the case over now Inspector Allswell has left?'

'Yes, I understand the lady was your Aunty, Miss Showers, and you attended as her companion?'

'That is correct, Sergeant. I'm calling you because I have some important additional evidence you should know about.'

'What is that?'

'I can prove a connection between Robin Steel, the hotel and the name on Aunty's invitation to the weekend at the hotel.'

'Excellent, Miss Showers; pop your evidence in the post and I will look at it when it arrives to verify how valid it may be to my investigation.'

'Can't I bring it to you? We could discuss the case and the fresh evidence?'

'Oh, no Miss Showers, you are far too closely involved with the case, Miss Birch was family. I haven't even ruled you out as a suspect. I'll have you know I've spent twenty-seven years as a police officer; I know how to investigate a crime. You just send me your evidence and I'll evaluate how relevant it is to the case. Now, if that is all Miss Showers, I have a lot of work to do; goodbye.'

I sat, staring at the telephone receiver in my hand, unable to believe how condescending and pompous that insufferable man had been, before slamming it down on its cradle. Whilst sitting and wondering what to do next, Holly knocked on the door and came in.

'Hi, April.'

'Holly, what are you doing? I thought you'd be getting ready for your starring role in Harrogate?'

'There's just one thing that we've forgotten about. When I go to Harrogate, I need to arrive in style as befitting a film star. The problem is, I don't have a car and I wouldn't know how to drive one if I did.'

'Yes, I see. I hadn't thought of that. Wait a minute, I've had an idea. I know someone with a fabulous car. I bet I can talk him into taking you there.' Flicking through my address book, I soon found Rex's home phone number.

'Hello; is that Mrs Barker? It's April Showers; I was hoping to speak to Rex.'

'He's at work; very well, I'll call him this evening when he gets home. If you don't mind, would you tell him I called, please?'

Once again, I laid out all the evidence of Aunty's murder on my desk.

'Is there anything I can do to help?' asked Holly.

'Yes, you can help me sort through this.'

'This is my list of suspects and the evidence gathered so far. As I sort through it and explain what I have found, you can tell me if it makes sense or not. I understand why Robin Steel bore a grudge against Aunty after the death of his daughter during the time he was in prison, but I haven't worked out how Faith Warlock and her husband fit in with Robin Steel and the murder of Aunty. Faith Warlock can't deny that they didn't know each other. She visited him in prison and her name is on the Steel's wedding certificate as a witness. Then there's Natalie West. I saw the Steels' leaving Natalie West's flat, so where does she fit in? What is it that Natalie West has brought to Robin Steel's murder plot? She's just a waitress?'

'Yes, but don't forget she worked in a bank. Maybe she did steal your Aunty's money after all. She could have been stealing money from the bank to pay for the murder in Harrogate,' suggested Holly.

'Yes, she could if she knew Robin Steel was going to kill Aunty Violet. We know Natalie West had a grudge against Aunty after she was accused of stealing Aunty's money, but what if Robin Steel already had a hold over Natalie that I haven't uncovered yet and was forcing her to steal the money?'

'Wow, you're right,' agreed Holly.

'Holly, that was an excellent suggestion.' I showed her the invitation with Elizabeth Milbank's name on it.

‘This is Robin Steel’s daughter’s name. He’s used a combination of her first name and her mother’s maiden name to disguise who the sender was.’ I handed it over to Holly. As the letter passed beneath my desk lamp, the light illuminated the paper briefly, highlighting the watermark. Snatching it back, I looked at it again, then took the sheet of paper with the directions to the petrol station in Harrogate out of my handbag and held that under my desk lamp. It too had the same watermark. Taking both pieces of paper to my office window, I held them to the glass. Lit up by the sun, both watermarks showed up clearly.

‘Holly, look, they are both identical! I got this paper with the map on it from the hotel in Harrogate. What are the chances of that?’

‘You can probably buy that paper from any stationery shop, it’s not proof,’ said Holly.

‘You may be right, but look, this is good quality paper; it’s going to be expensive, and that means it is traceable. There is a stationer’s in town, I’ll ask them if they’ve seen the watermark before. They may be able to tell me who the supplier is.’

After leaving the stationers in Driffield with the address of the manufacturer of the lion paper, I was ready to visit the paper manufacturer, so I set off for Leeds. When I arrived at Hemp & Sons, Superior Paper Manufacturers of Leeds, the office was at the top of a set of metal stairs above the print factory floor. At the reception desk sat a young, blonde woman, wearing a deep cut, frilly blouse. She was painting her nails and didn’t even bother to look up as I entered.

'Excuse me, I need some help. I've just started a new copy typing business and would like to buy a stock of high-quality paper; something like these.' I placed the sheets of paper on the counter.

The woman looked up at me but didn't leave her seat.

'Do you know the reference number of the paper?'

'No. I just have these two samples.'

'Sorry, love, I can't help you. I need a reference number to fill in the order sheet.'

'Well, can't you tell from looking at it what type of paper it is? I was told by a stationer that it is one of your makes.'

'I just take the orders, love. I don't know what the difference is between one bit of paper and another.'

'Is there anyone here who would know?'

'You need Bert. He knows all the papers just from the feel of them.'

'May I speak to Bert, please?' She finally got up. Wobbling on her excessively high-heeled shoes to a door at the back of the office, she opened it and yelled at the top of her voice for Bert. She left the door open and returned to her seat to finish her nails.

A tall thin man arrived wearing a brown work coat. He stared at the woman sat in the chair as he crossed the floor and didn't look at me until he arrived at the counter.

'Yes, Miss. What can I do for you?'

'A shiver of revulsion ran down my spine as I stared into his watery blues eyes, set into a pale, sweaty face, topped with thinning greasy ginger hair.'

'I'm thinking of ordering some of this paper for my office, but I want to ensure it is of the highest quality. I want to give a good impression when I write to my clients.' He paused before answering. Looked me up and down and licked his lips, before dipping into his breast pocket to pull out a pair of black horn-rimmed glasses. He held the sheets up to the light and licked his fingers before running them over the paper a few times.

'Lion brand, grade one, superior, heavyweight; exclusive. You have good taste, Miss. We don't sell much of this.'

'Who buys this kind of paper?'

'Don't know for sure; Carol here can tell you.' 'Who buys S.H.E. number one, Carol?'

'Do you want me to look it up for you?'

'Yes, please! If it's not too much trouble,' I clenched my teeth to stop myself from saying what I really wanted to say.

'Ah, it's no trouble. I've finished my nails, now.' She pulled an order book out from beneath the counter. 'SHE 1; we sell that to a few places. Some big stately homes buy it, judges, big hotels in London...'

'What about in Yorkshire?' I asked impatiently.

'Oh, that would be a couple of the big houses, two judges and a hotel in Harrogate.'

'A hotel in Harrogate. I like Harrogate. Which hotel would that be? I asked as innocently as I could'

'That would be the Yorkshire Dales Spa Hotel,' answered Carol. 'How much paper would you like to order, Miss?'

'Not now, thank you. Now that I have the reference number, I'll place an order over the telephone.' By the time I'd finished speaking, I was out the door.

On the way home, I couldn't help feeling pleased with myself. I'd made another link in my chain of evidence, someone at the hotel was involved in the murder. Hopefully, Holly would connect another link when she went to the Spa Hotel tomorrow. All I had to do today was telephone Rex this evening.

'Hello, Rex, it's April. I have a favour to ask of you. Would you drive Holly Starbrightly to Harrogate for me? Yes, that Holly Starbrightly... I'm sure she'll tell you everything you need to know during the drive... Yes, it is all to do with Aunty's death. Holly is helping me. Thank you, you can pick her up from my parent's house tomorrow morning, but you mustn't breathe a word of what you are doing to anyone. I don't want half of Driffield camped out in our front garden, hoping to catch a glimpse of Holly Starbrightly. What will I be doing? I will be following up a lead on another suspect. Thank you, Rex; I'll see you in the morning.'

Thursday.

Rex arrived looking like the perfect partner for a film star, young, handsome and wearing his new suit and with his hair swept back; his fabulous car adding the finishing touch to the illusion. Whilst father loaded Holly's luggage into the boot, Holly came out to meet Rex; she looked like a million dollars. The transformation from a young woman passing as my cousin and waitress to a glamorous film star was remarkable. I thought she looked a bit like Vivien Leigh and I could see from the expression on Rex's face that he was impressed by her looks too.

As I waved them goodbye, Mummy asked me what I had planned for the day.

'I have an unexpected suspect to visit. I will tell you more when I come home this evening. But first, I have a telephone call to make.' After kissing Mummy on the cheek, I got in my car and drove to the office.

I was still quite excited about seeing Holly dressed up in her Hollywood clothes when I arrived at the office and found it difficult not to tell Jennifer, Patsy and Annabelle about my film star friend.

Just as we finished our tea and a full packet of chocolate digestives a thought struck me. The Warlock's lived in Leeds during the time Robin Steel was in prison and Faith used to visit him.

'Jennifer, have you got a spare few minutes to help me?'

'Sure, April, any time.' She followed me into my office.

'I need you to make a telephone call to Leeds prison for me. I would do it only I can't take the risk of them recognising my voice from the last time I called. All I need you to do is say that you are calling on behalf of Faith Warlock and that she won't be able to make her next visit to the prison, then you tell me what they say.'

'Oh, I see,' said Jennifer. I leaned in closer to the telephone, trying to overhear what was being said on the other end.

'When was that?' responded Jennifer. 'I'm sorry, I can't understand why she asked me to call you if she's no longer visiting the prisoners. Maybe I got the name of the jail wrong. I will have to speak to her and check. I'm sorry to have bothered you.' Jennifer put the phone down.

'Well, what did they say?'

'They told me, Faith Warlock, no longer acted as a prison visitor at Leeds Jail, which was unfortunate as the prisoners used to look forward to her visits and still miss her coming to see them. They liked to talk to her about their problems. She would also help the trustee prisoners with gardening tips when they were allowed in the prison garden. She befriended one or two of the prisoners and she stayed in contact with them after their release from jail. Robin Steel was one of those inmates she befriended.'

'Brilliant, thanks Jennifer; that confirms a couple of points.'

After looking up the telephone number of the Church of England Diocesan Office in the telephone directory, I called them.

'Good morning, I wonder if you can help me. My name is Miss Showers, and I am a researcher for the Northern Gardeners and Flower Festival magazine. We have a lot of Christian readers of our magazine, so we are looking for someone from within the church community who can give us an interesting interview; someone who keeps an unusual array of plants or has a spectacular garden, or maybe, someone who is qualified as a gardener. Do you know of anyone who would be able to help us?'

'Thank you, Miss Showers. It is always a delight to be able to demonstrate the skills that many of our church community keep hidden under a bushel. We have a Reverend Doctor Wood, he's written several books on exotic trees and shrubs found on his missionary work in Africa. There is Bishop Lovelace, his speciality is Orchids.'

'Is there anyone in the North East of the country; our magazine is produced in Leeds, so it would be convenient for me to stay local for the interview?'

'Well, there is no one in Leeds that fits your requirements, but there is Mrs Warlock in East Yorkshire. She is a qualified Apothecary. She's done a lot of research into the medicinal properties of plants.'

'She sounds very interesting, just the type of person I am looking for. I think our readers would like to hear from her. Do you have her address and telephone number, please?'

I parked my car close to the vicarage and walked up to the garden gate. Before entering, I surveyed the garden. I didn't spend any time looking at it the first that I had come, but the garden was full of a wide variety of colourful flowers; as pretty as any painting I had seen. As I stood admiring the garden, Mrs Warlock stepped out from behind a rhododendron bush, spotting me immediately.

'Good morning. I was just admiring your garden.'

'Yes, it is nice. It's one of the few joys I have left. Haven't I seen you before?'

'As it happens; yes. My name is April Showers. I interviewed you a few days ago about the death of Miss Birch in Harrogate.'

'Oh, yes. But why have you come back? Do you think I did it?'

'No, no, of course not, but you know the person who may have killed her. His name is Robin Steel. He was in jail in Leeds during the time you were a prison visitor. Once he realises I am on to him, he may decide to kill anyone who could link him to the murder of Miss Birch and you certainly knew him in the past and you were at the hotel. You may be his next victim.' I hoped my spin on the truth would get a useful response from Mrs Warlock. She looked at me for a few seconds, weighing up what I had told her.

'You'd better come in and tell me what you have learnt about Robin Steel.' I felt like Daniel entering the lion's den.

'Where is Reverend Warlock?' I asked as I sat in an armchair whilst Faith Warlock poured out the tea.

'He's visiting a bereaved family. He will be conducting the funeral service for them in a day or two. Now tell me why you think Robin would want to kill me.'

'My Investigations have led me to believe that Robin Steel murdered my Aunty Violet. I have discovered that she was a very unpleasant person and took revenge on anyone who crossed her. Robin Steel seems to have suffered at the hands of Aunty Violet more than any of my other suspects. First, he lost his first wife and was left with a young child to bring up. He met Aunty Violet, who wanted nothing to do with the child but wanted to use him. She accused him of theft and had him sent to prison. Whilst in prison his only child died in tragic circumstances. So you see he has a good motive for killing Aunty. Also, when he married his second wife, I found your name on their wedding certificate as a witness, so obvious a link to Mr Steel must make you a potential threat to him.'

'Yes; I see what you mean. What do you think I should do?'

'Well, if I were you, I would go away somewhere, a holiday maybe and wait until you read in the newspapers that Robin Steel has been arrested.'

'Do you have enough evidence to get Robin arrested?'

'Oh, yes. I have one or two loose ends to tie up, but then, I will hand all the evidence over to the police. It won't be long before Robin Steel is back behind bars.'

'Well, Miss Showers, thank you for the warning. I will certainly take everything you have said into consideration and talk it over with my husband.'

Mrs Warlock got to her feet. 'The reverend will be home soon, I think it best that I tell him what has happened, in my own way. He is not used to cloak and dagger stuff.'

'But, you are, Mrs Warlock?'

She looked surprised at my poorly cloaked accusation but deftly fended it off.

'Being a prison visitor toughens one up, dear. One gets to hear all kinds of horror stories from the inmates.'

'Yes, I expect you do. Please don't delay in acting on what I have told you.'

I won't, dear; thank you.' She closed the front door behind me and I hurried down the garden path to my car, trying to hold back a smug smile.

When I got back to my office, I'd only just settled when the phone rang.

'Hello, is this Miss Showers, this is Sergeant Duffy.'

'Sergeant Duffy, what a surprise. How may I help you?'

'I thought I'd give you an update on my investigation. I tracked down the occupants of room 222 at the Yorkshire

Dale Spa Hotel, the room where you overheard two people arguing after your Aunty's death. They are a young married couple who were on holiday. The argument they were having was a misunderstanding over something that had happened earlier in the day; nothing to do with your Aunty. But more interestingly, after an anonymous tip-off, I went to the hotel and found a bottle of Cyanide in the headwaiter's room. He denies using it to kill your Aunty, but then he would, wouldn't he? Anyway, I am holding him for questioning.'

'But, Sergeant, I was led to believe Aunty died from Aconitum poisoning.'

'What! Really! Who told you that?'

'I'm not at liberty to say, but I think if you check the pathologist's report you'll see it is on there.' The line went dead with a loud click.

'The man's an idiot,' I told the telephone receiver. 'Inspector Allswell, where are you when I need you?'

Chapter Eighteen

Friday.

Over tea and biscuits in the office kitchen before starting work, Patsy, Jennifer and Annabelle wanted an update on how my murder case was going. So I told them everything I'd learnt so far.

'So where does Natalie West fit into the story?' asked Patsy.

'That's just it, I don't know. She knew Aunty Violet. She knows Robin and Heidi Steel, but she doesn't seem to know any of the other suspects. I know she is important because the Steel's visit her.

'Maybe she's the mastermind behind it all,' suggested Annabelle.

'No, I don't think so. She doesn't come across as intelligent or strong-willed enough to plan a murder this complicated with so many people involved. But, you may be on the right tracks. She may have helped provide some of the money. I'm going back to Bridlington to watch her; she may provide me with the key to solving the entire case.

By ten o'clock I was parking my car in a car park next to Bridlington harbour. The smell of wet fish was strong. As I looked towards the harbour it looked like every hungry seagull from miles around was soaring above it, eyeing the crated fish from the previous night's trawler catch. The rest of the seaside town was just coming to life, hoping to attract the early tourists. Making my way to the Italian style cafe to find Natalie West, I approached the cafe from the corner of the street instead of crossing the road directly in front of it. I had to know if Natalie was already at work without her seeing me. After a sneaky look into the cafe, I caught sight of the cafe waitress. She was standing by the window serving a drink to a customer, but the waitress wasn't Natalie West.

Going into the cafe, I spoke to the man behind the counter. 'Excuse me, when does Natalie come on duty?'

'Not today. Today, her day off.' He returned to filling glass tumblers with folded paper napkins. I left with no choice, I had to go to her flat to try and find her.

From the end of the street where Natalie lived, I looked down the street to ensure there was no big black car parked at the kerb. Luckily, the street was free of parked cars. There was just a street cleaner sweeping the paths. It looked clear enough to risk going down to the house. As I got closer I could see that her curtains were still closed, so I strolled past the house and carried on for about another hundred yards where I found a corner newsagent's and sweetshop, so preparing myself for a long wait, I popped inside and bought some sweets and a magazine. Opposite the sweetshop, just across the street was a public bench. From there I would have a view of the entire length of Natalie's street. So, taking up my position, armed with my magazine and a bag of chocolate-covered toffees, I settled in to wait for her to show.

I was on my third toffee and partway through the magazine when I looked over the top of the pages and saw Natalie coming up the street. Using the magazine to hide my face, I spied over the top of it to see how much closer Natalie had come. With my last look, I saw her enter the shop. I left my seat. If I hadn't, Natalie would surely have seen me as she left the sweetshop. I crossed the road to a house on the opposite street corner which was bounded by a tall hedge and took up position there. The shop was just out of sight, so once again I had to break cover and risk frequent looks to spot when Natalie came out of the shop. I didn't have to wait long. I spotted her walking back towards her flat with a carrier bag in her hand. Following at a safe distance, the magazine open in front of me, ready to hide my face, I trailed her back. Once she had entered the house, I continued along the street, noting the curtains to the flat were now open. The problem I had was there was nowhere to hide at this end of the street and still keep a watch on Natalie's front door. So I retraced my steps back to the public bench at the other end of the street. I'd just about made it back to the bench when an elderly lady came towards me.

'Are you lost, dear? What's the address you are looking for?' she asked.

'Oh, no, I'm fine. I'm just taking a walk whilst I wait for a friend. It's nice around here, isn't it?' I replied.

'Well, not like it used to be. It used to be quite a posh street at one time. Then the decent people moved away, and the houses were turned into flats. Holidaymaker's mostly. Always people coming and going; all times of the day and night. I'll be moving out soon. I've found a nice little bungalow on the edge of town. Sorry, dear, I mustn't keep you. You don't want to listen to the ramblings of an old woman.'

'No, no, it's all right. I was just wondering. Do you know all the people down this street?'

'Mostly by sight, if not by name, why?'

'Well, I'll let you into a secret, I'm really a private detective and I'm on a case. I can't tell you what it is, but it involves the woman who lives it that flat over there.'

'A private detective, like you hear about on the wireless. I thought private detectives were all men?'

'Oh, no, the best ones are women because no one suspects them of being a private detective.'

'Um, yes, I see what you mean. You're talking about Miss West. I've seen her out and about a few times. She works at that cafe near the seafront.'

'Yes, that's her. My client thinks she is having an affair with the owner of the cafe. Have you seen him coming or going from her flat?'

'Old Luigi from the cafe? He never would. I see him and his wife at the dance in the church hall every Thursday night. He's not the type to chase other women. But, Miss West does have a fella living with her. He doesn't say much. I think he's foreign; he's got a bit of an accent, though I can't quite place it. However, I'm sure it's not an English one, even though his English is good. Look, here they come.'

Instinctively, I turned to look at them before checking myself and turning back, praying they hadn't recognised me. Keeping my back towards Natalie and her friend, I continued to talk to the old lady. Once they had turned the corner. I thanked the lady and said 'goodbye.'

Racing across the street to the shop, I paused for a second then risked a look; they were heading for the seafront. With my heart racing, I had to force myself to stay calm and keep my distance as I followed them. If they turned around now, I had nowhere to hide. As they reached the road that ran along the promenade they stopped and, hand in hand crossed to the seawall. I turned my back to them and waited. They could only turn left or right, so whichever direction they took, I would be able to see them once I reached the corner of the road. When I looked back, they were gone. Quick stepping it to the end of the road, I saw them a little way ahead, still, hand in hand and walking towards town. Staying on my side of the promenade road, I followed them. They passed various shops selling buckets and spades and boxes covered with shells. They ignored the ice cream and candy floss sellers. They were heading into the town centre, away from the touristy spots. They didn't stop until they reach a jewellery shop. They looked through the window, taking it in turns to point to items on display, but I was too far away to see what was that caught their attention. It ended when Natalie turned towards her companion and, with her arms around his neck, she kissed him. They turned away from the jewellery shop window and headed back towards the seafront.

'You're not going to treat her to the ring today then,' I muttered under my breath. 'Where are you off to now, I wonder?'

I got closer to them now we were in town. The streets had places for me to hide at a moment's notice, and the extra people allowed me to blend in with the rest of the shoppers. The day was warming up, and I was ready for a drink. I looked at my watch, twelve forty-five. With a bit of luck, he would take Natalie to lunch. They returned to the seafront and bought an ice cream each before heading back in the direction from where we had come. After walking for a few minutes, it was clear they were heading back to Natalie's flat.

'Who is your friend, Natalie? Is he one of your gang of murderers?' I followed them back to the flat and wondering how long I would have to wait before they would come out again. As I looked up towards her window, the man came into view. He reached up to the curtains and closed one before Natalie came into view. She put her arms around him and kissed him for a few seconds before saying something. He closed the second curtain, and they were gone.

'What? In the middle of the day? Really!' I wasn't going to hang around like a peeping Tom, so I made my way back to the seafront and found a cafe to get a cold drink and something to eat.

Opening my now crumpled magazine, the pictures and stories were all about love and romance. How to get your perfect man, keep your man happy, and what to do if things weren't working out with your man. I didn't want a man; I had a career to think about. Reading my horoscope on the inside of the back page was the last straw; 'the man of your dreams is not far away.' Closing the magazine, I asked the waitress to put it in the rubbish bin for me.

I allowed myself forty-five minutes before leaving the cafe and heading back to Natalie's flat. The curtains were open and a big, black car was parked at the kerb. Retracing my steps to the shop at the end of the street, I bought a newspaper and took up my post on the bench I'd used that morning. It wasn't long before I was joined by the same lady I'd spoken to earlier. She sat next to me and looked down the street.

'Still, at it, I see,' she said, smiling at me. 'One of the benefits of getting old; no one sees you and you have the time to watch the world go by. Comes and goes all the time, that car. Sometimes there are two of them in it, other times, like today, there's just the one, a woman.'

'Maybe I should put you on the payroll,' I said humorously.

'Not likely. I don't mind sitting here on a nice day, but I'm too old to be wandering the streets at night or when it's raining. Anyway, I'd get bored with this sitting around and waiting. The car arrived about ten minutes ago.'

The elderly lady had no sooner finished speaking when Heidi Steel came out of the house, followed by Natalie West's boyfriend. He got in the passenger side seat, though Natalie stayed on the doorstep, still wearing a dressing gown and waved to the car as it drove off. The car came towards my bench. I put my hand on the elderly lady's shoulder and I made it look as though I was comforting her but hiding my face at the same time. After the car passed by, I looked up.

'Sorry about that, I didn't want them to recognise me.'

'Don't worry, dear. This is the most excitement I've had in a long while.'

The sound of another car with a powerful engine made me look up. At first glance the car looked old, nothing special, but as it turned the corner to follow Heidi Stone's car, I got a look at the driver, it was Rex.

Jumping to my feet, I watched both cars turn left at the end of the road.

'Bother! Next time, I'll park my car at the end of the street.'

At home that evening, I was just about to telephone Holly to ask her if she had learnt anything from the hotel staff when Mummy came into the hall insisting that I come to listen to the wireless. The announcer was making a dramatic broadcast.

HOLLY STARBRIGHTLY HAS ABSCONDED FROM ANOTHER HOTEL WITHOUT PAYING HER ROOM BILL. - THE BRITISH ACTRESS WHO HIT THE BIG TIME IN AMERICA HAS GONE MISSING FROM HER HOTEL IN HARROGATE. - OUR BBC REPORTER AT THE HOTEL SAID THE HOTEL MANAGER HAD BECOME SUSPICIOUS WHEN HE RECEIVED REPORTS FROM HIS STAFF THAT THE FILM STAR HAD NOT BEEN SEEN ALL DAY, AND THAT WHEN A CHAMBERMAID WENT INTO HER ROOM TO MAKE HER BED, MISS STARBRIGHLY WAS NOWHERE TO BE FOUND. - FILM CRITICS SUSPECT THAT THIS IS JUST ANOTHER PUBLICITY STUNT TO IMPROVE CINEMA TICKET SALES. - A FILM STUDIO SPOKESMAN AT THE HOTEL DENIES ANY INVOLVEMENT IN A STUNT AND

EXPRESSED HIS CONCERN OVER WHAT COULD HAVE HAPPENED TO MISS STARBRIGHTLY. Here are the latest cricket scores from Lords...

Daddy switched the wireless off, 'Did the two of you set this up as a publicity stunt?' he asked.

'No, of course not! She is helping me gather evidence and discover who killed Aunty Violet. Holly would never do anything like this without telling me first. If she has disappeared, then it is because she has discovered something. Wait and see, she'll be in touch with me very soon to tell me about what she has discovered.'

Seconds later the telephone rang, making us jump. I ran to the phone, snatching it up, 'Holly?'

'No, it's Rex. I've just heard the news on the radio. What has happened to Holly?'

'I don't know. I've only just heard the news, myself. I thought this call might be from her.'

'I'm coming over. We'll drive to Harrogate tonight. I'll be there as quick as I can.' There was a loud click as he put the phone down.

'Mummy, Daddy, Rex is coming over. We're going to Harrogate tonight. Hopefully, we'll find Holly and find out what's going on.'

'Shouldn't you telephone the police first?'

'Mummy, the police will already know that Holly is missing. I need to know why. I don't believe she would willingly abandon the job I sent her to do; remember, she sees it as a debt of honour for us helping her after her husband died.'

It was getting dark as Rex drove the two of us along the road to Harrogate. The hood was up on his Jaguar. Its large headlamps illuminating the road ahead; its powerful engine eating up the miles as we raced through the countryside.

'Thank you for taking me to Harrogate. If I'd used my car, it would have taken twice as long.'

'It's no problem. I'm as concerned about Holly as you are. She's a nice girl and a pretty talented actress; I've already been to see her film. What do you think has happened to her?'

'I don't know. She was happy enough to help me when I asked her to. I fear that she's asked one too many questions and someone has got wise to what she is doing and kidnapped her or worse.'

'No, I don't think it's that bad, said Rex reassuringly. She may have uncovered the identity of your Aunty's killer and gone into hiding until you show up? This disappearing act maybe how she is telling you to come to Harrogate and rescue her.'

'Then, why didn't she just telephone for help?'

'I don't know; there could be any number of reasons. We will know why once we find and speak to her.'

Rex parked the car about a hundred yards from the hotel. There was nowhere closer to stop as the street was full of cars and reporters blocking the road outside the hotel. With Rex taking the lead, he ploughed a path through the throng of reporters whilst I followed in his wake. Once inside, I led the way to the reception desk. Perkins was on duty and recognised me immediately.

'I'm sorry, Miss Showers, Mr Bunkhouse is too busy to speak to you right now. I'm sure you understand.'

'We are here because Miss Starbrightly is missing. It's important that I speak to Mr Bunkhouse about her, now!'

The poor man looked at me and then at Rex and folded without further resistance. He tapped lightly on the manager's door before entering the room. He was only gone seconds before the door flew open and Mr Bunkhouse came stomping out.

'Miss Showers, I cannot drop everything I am doing every time you demand my attention.'

Rex lifted the hatch in the reception desk and passed through. Taking the hotel manager by the shoulders, he spun him around and marched him back into his office.

'I'm sorry, Perkins, hopefully, we won't keep Mr Bunkhouse for very long. We are just eager to find out what has happened to Miss Starbrightly.' I closed the manager's office door and went to sit at his desk. Rex directed the manager to his chair and lingered close by in case Mr Bunkhouse tried to leave.

'Mr Bunkhouse, I am going to be straight with you. Over the past few weeks, Miss Starbrightly and I have become good friends. Miss Starbrightly, Holly, was here at my request. She is helping me to investigate the death of my Aunty at your hotel. So I don't believe Holly's disappearance has anything to do with a publicity stunt. During my investigation, there has always been one common thread –

this hotel, which means you are involved. Now, Mr Bunkhouse; where is Miss Starbrightly?'

The hotel manager went pale and his mouth dropped open. He struggled to speak for a few seconds whilst trying to think of an answer and then began to bluster.

'This is outrageous. You cannot burst into my office and make claims like that. I'm going to call the police.' He leant forward to pick up the telephone, but Rex's hand landed on his shoulder. The manager whined in pain as Rex squeezed. His outstretched arm dropped to the desk and he slumped back into his chair.

'Mr Bunkhouse, I know about your connection to Mr Steel, Faith Warlock and Natalie West, so you may as well release Holly before you have a second death to account for.'

'I don't have your friend. You must know by now that Aunty was an evil woman; she deserved to die after what she did to all of us.'

'Where is Holly?'

'I've got no idea where she is and I don't care. I going to be ruined after all this gets back to the hotel owners and the police. I didn't want to get involved in the first place. It's Steel who is behind it all. I expect he's the one who has Miss Starbrightly.' The manager's voice changed and took on a more confident demeanour. Shaking himself free of Rex's hand, he straightened his jacket.

'Get out, the pair of you. If you really had all the evidence you said you do, you would have come here with the police and arrested me. So you have nothing against me. All you have is guesses. I didn't kill your Aunty and I haven't had anything to do with that second-rate floozy's disappearance. I've got a hotel full of staff to prove it.'

Getting up from his chair, he crossed to the door to open it. As he grasped the door handle, I noticed a button on his jacket cuff had been replaced. The criss-cross stitching was poorly done and there was far more thread holding the button on than with the other buttons. The button had been crudely replaced by a man. No woman would have sewn a button on that crudely. So, it was Mr Bunkhouse who had attacked me during the night. As Rex and I returned to the hall through the reception desk, Mr Bunkhouse was hard on our heels.

'As you are not residents, I must ask you to leave,' he instructed politely but firmly.

As we sat in Rex's car, he turned to me, 'you only had to say the word and I would have made him tell you his entire life story. Why did you let him off so easily?'

'Because it occurred to me that the manager not only knows who took Holly but where and why. Holly must have asked too many questions, too soon or inadvertently tipped off someone, probably the manager, that, she was searching for clues into my Aunty's murder. I'm pretty sure they won't have killed Holly, yet. Her body would raise too much publicity and another police investigation. I suspect they've kidnapped her and will try to use her to make me drop my investigation or lure me into a trap where the pair of us will meet a tragic accident. We should go home and wait. If I am correct, Robin Steel will get in touch shortly to arrange the return of Holly and then, when I go to get her back; that's when he'll spring his trap. But I'll be ready for him. Are you prepared to continue helping me?'

'Try stopping me; I quite like having a film star as a friend.'

'Very well, let's go home. When Steel's trap fails his next step will be to try and kill me or threaten me or, more likely, threaten to kill Holly if I don't do as he says. So I'll agree to his demands and then try to stall and hinder him until I can get a message to you. The more pressure we can put Robin Steel under, the more likely he is to make a mistake. The only thing I can't figure out is what Natalie West has to do with Robin Steel and the murder, but she's definitely involved somehow.'

'I may have the answer to that question, but I can't tell you just yet, there are people I need to speak to first.'

'What people?'

'Give me a day or two. Just remember, call me if you need me, any time of the day or night. If Steel has Holly, he will call you or be in touch, soon. Go to the office tomorrow and wait for him to contact you.'

Chapter Nineteen

Saturday.

At my desk for eight o'clock, it was hard to concentrate; the constant worry about what had happened to Holly had kept me awake most of the night. I blamed myself, I should never have sent her to Harrogate; I should never have got her involved, but it was too late, she was involved and it may very well cost her her life. I'd told my office friends what had happened to Holly and promised to keep them up to date with developments. Patsy agreed to cancel all her music lessons for the day, so I wouldn't have to leave my office. As I sat alone in the silence, I kept staring at the telephone, wishing it to ring and put me out of my misery. I was ready to agree to just about anything, so long as I got Holly back, safe and sound. Heavy footsteps in the hall made me look up from the telephone.

'Just the one for you today, Miss Showers; how come you're in on a Saturday? Hey, I have to ask; you been out all night chasing villains? You don't look like you've slept at all, last night,' said George the postman.

‘Thank you. George; you are a real boost to a girl’s confidence. Does your wife appreciate your honesty after she’s had an awful night?’

‘I’m sorry, April. But you’re right, my wife left me a couple of years back. No sense of humour that woman.’

‘Goodbye, George.’

I opened the letter without taking much notice of the envelope until I read what was inside. It was from Holly.

Dear April

I’ve settled into the hotel and there is quite a positive response from the local press about my new film, thank you. I decided to write to you instead of telephoning because my call would have to be routed through the hotel reception and I didn’t want to risk anyone listening in.

You were right; the hotel staff are ready to gossip about what goes on behind the scenes here. Working as a waitress at the hotel in Driffield has been a big help in getting the staff to talk to me. I tell them stories about when I worked in Driffield and they tell me what happens here. But, when I tell them a bit of Hollywood gossip, they respond by telling me more intimate secrets that they know about each other. I’ve heard some interesting gossip about the hotel manager that I’m going to investigate tonight. When I know more, I'll write to you again about what I find out.

Love Holly.

'Oh Holly; be careful.' I said aloud as I laid the letter on my desk. Whilst wondering what had happened to Holly, the phone rang.

'April Showers, Private Detective Agency.'

'Is that Miss Showers?'

'Yes.' I recognised the voice, it was Heidi Steel.

'What have you done with Holly?'

'Be quiet, and listen.' I concentrated on what she had to say, pencil at the ready. 'I have your friend. Do you want her back, dead or alive?'

At first, after hearing the evil edge in her voice, I had trouble answering.

'Well,' she demanded.

'Alive and unharmed; what have you done to her? What do you want?'

'She is safe, for now. To keep her that way and to get her back in one piece, you must first arrange for Miss Starbrightly's hotel bill to be paid. Then, you will contact the press and inform them that Miss Starbrightly's disappearance has been a publicity stunt and that she is sorry for causing a nuisance. Collect her luggage. If there are any members of the press still waiting at the hotel for her to return, tell them she had gone into hiding until she feels confident enough to speak to them. In return, I will arrange for her to send a letter to the Yorkshire Post newspaper confirming your statement. Once the press has denounced her disappearance as a stunt, I will be in touch again. Just remember; if you go to the police, you will never see your friend again; not in one piece anyway.'

'Let me speak to her, I want to know that she is alright.' Over the telephone, in the distance, I heard a woman cry of pain, Then Heidi put the receiver down.

I dropped the telephone receiver onto its cradle and ran over in my mind what Heidi Steel had demanded. Picking up the telephone again, I dialled the number for Sergeant Duffy in Harrogate, but stopped partway through the process and put it down again. With no idea where Holly was being held, it was pointless bringing in the police at this stage. For now, I had to comply with Heidi Steel's demands, so I phoned the Yorkshire Post and a couple of other Yorkshire newspapers offices and told them that Holly's disappearance was a publicity stunt and that I had been hired to handle her affairs until she was ready to talk to the press. Then, I telephoned Daddy at the bank and told him what had happened. He said he would arrange for Holly's hotel bill to be paid. I also explained to him that I was going to contact Rex and ask him to go with me to Harrogate to collect Holly's luggage. It was now time to see if Rex was as good as his word. I telephoned his house, but he wasn't there. I informed his mother that I needed his help and that as soon as he got home, he had to telephone me at my office. She seemed a little put out by my curtness, but I had more important things to worry about. I would apologise to her, later. I left a note on my desk pad for Jennifer in case I hadn't returned before Monday, saying that I was going to Harrogate to collect Holly's luggage. I waited an hour and telephoned Rex's house again; there was no answer, so I decided to go to Harrogate on my own.

Whilst speeding up the road towards York, a thought struck me. If Heidi Steel has taken Holly, the last place she would take Holly was to her home in Helmsley. This meant, the Steel's must have a second home or hideout somewhere else and the house in Helmsley would be empty.

Parking outside the Steel's house, I watched it for a few minutes. Now I was here, I was less sure that breaking into the house was a good idea. What would I do if the property was still occupied? It was the milk bottles that tipped the balance. It was gone midday and two bottles of milk were still standing by the front door in their wire basket. Going to the front door I knocked; no answer. Walking along the street to the end of the row of eighteenth-century cottages, I turned down the street I turned down a lane that gave me access to the back of the properties. Having reached the Steel house, I found the rear garden was long and narrow; half laid to lawn the rest flower beds of various types. An extension had been built onto the back of the house, but they had used redbrick which detracted from the character of the older original building. But the modern extension worked in my favour. It meant the neighbours could not overlook the backdoor. A long-handled broom I found propped up against the wall was all I needed. A sharp wrap with the handle broke a small pane of glass in the kitchen window, which allowed me to put my hand through and unlatch it. Then, using an upturned metal bucket as a step, I gathered my skirt up around my waist and climbed in. After sending two cups, left on the draining board, crashing to the floor, I reckoned that if no one heard the shattering cups, the house must be empty. I started to pick up the broken cups, then stopped. What was the point, I'd already broken the window? It wasn't as though I could hide the fact that someone had broken in.

Going through the kitchen door took me to the room where I had interviewed Robin Steel. I still liked the decorative style of the house, but there was no time to admire the decorations. I checked all the drawers and the cupboard in that room and the rest of the house. They had left most, if not all of their processions behind, clothes still hung in the wardrobes and underwear was still in their drawers. I suspected that they would be back to collect them once they had got rid of Holly and me. I found nothing that gave a clue as to where they had taken Holly.

Standing in the hall next to the front door, I felt deflated at finding nothing to help me locate Holly after so much effort. Looking at the telephone on the hall stand and the notepad beside it, I wondered. It was an old trick, but it was all that I had left. Running a pencil back and forth over the top page of the pad, it highlighted the message from the previous page; Lucky Lady, Whitby, 07:45, 26th. Are they taking Holly to Whitby? The 26th is just a few days away. Who or what is Lucky Lady, or is that a code word for Holly? Could 07:45 be the time of the train? No, they wouldn't take her by train. They had to be in Whitby at 07:45 to meet someone, but who? I ripped the page from the pad, turned the knob on the Yale lock and left the cottage by the front door. Sitting in my car, I tuck the message into the car's glove box, before starting the engine and driving away.

When I arrived at the Harrogate hotel, the receptionist informed me they had received a telephone call from their bank to confirm that Holly's outstanding room bill had been paid and that I was on my way to collect her luggage. The receptionist asked me if I wanted any help packing Holly's clothes, but I declined. If Holly had left me a message, I didn't want someone else finding it first.

Holly's room was a mess, either Holly had had a hissy-fit and thrown her clothes and possessions all over the floor or else someone had been here before me and searched the room. Opening one of her suitcases, I began to pick up and pack her clothes. I didn't hear the door open, only when it closed with a click. I didn't look to see who it was, assuming it to be a member of the hotel staff.

'I told the receptionist, I can manage on my own, thank you. I won't be long and then you'll be able to clean the room.' The sound of someone clearing their throat made me turn around. Unfortunately, instead of seeing a chambermaid; it was Heidi Steel, with two men and she was pointing a small automatic pistol at me.

'Not a word or I will shoot you here and now.' The two men came towards me; one held my arms behind me, the other held a cloth over my mouth and nose. As I breathed in the smell reminded me of hospitals, then my head went fuzzy and I passed out.

When I came too, I was lying on an old sofa which stank of cats. However, the awful smell had helped clear my head of the effects of the drug. I tried to move my arms, but they were tied behind me. Sitting up, the first thing I spotted was Robin Steel sat in an armchair a few feet away.

'Where is Holly, what have you done with her?'

'Not so fast, Miss Showers. She is safe for now, but first, you and I must come to an agreement. You have to understand that it would be so easy to kill the pair of you and be gone. Only she is too well known for the police not to put in a lot of effort into tracking down her killers. If she hadn't been so nosy at the hotel, Heidi and I could have slipped away discreetly. You would have found your murderers, Miss Starbrightly would have promoted her new film and everyone would be happy, but your little friend stumbled onto something that needed to remain secret and that changed everything.'

'What do you mean? Have you murdered someone else?'

'Nothing that simple. It's more to do with international ideology and power; returning power to the people and not the unelected industrialists who manipulate corrupt Politicians so they can exploit their workers to become even richer.'

'You're mad!'

'No, Miss Showers. Prison has a way of showing you how unequal the world is. It showed me the forgotten, the lost, the uneducated and all those who are mentally scarred and discarded by society, just because they are too inconvenient and expensive to deal with.'

'It also gave you an education.'

'I was lucky, that's all. Just one amongst the thousands of lost and forgotten, but you'll never understand that. You are just like the rest of the people in this country; you don't want to know what life is like for the less fortunate. So long as society hides them away, you don't give them a second thought.'

'You may be right in some of what you say, but I can't change the way society works, so what makes you think you can?'

'I agreed to work for the people who can make those changes.'

'Who are they?'

'People with connections to countries where everyone is equal.'

'In that case, I hope you are both happy in your new utopia, but where do Holly and I fit in with your plans?'

'You two are our tickets to freedom. You never know, Hollywood may even turn your adventure into a film. Instead of 'the one that got away,' it would be 'the two that got away.'

'Where is Holly, I want to see her?'

'You are in no position to make demands, Miss Showers. All you need to know is that she is safe and well. You will see her again when the time is right. At the moment, it is better that we keep you apart.'

'Your wife, Heidi, has her, doesn't she?'

'Yes, and be grateful, she doesn't have you too; she's really taken a dislike to you. You've got in our way more than you know. It's funny, but it's true, it's always the blundering idiots that foul things up.'

'I'm pleased to know that I got something right.' I should have expected the slap across the face that came after saying that, but I was too angry at being drugged, kidnapped and kept tied up to think straight. The taste of blood from my split lip kept me quiet for the next couple of hours. I looked around the room, hoping to spot a clue to where I was being held. The room was clearly in a house; there was a fireplace, carpet and curtains at the windows. The curtains were closed so I couldn't see outside. There were two armchairs; in one, sat Robin Steel, reading a book. The other was empty. A shabby, old dining table with four mismatched chairs was at the other end of the room and I could see two doors in the wall opposite me; one I supposed led to the hall, the other the kitchen. I lay down on the sofa as though going to sleep; I needed to think. My best chance of getting out of here was whilst there was just the two of us. Glancing across at Robin Steel, I noticed his head nod as he read his book. Then it happened again. He was getting tired. I looked for a clock but there wasn't one. That's when I noticed that there were no pictures on the walls or any ornaments to show that the house was a regular home. It had to be safe-house, for use in times of need. I had no idea how much time had passed whilst I had been unconscious. I couldn't see my wristwatch, I could only assume that as the curtains were closed and the lights were on, it must be late and dark outside. I wasn't tired because of my earlier drugged sleep. Nevertheless, I pushed off my shoes and made a show of getting comfortable as though going to sleep. Robin looked across at me for a second and then went back to reading his book. I let my eyes close and forced myself to relax and breathe slow and steady. Opening my eyes just enough to spy on my captor. I watched as his head nodded and his hands struggled to hold his book as he fought back the need to sleep. Until finally, he put his head back and let the weight of the book take his hands to his lap.

Moments later, a soft snore confirmed he was asleep. Bending my knees up to my chest I brought my tied hands past my feet and around to my front. Able to reach the knot in the rope around my ankles, I pulled at the bonds. It was tight, but picking at it with my nails loosened one strand of the knot and then another until I could unwind the cord. Leaving my shoes by the sofa, I crept to the door praying it would lead into the kitchen where I would find a knife to free my hands. The door opened easily and silently; closing it behind me, I flicked the light switch with my chin. The lino covered floor was icy cold on my stockinged feet. The kitchen was as just as Spartan as the room that I'd just left. A deep, white, rectangular, ceramic sink with one tap and wooden draining board was set beneath the window that looked out over the back garden. Next to it was a dark green, enamelled gas stove and next to that was the door to the back garden. Against the wall opposite the window was a square kitchen table, and against the far wall was a large cupboard that had three large doors above three drawers and three smaller cupboard doors below them. If I was going to find a sharp knife, it would be in one of the drawers. The drawers all had different items in them, but no knives. Frustrated by my disappointment, I turned around to look for another drawer. There was one in the kitchen table. Dragging out the drawer provided I found a knife. Only I soon found that holding a dull knife with only your fingertips makes little impression on a rope. I needed to find somewhere that I could wedge the knife so I could rub my bonds against it.

There was nowhere in the kitchen to wedge the knife that wouldn't make a noise, so I made for the backdoor.

The key turned smoothly in the lock as the bolt slid back. The latch lifted out of its resting place without a sound. Opening the door I was greeted with an inrush of cool night air. As I stepped into the back garden from out of the darkness stepped Heidi Steel blocking my path, her little, black automatic pistol in her hand.

'Going somewhere, Miss Showers?'

'I couldn't sleep, so I thought I'd take a stroll in the garden.' She indicated with her gun for me to return inside. As she entered the kitchen, she called to her husband.

'Robin, Robin, are you there?'

The door to the lounge swung open and Robin Steel stumbled through. The look of relief on his face when he saw me was unmistakable. However, his wife wasted no time in deriding his inability to watch over me as his gaze traversed from me to her. Heidi pushed me forward. Robin relieved me of the kitchen knife, then took me by the arm and led me back to the sofa where he bound my legs together and fastened my arms to my sides with a rope around my upper body. Whilst Robin dealt with me, Heidi paced the room berating her husband.

'Why I allowed you to take revenge on that woman I'll never know! You have put all my work here, in jeopardy. How am I going to explain this mess to Comrade Colonel Spion?'

'You're exaggerating again, calm down. No one knows we have the actress and this one. The press thinks it's all part of a publicity stunt for the star's film. No one is seriously looking for them. By the time their bodies are found, we'll be long gone. Has the boat been arranged?'

'Yes, for tomorrow night.'

'Good, then there is nothing to worry about. We can move on and their bodies will not wash ashore until we are safely away.'

'We wouldn't have to leave at all if it weren't for your insistence on killing that old woman.'

'Well, it's too late to worry about that now. You keep watch on her, I going to get some sleep. Wake me in a few hours.'

Knowing Holly and me were going to meet a sticky end kept me awake for most of the night. However, I must have dozed off because I kept having nightmares of various ways to die with Robin and Heidi standing over my body.

Sunday.

I awoke to the smell of coffee and fried bacon. The cramp bit into my arms and legs, making me cry out and Heidi Steel come rushing into the lounge to see what was happening.

'Help, I've got the cramp. I need to stretch my legs.' As I writhed in pain on the sofa. Heidi stared at me for what seemed an age before coming over and untying my legs.

'Put your toes against the arm of the sofa and push,' she instructed. I did as she said, and the pain in my calves eased instantly.

'Thank you,' I breathed with a sigh of relief. 'I'm really desperate for the bathroom, please?' She took me by the arm and led me upstairs. At the bathroom door, she untied my hands. As I tried to shut the bathroom door, she pushed it open again.

'Get on with it. In East Germany, we don't need privacy for such things.'

I looked at her, astonished. If I hadn't been so desperate to go, I would have waited till later. Feeling a whole lot better after washing my hands and face, the aromas coming from the kitchen made my stomach rumble.

Back downstairs, before Heidi retied my hands, I asked for some breakfast. Robin brought me a bacon sandwich and a mug of black coffee, which was not quite what I'd had in mind, but it had to do.

'Where is Holly?'

'She's safe,' replied Heidi.

'You keep saying that, but if you two are here, who is looking after Holly? Have you left her with those two muscle men of yours?'

Heidi laughed. 'She is being taken care of, that's all you need to know.'

'Will I be able to see her, speak to her, before you kill us?'

'Not today. Tomorrow; maybe.'

The rest of the day passed painfully slowly. Robin put on the wireless and continued reading his book. Heidi came and went from the house. I heard what sounded like her unpacking a shopping bag with tins and packets being placed on the kitchen table and then cupboard doors opening and closing. *So, we are within walking distance of some shops, maybe we are still in Harrogate*. Twice she went upstairs, the creaky floorboards giving away her movements. During one instance, I heard a rhythmic tapping, which went on for only a couple of minutes before she returned to the living room and showed Robin a piece of paper. He responded to it by saying, 'Good, the sooner the better.' It was then that I realised they must have a radio transmitter set upstairs.

No matter how hard I struggled against my ropes, I couldn't loosen them and I wished I'd waited for Rex before setting off to Harrogate. Thinking back to Aunty's death had I known there was more to this case than I could handle, I would have asked Rex for help right from the start. I know I wanted to solve this case all on my own, but I hadn't thought that there was more to it than someone with a grudge against Aunty Violet. What East Germany had to do with Aunty, I didn't know. Even though she had turned out to be a thoroughly horrid person, I couldn't imagine she would ever consider being a spy for a foreign power.

I consoled myself with the thought that at some point they would have to leave the house and hopefully, they'd take me with them. That would be when I'd get my best chance to escape. However, for now, the best thing I could do was listen to everything they said and learn as much as possible about their plans.

Chapter Twenty

Monday.

Yesterday passed slowly, Heidi was unwilling to enter into conversation, except to complain about their current predicament and Robin was not allowed to do so whilst she was around. However, on Monday, we were all up early. Robin and Heidi were busy preparing to leave as they carried suitcases and bags out of the house, obviously loading a car.

'We all going for a nice day out?' I asked.

'Unless you change your attitude, it'll be the last day out you ever get,' snapped Heidi.

'I thought that was the idea?' Heidi ignored me but as she left the room Robin lowered his voice and said, 'She'll be waiting for us when we get to Whitby.'

I almost responded with a quip about going to the seaside for the day but thought better of it. When it came to my turn to be loaded into the car, I was shocked to learn that the back seat of their car was filled with luggage and that it was me who was going into the boot. I backed away, but Heidi came up behind me and placed a cloth over my mouth. As I gasped for breath, my mouth filled with the taste of the chemical on the cloth again and then I blacked out.

I awoke to darkness, a gentle rocking motion and the sound of a car engine. As my mind cleared, I realised I was still in the car's boot. I had a gag over my mouth and my hands were tied, but my legs were free. Unfortunately, I could smell exhaust fumes seeping into my confined space each time the car slowed, making me feel sick. Desperately, I rubbed the side of my face against the fabric of the boot floor until I could clear my mouth of the gag. Shouting for help and kicking with my heels against the inside of the car made the car slow down abruptly and swerve to the side before stopping. The lid of the boot opened and Heidi and Robin stared down at me, Heidi was holding her gun at the ready. From what little I could see, we had pulled to the side of the road somewhere out in the country.

'I can't breathe in here; it keeps filling with exhaust fumes!'

'Be quiet, there's not much further to go,' demanded Heidi, then she slammed the boot lid closed.

I started kicking and shouting again. 'I'd rather be shot than suffocate in the boot!'

I heard Robin and Heidi exchange words just before the lid opened again.

'Get out,' demanded Heidi.

I struggled to get my legs over the rear lip of the boot so Robin helped me. My back and legs ached painfully when I tried to stand up. Giving in to the pain, I fell onto the grass verge. Seconds later another car went past us. As Robin bent down to help me up, I heard Heidi say, 'Oh, hell, he's stopping. Quick, get her on her feet and untie her hands.' 'If you say a word to warn the driver, I will shoot him, and you can watch him die, knowing it was your fault.'

As the man approached, Heidi stood behind me. With one hand, she held my left arm with the other hand she pressed the muzzle of her gun into the small of my back. Robin stood to my right, holding my other arm.

'Do you need any assistance? I'm a St John's First Aider. I saw you fall. Are you in need of medical help?' He smiled and looked hopeful as he glanced at each of our faces. Heidi gave me a prod with the gun, showing that I should respond.

'No, I'm fine, just a little car sickness. We stopped to look for some travel pills. We are on our way to Whitby, we'll soon be there and I'll be able to get some for the drive home.' As we all stared at the Good Samaritan, I put on my most fearful expression and silently mouthed as clearly as I could, 'HELP ME.'

His eyes held mine for the briefest moment before he smiled.

'Well, if there's nothing I can do, I'll be on my way. Enjoy your trip to Whitby.'

He turned and began making his way back to his car. I didn't feel her move, I just heard the gun go off and then saw the man ahead of us fall to the road. Heidi spun me around and pushed me up against the car.

'What have you done that for?' screamed Robin.

With me pinned against the car, Heidi yelled at me. 'I warned you. Why did you mention Whitby? You signalled him, didn't you?'

Stunned by what I'd seen and Heidi's rage my mouth just opened and closed with no sound coming out. I stared into Heidi's cold, deadly eyes expecting her to shoot me next. Instead, she shoved me towards the back of the car and back into the boot. I didn't resist; I was just thankful to be alive. The boot lid slammed shut; however, from inside, I could still hear the two of them talking about the dead man.

'What do we do now?' protested Robin.

'We'll put him in his car before someone else comes along. Make him look as though he is having a nap.'

All went silent for a few minutes, until a few minutes later when I felt the car rock as Heidi and Robin got in the car. We pulled away quickly but the pace eased for a while. Until I felt the car slow down once again and come to a stop. I felt the car move as Robin and Heidi got out. Time passed slowly, my heart thumped, my heading buzzed as I feared if this was about to be my final destination. Then I heard voices just before the boot was reopened.

'Get out!' demanded Heidi, brandishing her gun.

As I stepped into a different lay-by, my knees were shaking; I couldn't take my eyes from Heidi's gun. She used it to indicate that she wanted me to move away from the car boot. That's when I saw Robin was emptying the back seat of the car of its luggage. I looked from Robin to Heidi, confused by their actions.

'You are going to sit in the back, next to me for the last part of the journey. I will have my gun on you at all times, so don't try to signal anyone again or you'll be the first to die this time,' said Heidi.

I nodded my understanding. Once the back seat was empty, I got in, followed by Heidi. Robin checked the lay-by for anything that may have been dropped then got in. No one spoke, as we set off. I thought about the dead man left in his car. It would probably be hours before anyone checked on him.

It wasn't long before I saw a signpost for Robin Hood's bay and realised we'd soon be in Whitby. In the distance, the sun glinted off the water as I got my first glimpse of the sea. Then the scenery changed from farmland to open moor with fell-sheep roaming free in the heather. Before the scenery changed back to farmland and the occasional house by the side of the road. A mile or two later we entered the outskirts of Whitby. I looked at Heidi, her face was hard and fixed; she must be feeling just as tense as I was as we neared our journey's end. As we entered the more built-up areas of the town the car slowed. Heidi pushed her pistol deeper into my side as if I needed reminding to behave myself.

As we drove further into Whitby, we followed the road that ran alongside the River Esk. Shortly after passing the Fleece pub, we turned into a car park at the river's edge. Robin drove around the car park before spotting two men standing at the rear of a car; one raised his hand as he recognised Robin. He parked our car next to theirs and got out to speak to them. I recognised them as the men who had accompanied Heidi when they abducted me from Harrogate. I wondered if they had Holly with them and looked around to find her.

I didn't notice anything at first until Heidi took her eyes off me to look out of the window for the first time since we'd got in the car together. She stiffened in her seat then, twisted around to look at Robin and the two men outside, before tapping on the glass with the muzzle of her gun. Robin turned to see what Heidi wanted, but the car door was already opening and she was getting out.

'IT'S A TRAP!' she yelled at Robin and the men.

I looked around frantically to see what she meant. Men running towards us from all directions, I spotted Rex chasing Robin Steel along the street in front of the car. Heidi was running between parked cars. Seconds later my car door opened and a uniformed policewoman was asking me if I was alright and that it was safe for me to get out of the car.

Sitting in an interview room in Whitby police station, the uniformed officer who'd rescued me from the car put a mug of tea into my hands.

'Here, drink this; you look like you need it.'

'Have you found Holly?'

'I'm sorry, Miss Showers, I don't know. Inspector Allswell will explain everything to you later. At the moment, he's doing some preliminary interviews with the men captured at the quayside.'

'Men; you mean you didn't capture Mrs Steel?'

'We have three men in the cells. I know nothing about a, Mrs Steel; maybe they took her somewhere else.'

'What about Rex Barker; I saw him chasing someone down the road.'

‘I’m sorry. I don’t know any police officer at this station called Rex Barker.

‘Did you find the dead man in the lay-by?’

‘I don’t know anything about a dead man being found, but I will mention it to my sergeant. You sit there until the Inspector comes, I’m sure he’ll be able to answer your questions.’ The constable left me and returned to the depths of the police station. One sip of the overly sweet, strong tea reminded me of the police tea in Harrogate, so I set it down on the seat next to me and left it.

Twenty agonising minutes later Inspector Allswell came to find me. As he entered the interview room, I got to my feet with a head full of questions for him.

‘Where is Holly? I want to speak to Rex Barker? Did you get Mrs Steel? What has Robin Steel told you? How did you know we were in Whitby?’

The Inspector raised both hands in the air in defence. In one hand he held a buff coloured file.

‘One thing at a time, I have to ask you some questions first? Where have you been? Where did they keep you over the past forty-eight hours?’ He sat at the interview table, opened the file and beckoned me to sit in the chair opposite him.

‘I don’t know. They kept me drugged in a house somewhere so that I would sleep a lot of the time. The one time I did get close to escaping, Heidi Steel came in and found me. The only thing I know for sure about where I was being kept was that Heidi Steel walked to the shops. She didn’t take a car, so the shop must have been close to the house. The next day, when it came time to leave, I had to travel in the car's boot. All I got to see of where we were was the back of the house. Later, just before we reached Whitby, they let me out. I was so stiff from being cramped up; I nearly fainted; that's when a passer-by stopped to offer help. Did you find the man in the lay-by? Heidi Steel shot him in the back.'

'No. We know nothing about a man being shot. I'll send a patrol car to investigate. We don't know where Holly Starbrightly is, and we didn't capture Heidi Steel. Rex is out looking for her, right now. Robin Steel and the other two men we captured are not talking. I wouldn't ask this of anyone else who had been through the things that you have, but time is short and we're worried about Miss Starbrightly. Would you be willing to speak to Robin Steel? He may let something slip if you ask him a few questions. Don't worry, I will be sat beside you and there will be another officer at the door.'

'Yes, of course, I will, but what about the hotel manager, Natalie West and Faith Warlock? They are just as involved in my Aunty's murder as the people you have captured.'

'They can wait. I will send officers to arrest them later. Are you ready to meet Robin Steel?'

'But, but...' Allswell marched off, and I followed him.

In an adjacent interview room, I found Robin Steel sat at a table wearing handcuffs. Hesitating in the doorway before stepping through, he looked up to see who was entering and smiled at me. A shiver ran down my spine. His cold blue eyes meeting mine, and I wondered if I could go through with it. The Inspector placed his hand on my shoulder and whispered in my ear, 'you'll be fine; you can leave any time you like.'

The Inspector took the seat directly opposite Steel, and I sat next to the Inspector. Robin Steel leaned back in his chair and eyed us both, waiting for one of us to speak. Allswell opened his file and started the proceeding by reading its contents then, letting the silence linger.

'What have you done with my wife?' asked Robin Steel.

The Inspector took his time before answering.

'She's not here; she escaped, but I have men out looking for her. It won't be long before we get her too.'

'What have you done with Miss Starbrightly?' he continued.

Steel sat upright in his chair, 'I want a solicitor.'

'No, I don't think so, not yet, anyway. You see, you are implicated in matters of National Security, which means I can do what I like with you. Later, when you are found guilty of treason, you'll be hanged.'

The Inspector closed his file and continued. 'You see, we've had you all under observation for a long time. Your two compatriots are in another room. They are cooperating and telling us all they know. They don't want to go back to East Germany, so they are prepared to cut a deal.'

'Let me go, and I promise, I will tell you where Miss Starbrightly is before it's too late. If you don't, she'll be dead before you find her. Time is running out if you want to see her again.'

Desperate to find Holly, I asked the next question.

'Where is Holly? She knows nothing about your dealings with East Germany. She went to the hotel to help me find my Aunty's murderer, not get involved in international spying.'

The look of self-satisfaction on Steel's face made my skin crawl. I took all my willpower to stop myself from slapping his face as he had done mine.

'You should have accepted your aunt's death as natural causes and left it at that. You weren't even supposed to be at the hotel.'

I turned to face Inspector Allswell. 'You know it's ironic, Inspector. Would anyone have imagined it, the psychologist who helps other people, but is in need of psychological help himself?' Looking directly at Robin Steel I said, 'You need help to get over the death of your daughter.'

Steel sprang from his seat, 'My daughter was innocent. She wouldn't have died if I'd been there for her. That woman killed her as surely as if she had started the fire herself!'

I smiled vindictively. 'It's unfortunate that it took me so long to realise that it was a variation of your daughter's name which was on the invitation to the weekend in Harrogate. I didn't make the connection until I laid out all my notes and the names of the suspects on the table and looked for links between them. You didn't live in the same town as Aunty Violet, but it didn't stop you from visiting one another. Then, after concluding that someone at the hotel was involved; which could only be Mr Bunkhouse, the hotel manager; because he had the authority to make the bookings and cover his tracks, things started to fall into place. It was him who turned out the lights during dinner, allowing Faith Warlock to administer the poison. It was the hotel manager, who was still up and about late at night, who attacked me in my room during the night, using the fire escape staircase to leave the second floor unseen by the other guests, because he knew the hotel staff weren't allowed to use those stairs. The button found in my pillow matched the ones on the cuff of his jacket. I noticed one of the buttons on his jacket cuff had been replaced. He must have sewn it on himself; a woman would have made a much neater job of it. He also provided the paper for the invitations, the free hotel rooms and the dinner. I traced the manufacturer of the paper; they don't have many customers for such an expensive and exclusive brand. The Yorkshire Dales Spa Hotel was the only hotel in this part of the country to use it.

After making friends with Faith Warlock and learning about her husband's run-in with my Aunty, you collaborated with Faith, an amateur apothecary and Henry Bunkhouse in the murder of Aunty Violet. Only, as you say, you hadn't counted on Aunty Violet asking me to accompany her that weekend. You are the only one who has the skill to coerce the others to help you with a good enough reason for taking revenge on Aunty Violet.'

'True, but you still don't know where your friend is hidden. I don't care if she lives or dies. The penalty for two deaths is the same as for one.' He looked at the Inspector once again. 'So Inspector, let's make a deal. I'll tell you where to find your film star in return for no death sentence?'

'Sorry, Mr Steel, no can do,' said Allswell. 'I think we are finished here, Miss Showers.'

The Inspector got to his feet, leaving Robin Steel and me looking at each other. I jumped up and followed the Inspector to the door, ready to protest and ask him why he didn't push Steel harder for information.

'Inspector, Holly's life is at stake. You must offer him something.'

'I know what I am doing, Miss Showers.'

'But, but... And, what have East Germans and National Security got to do with Aunty Violet, Inspector?'

He stopped and turned to face me, 'everything and nothing.'

'You mean Aunty Violet was a spy?'

'No.'

He took me back to my interview room and asked me to wait. However, sitting alone at the table with nothing to do but worry about Holly and wondering when the Inspector would come back was too much to bear. With a quick look at my wristwatch, I left the room. It was time to take matters into my own hands and find Holly. As I entered the entrance lobby to the police station, I smiled at the desk sergeant and made for the exit.

I'd lost my handbag and purse sometime over the past two days, so with no means of buying a bus ticket, never mind a train ticket, home, I headed for the main part of town. I knew daddy's bank had a branch here, so all I had to do was ask them to contact him and he would ask them to release some money to me so I could buy a train ticket home. After the manager of the Whitby branch had finished speaking to Daddy, he passed the telephone to me. After repeatedly reassuring Daddy that I was unharmed and that I was about to make my way home, he said 'goodbye.' The bank manager opened his wallet and handed me five pounds.

'Your father is an old friend. I know he would do the same for my daughter if she needed help. He'll send me a personal cheque rather than risk getting the bank involved in your investigation.'

'Thank you, this is very kind of you. I'll make sure I let my father know how helpful you have been, goodbye.'

Armed with my train ticket, all I could do was wait for the train and hope I got to Scarborough in time to change to the Driffield train.

It was the middle of the afternoon by the time I got to my office. Two seconds after walking through the door, Jennifer came in asking me where I had been.

'Not now, Jennifer, please! I've got too much to do and no time to do it.' Picking up my case notes, I was out the door and on my way to the taxi stand opposite the hotel before the others could slow me down.

As the taxi pulled onto the drive, my car was parked to one side. Confused, but pleased to see it there, I figured Daddy must have arranged for it to be collected and brought it home. Mummy and Daddy came to the front door as I paid the taxi driver, and as the taxi drove away, Mummy came to greet me.

'April, where have you been, we've been so worried?' cried Mummy.

'I'm sorry Mummy, but I can't stay and explain just yet, I still need to find Holly.'

'That's a job for the police,' interjected Daddy.

'As far as I can tell the police are not interested in her. They have National Security issues to think about.'

'Stop talking in riddles and tell us what is going on,' demanded Daddy.

'I can't, there isn't time. I have one hunch to work on. If I'm wrong, Holly is as good as dead, so I will not sit back and do nothing and let that happen. I'd never forgive myself if I could have helped her but did nothing.'

'Well, where are you going?' demanded Mummy.

'Easington!'

'What?'

'I'm going with you,' declared Daddy. 'We'll take my car.'

I was about to protest, but then realised how tired I was. I could let Daddy drive and it would be good to have him come along in case I ran into problems.

Daddy parked the car at the Warlock's vicarage gate. As I opened the car door Daddy removed the keys from the ignition, 'you're not going in there without me.'

'Come along then, Sherlock Holmes, we have a case to solve.' Daddy relaxed and smiled at me.

'You can be Sherlock Holmes, I'll be Doctor Watson,' he countered.

After knocking on the vicarage door, it was opened by the Reverend Warlock.

'We are sorry to bother you,' I said as politely as I could. 'We were hoping to speak to your wife, Faith. I understand she used to be an Apothecary.'

The reverend's shoulders slumped. 'Alas, she's not here. She received a telephone call around midday, then she packed a small suitcase and left. She wouldn't tell me where she was going. When you knocked on the door, I hoped it was Faith coming home; you see, she left without taking her house key.'

'I see. I'm sorry. Do you have any idea where she may have gone?'

'No. I tried telephoning friends here and in Leeds, but no one has heard from her.'

'Has she had any visitors lately?'

'Why are you asking these questions, are you the police? I thought you were interested in her as an apothecary.'

'I'm sorry, Mr Warlock. I am interested in your wife's apothecary skills, but I'm also a private detective.' The statement seemed to trigger the reverend's memory.

'You've been here before; more than once.'

'Yes, the last time I was here you found me in the churchyard, I was not feeling well and stopped to talk to me until I felt better.'

'Why are you really here? What has it got to do with Faith?'

'You mean, you do not know what she has been up to?'

'No; she's always kept herself busy; sometimes it's church-related, but she also has her own interests. I don't always know what she is doing. This may be a small village, nevertheless, I'm kept very busy. It's hard to get an assistant in these remote parts of the country. I suppose it's a sign of the times. So few people want to become priests these days, Faith and I have to do all the work ourselves. But why is a private detective interested in what we do here?'

'It's complicated and I don't have all the answers, it's just that your wife is involved with some dangerous people. I'm here looking for a lost friend. That's why I asked if you'd had any visitors.'

'Dangerous people! What do you mean by that? She hasn't been a prison visitor since we came to this parish. Though I have to admit, Faith has been acting out of character lately. She's been very tense. For the past couple of nights, she has been going into the church to pray when normally we would pray together at home; except Sunday's of course.'

'Is there any reason why she would want to pray in the church at night?' I asked.

'Not especially, though one does feel closer to God when one prays in church. You must tell me what you mean by, she is involved with some dangerous people?'

'During my investigation into my Aunty's death I have discovered that your wife was a witness at the marriage of Robin Steel and Heidi Katin; I have a copy of their marriage certificate to prove it.'

'Yes, that is correct, but she has also been a witness to the marriages of many other couples. I have even been the presiding priest over some of them. It doesn't make them dangerous people.'

'Please, allow me to continue. Robin Steel and his wife Heidi have kidnapped a friend of mine. Two days ago they kidnapped me, but the police found me earlier today. Right now, Robin Steel is in jail in Whitby. When the police rescued me, Heidi Steel escaped; the police are out looking for her. They kidnapped Holly Starbrightly from the hotel in Harrogate a few days ago. I need to find Holly before anything worse happens to her. Robin Steel said the police would never find her before she died. He is using Holly's disappearance as a bargaining chip to get a lighter sentence.'

'But what has Faith to do with all this?'

'I have also learned that many years ago, you and Faith have had an unfortunate encounter with Aunty Violet, which prevented you from becoming a bishop and brought about your transfer to this parish. Your wife is an apothecary; she knows how to transform garden plants into sleeping drafts or deadly poisons. Your garden is full of such plants. Robin Steel is using Faith to help him. I'm guessing that by the time police get around to coming here to search for clues, Holly will be dead. Now, I don't suspect for one minute that Holly is in this house or that you are directly involved in the death of Aunty Violet or else you would have fled with your wife. But, of all the places I have visited, this house, its grounds, the church, its remoteness, make it the only place where a person could be hidden for any length of time and not be found. Is there an attic or cellar in the house or rarely used outbuildings where someone could be hidden? I am convinced Holly is here somewhere.'

'The house doesn't have a cellar, and the attic is difficult to reach; you would need a ladder to get up there. The only outbuildings we have are a shed and a chicken hutch. When did Miss Starbrightly go missing?'

'Two, maybe three days ago.'

'That's when you said your wife started acting strangely and began going to the church to pray on an evening. Does the church have a crypt?' interjected Daddy.

'Yes, it does. But it is very cold and damp down there. It's not somewhere that you would hide from anyone,' said Reverend Warlock.

'Yet, your wife made a point of visiting the church each evening for the past two days. We need to look,' I insisted.

When we went outside, daylight was fading, giving way to the onset of evening. As we approached the western end of the church it was lit by the setting sun like a scene from a horror film. I felt my fear of churches return the closer we got to it; that overwhelming feeling of dread and doom. I stumbled and nearly fell as we went through the churchyard gate. So Daddy took my arm. Now, more than ever, I was glad that he was with me. As the Reverend Warlock unlocked the church door, I tightened my grip on Daddy's hand.

'You can stay outside if you wish,' said Daddy. 'If Holly is inside, well, it may be better that I find her first.'

'No, I'm coming in with you. This is my investigation. I got Holly into this mess. I need to deal with my own fears.'

The reverend switched on the church lights, then led us up the Nave towards the Chancel before turning right and stopping at a curtain.

'The entrance is here' He took a three-branched candlestick from a shelf and lit the candles before holding the curtain open for us to enter.

'If you would be so kind,' the reverend indicated to a trapdoor in the floor, 'it should open easily enough.'

Daddy gave me a questioning look, I nodded, and he released my hand to open the trapdoor. It swung back without a sound and rested back on the floor. A damp, musty smell wafted upwards to greet us. But instead of seeing a dark hole in the floor of the church, we were greeted with a faint glow.

'I'll go first,' said the Reverend. Daddy went next, and I followed. The steps were steep and turned left at the bottom. I felt like sitting on them and inching my way down one step at a time, but I didn't want to get left behind. The light from the crypt grew stronger as the Reverend added his light to the one below us. As Daddy led the way into the hole in the floor, I felt sick, my hands and knees trembled. With my hands pressing against the walls of the narrow passage, we descended into the small damp chamber. As I turned the corner at the bottom I got my first glimpse of Holly. She lay, unmoving, wrapped in blankets, on top of a stone sarcophagus. A jug and a cup had been left on the floor next to her. The instant I saw her I rushed across to her, my fear of churches forgotten.

'Go call an ambulance and the police,' Daddy instructed the reverend.

As I took Holly's hand it was cold, and she made no response to my touch. I thought we were too late, but I could see a faint mist of breath from her mouth as she breathed.

'We need to get her out of here. Take her arms, we must get her to the house and warm her up.'

Before taking her away, the ambulance medic reassured me that he couldn't find any physical injury on Holly and went on to say the hospital doctors would counter the effects of the drugs she was under. Whilst giving my statement to the local police, I insisted that they telephone the Whitby police to corroborate our story and inform Inspector Allswell that Holly had been found and that she was on her way to the hospital in Hull. Daddy and I were free to go home, but unfortunately for Reverend Warlock, the local police insisted on taking him in for further questioning.

Chapter Twenty-One

Tuesday.

I awoke with Holly on my mind. Even though the ambulance crew had assured me she hadn't been physically harmed whilst in captivity. It was little consolation knowing Holly was now safe, I still blamed myself for getting her into that situation. The events of the previous few days had taken their toll on me; I was exhausted, even after a goodnight's sleep with the aid of a glass of warm milk with a hefty shot of whisky in it. As I got out of bed and dressed, I cheered myself up with the thought of visiting Holly later that day.

Over breakfast, my parents pleaded with me to give up the detective business. Too tired to argue with them, I only put up a feeble defence as to why I should continue with my chosen career. The telephone ringing saved me as Daddy went to answer it.

'It's for you; it's Rex,' said Daddy as he stood in the living room doorway with a disapproving stare. Moments later, after a brief conversation with Rex my fatigue was forgotten, I grabbed my handbag and jacket.

'Sorry I must dash, Rex wants me to return to the Whitby police station; he needs to talk to me about something important.'

I couldn't help but slow down and stare as I drove past the lay-by where Heidi Steel had shot my Good Samaritan. It sent a shiver up my spine knowing that I could never pass this place again without the image of that poor man falling to the ground coming to mind.

Parking my car in the police station car park, I found Rex waiting for me as I entered the station reception.

'Thank you for coming so promptly. How are you feeling?'

'I try not to think about it too much in case I want to run away and hide until it's all over.'

Rex laughed, 'Never, you're not the type of girl to do that; you'll see this through to the bitter end.'

At that moment, I wasn't so sure. As we entered one of the station's interview rooms, I asked the questions he wouldn't answer over the telephone.

'Why have you dragged me back to Whitby? What are you doing here? What have you got to do with Robin Steel and Aunty Violet's murder? I know I've asked you to help me a couple of times, but I feel you're more involved in what's going on than you are telling me.'

'I've been following you,' answered Rex, as though it was the most natural thing in the world to do.

'What! why? This is a police matter.'

'Well, yes, it is, and no it isn't. It is a bit bigger and more complicated than the police can handle.'

'What do you mean by that, I don't understand? Why are you involved in something you say the police cannot handle? You work for the BBC?'

'Well, you're going to find out sooner or later, you're so deeply involved in my investigation. Let's just say, I don't work for the BBC, but another government agency linked to my old army job.'

I stared at Rex; for once in my life, I was speechless. Questions about Rex, his new job, who he was and everything that had happened to me tumbled through my mind in a muddle as I tried to make sense of it all. I had a million questions I wanted to ask him but didn't know where to start. A police constable entering the room interrupted my interrogation of Rex.

'He's ready for you now, Sir,' said the officer.

'Thank you, we'll be through in a minute,' answered Rex.

'What's going on? Why am I here?'

'We have arrested a group of foreign agents that we've been watching for some time. We didn't know who their minders were until you started to investigate your Aunty's murder and made the links that we didn't spot. We didn't know who was bringing the spies into the country or how. We now know it was Robin and Heidi Steel who picked them up from Whitby and arranged for them to quietly settle into the area to learn our customs so they didn't stand out before they started their spying. If Robin Steel hadn't ended up in jail because of your Aunty Violet, met Faith Warlock and later met and married Heidi Katin, we may have been searching for this spy network for years. But, thanks to Robin

Steel and his desire to get revenge for the death of his daughter, he inadvertently dragged you into the mix.'

'But all I wanted to do was find Aunty's murderer.'

'Yes, and in doing so you made the links we had missed. The problem is Heidi Katin or, Steel as you know her has escaped.'

'What about Faith Warlock; she had left by the time I got to her house.'

'Don't worry, the police in Hull arrested her at the railway station trying to board a train to London. It's Heidi Katin we need to find.' He paused and looking at me with hopeful eyes asked, 'I would like you to talk to Robin Steel. Rattle him if you can. Get him to say something in anger that can help us find his wife. Are you up to it?'

The image of the Good Samaritan came back to me.

'Yes, I'll do it.'

'You're a murderer.' I told Robin Steel as I sat opposite him.

'Wrong, I haven't killed anyone. You saw Heidi shoot that man when we stopped in the lay-by.' He sat back in his chair a smug expression on his face.

'I didn't mean that poor man, I meant my Aunty Violet and Holly Starbrightly.'

Sitting bolt upright in his chair, he looked shocked at my accusation. 'I didn't kill them; who told you that?'

'Faith Warlock was arrested yesterday, trying to catch a train to London. The police in Hull are amazed by what she is saying about you and your wife. She's told them that it was you who delivered Holly to their church and told them to hide her body after you had suffocated her.'

It's lies; she's lying. Heidi said that Miss Starbrightly was alive, and well when she delivered her to the Warlock's house. It was Faith Warlock who made the sleeping draft for the actress and the poison that was used on your Aunty.'

'That may or may not be true, however, when you all go on trial, given the choice, who is the jury going to believe, a sweet old lady married to a vicar or a criminal who has already done time in jail? It was you who planned the murder and co-opted all your helpers. You knew exactly what was going to happen and when. You arranged it that way, to get revenge on Aunty Violet for the death of your daughter when you were in jail. When I turned up at the hotel in Harrogate, you came to my room and tried to kill me, and when Heidi and I were alone, she confessed to me that the pair of you were only in this mess because of your overwhelming desire for revenge. You've blown her cover as a spy and wrecked her mission in England. I wouldn't be surprised if the East Germans don't send an assassination squad to kill you for messing up their operation in East Yorkshire.'

You've got it all wrong, yes, I arranged the get together in Harrogate, but it wasn't me who tried to kill you. It was that idiot of a hotel manager's idea. He's spotted you when he and the headwaiter were having five minutes alone with each other. He feared you would report him to the hotel owners and the pair of them would get the sack. It's not the first time that someone has caught the two of them together.'

'It seems to me, that the only person who can corroborate what you are saying is Heidi; where is she?'

He was looking worried as he answered, 'I don't know.'

'You shouldn't be protecting her. When you were asleep at the house she said she blamed you for everything going wrong. Ask yourself, where is she now? Is she trying to rescue you or is she safely on her way back to East Germany, just as fast as she can and leaving you to take the rap for all that has happened? I wouldn't be surprised if she hasn't left evidence at your house in Helmsley which proves you are the chief spy in this part of the country.'

'You're mad. Heidi would never do that to me.' Sweat was building on his forehead and upper lip.

'Then, answer this. What do you think she is going to say when she gets back to East Germany, 'Sorry Comrade Commander, I messed up years of spying, it is all my fault or it was Robin Steel and his hair-brained plan and fixation on getting revenge on an old woman?'

Robin Steel stared at me and then at Rex. Rex shrugged his shoulders and then leaned forward onto the table, 'sounds like the little lady has got it all sewn up to me. With the evidence she has collected and what I have on you. I expect they'll do what happens to all traitors and chop your head off at the tower of London.'

'I want a deal. I'll tell you everything, where I think Heidi is and how she runs the network in East Yorkshire in exchange for no trial and no death sentence.'

'Thank you, I'm sure I can arrange that,' said Rex.

Jumping to my feet, I screamed at Rex.

'What! You're going to let him go free, after all, he's done. I don't believe it. You tricked me into helping you.'

Feeling that he had won a significant victory, Robin Steel sneered at me, 'Ha, discovered by a silly little girl like you, playing at being a detective, all because of a tragedy that happened to me years ago that I couldn't forget. All this is your Aunty's fault, and now, after you've done all the work to get me arrested, you find I'm going to get away with murdering her after all. You're out of your league little lady. Go home, get married and have babies. Do something you may be good at.'

As I turned to attack the scum on the far side of the table, Rex grabbed me by the upper arms and forced me from the room. A policewoman waiting outside put her arm around my shoulder and led me away shaking with rage as I yelled 'I hate you,' at Rex. Shrugging off the police woman's arm I turn towards the door.

'I'm sorry Miss, but you can't leave without permission.'

'Try stopping me,' I demanded. She took a step forward, hesitated, and then backed off. Not waiting in case she went for help, I was out of there in a trice and didn't look back.

After pulling out of a junction and narrowly missing a car I hadn't noticed, I stopped the car at the roadside to calm down before heading for home. Looking for a sweet in the glove compartment, I found the note that I had made from the Steels notepad in Helmsley.

Lucky Lady, Whitby, 07:45, 26th.

The 26th was yesterday when the Steel's brought me to Whitby. It was early morning when the police rescued me in the car park, next to the quay, which can only mean the Lucky Lady is a boat. The police jumped us too soon; they don't know about the boat. I bet that is where Heidi is hiding. Driving back to the car park we stopped in yesterday. I parked my car at the side of the road before reaching the car park, figuring it would be better to approach it on foot. Because the Steel's had driven to that car park, the Lucky Lady was probably moored close by. It was a long shot, Heidi Steel maybe somewhere completely different or the boat could have left with Heidi yesterday. No, the police may have guessed that a boat was part of the Steel's escape plan, but apart from Robin and Heidi, I'm the only one who knows the name of the boat. The police may have searched all these boats, but they didn't find Heidi, she had escaped. She will have waited until the police had gone and then come back. What safer place could there be than a hideout that the police have already searched. That's what I would do.

Chapter Twenty-Two

As I made my way along the quayside, there must have been more than a dozen boats moored to the wooden platform, with more boats further upriver. Luckily for me, they were all moored facing downstream towards the mouth of the harbour, their names painted on their bows. I soon found the Lucky Lady.

She was about thirty feet in length, painted blue and white, and was definitely no pleasure craft. There was a large area of open deck at the back and a covered cockpit come cabin area at the front, with a forest of aerials sprouting from its roof. It wasn't the escape vessel that I had expected to find; it didn't look sturdy enough for a long sea voyage. However, it would get you far enough out to sea to meet a bigger boat without being seen from the shore. I got close enough to the boat to see that there was no one on deck, but I daren't get any closer in case someone inside spotted me. If I was going to keep watch on it, I needed somewhere to hide. The Captain Cook Museum next to the car park looked like the right place. At the river's edge, it had a low wall and over it, I could see shrubs. The museum had a garden at the rear.

A ticket to the museum cost me a shilling and the tearoom at the back had seating in the garden next to the river. Keeping watch on the Lucky Lady over the wall whilst I enjoyed a cream tea treat, seemed like a very nice way to carry out surveillance work. I could have stayed there all day in the sheltered walled garden. So I made a mental note to bring Mummy here one day, she'd love it.

I wasn't sure at first. It was just a slight tilting of the boat's deck that made me look harder. It may have been caused by a ripple in the water, but then it happened again, only the movement was more pronounced. There was someone on board the boat moving about. I couldn't see who it was. There was no one on deck, and the curtains at the cabin windows were closed. If Heidi Steel was onboard as I suspected, how was she going to leave? If the boat left port so soon after being searched, it would raise suspicions and get searched again before leaving the harbour. That's why it hadn't left already. Heidi was trapped onboard. How then, is she going to escape; how would I escape? I couldn't use the boat to get away, which means either walking away or driving away. Walking would be too risky, too slow. I'd drive. At night? No. That would be suspicious; it would have to be during the day. In a car? No. If anyone was watching the car park they would see me leave, but in a van, I could hide in the back unseen. That's what I would use.

As I watched the boat I saw the curtain twitch. My brain went into overdrive with excitement, she's looking for something; she's waiting for the van to arrive. I was about to find a telephone and call the police but stopped.

‘They’ll probably let her go if she promises to help them as they’ve done with Robin Steel. No, I wanted to get her.’

I needed my car. In my rush to leave the garden, I knocked my chair over but didn’t stop to pick it up, I didn’t have time. To the amazement of the cafe staff, I fled the building and headed up the street, rummaging in my handbag for my car keys as I did so.

Having driven up and down the street a few times until a parking place became vacant opposite the quay and the Lucky Lady; I waited for the van that I hoped would soon arrive. I didn’t have to wait very long. After a couple of false alarms, a small, white van turned up with the picture of a fish on its side. It stopped in the car park alongside the quay where the Lucky Lady was moored. One man wearing a white coat got out, opened the back of the van and unloaded stacks of orange coloured, empty plastic tubs. After placing six stacks side by side, he was mysteriously joined by a second person in a white coat who had appeared from nowhere. It had to be Heidi Steel in disguise, using the van as cover to leave the boat. As the man finished unloading the tubs, he closed one of the rear doors of the van, and let his mysterious companion jumped in before closing the second rear door. After a quick look around, he got back in the driving seat and drove out of the car park. I followed it in my Morris. The fish van was soon making its way out of town and heading inland. I stayed on his tail as we went through village after village until we reached Grosmont. Then the fish van turned onto a minor road. I dropped further back so as not to be noticed. Only being able to see the van ahead of me when the road was straight enough, my heart skipped a beat when along one section of road, the van had gone. I jumped on the brakes and pulled to the side of the road. Looking left and right from my seat, I looked for the van hoping to spot where it had turned off the road, but I couldn't see it.

Turning the car around I drove back the way I had come. Finding a lane between dry stone walls, I followed it for about a mile. Before, in the distance, parked next to a small cottage, I spotted the fish van. Coming to a stop, I watched the house, wondering what I was going to do next all alone in the middle of nowhere. I couldn't arrest Heidi; she had a gun and the protection of the man in the van. There wasn't enough space to turn the car around, so I reversed back between the dry stone walls to the top of the lane and then drove to Grosmont. In the centre, close to the railway crossing, I found a public telephone box and phoned the police, telling them where I was and the location of Heidi Steel. They told me to stay by the telephone, but I refused and made my way back to the top of the farmer's lane down which the cottage was located. My intention was to stop the police from driving past the lane as I had done.

With my car parked in the lane, I looked at my watch and estimated how long it had taken me to arrive here from Whitby. I guessed at somewhere between half an hour and three-quarters of an hour, so it would take the police about the same amount of time to arrive.

Sitting in my car, I couldn't help but clock-watch as I waited for the police. With nothing else to do, minutes felt like hours as the anticipation of their arrival grew torturous. Ten minutes passed, then twenty. At thirty minutes I could feel my heart thumping and I wondered if I had given the police the correct directions to the cottage, surely, they would be speeding along faster than I had done. Why couldn't I hear the warning bells on their cars? Winding down my car window, I listened for any sound of their approach. Instead, I was greeted with the faint sound of a car starting and moments later the sound of a car engine getting louder. The sight of the white van coming up the lane made me jump. 'No, no, no,' I repeated to myself. Starting my car I headed down the lane towards the approaching van. As soon as the driver saw me he began tooting his horn. What had come over me I will never know, but I was determined that Heidi Steel would not escape again. Putting my foot down harder on the accelerator, I pushed on. With the dry stone walls on either side of us, there was nowhere to turn off the lane. Neither of us slowed as I ploughed on. Bracing myself for the impact, I rammed my car into the van. The impact came with a great bang and crunching of metal. I felt myself being lifted out of my seat and hitting my head on the roof of the car interior. Steam and boiling water poured into the car's footwell, and black smoke billowed from beneath the crumpled bonnet. It took me a few seconds to regain my thoughts and stagger from the car. Apart from a headache, I felt in one piece. Looking at my car, my first thoughts were, 'What is Daddy going to say?'

Supporting myself against the dry stone wall, I looked at the white van. It had hit the wall before I had run into it, the driver must have turned his steering wheel at the last moment so that my car had rammed into his right-wing and wheel arch. As I looked at the mass of crumpled wreckage, I realised how lucky I had been. If it had been a head-on collision, I wouldn't have got out of my car so easily. It was then that I noticed there was no passenger in the van; the driver was slumped over the steering wheel with blood trickling from a head injury, but there was no sign of Heidi Steel. Opening the back of the van showed it to be empty; Heidi must still at the cottage.

I followed the lane down to the whitewashed cottage. There was no garden at the front just a neatly cut circle of grass, with a gravel track around it where cars could turn around. From behind the dry stone wall, I looked for signs of life from within the cottage. I was sure Heidi would have come outside if she'd heard the crash.

'What are you doing here?'

I didn't know where she'd come from, but I recognised her voice instantly, and the hard metal object pressing against my back as her gun.

'It's over Heidi; Robin has told the police everything they want to know. They are on their way; I telephoned them your location before I come looking for you. You can't escape; turn yourself in and make a deal with the police. That's what Robin has done.'

As I slowly turned to face my captor, I cautiously and slowly raised my hands in surrender, bringing them up in front of me, maintaining eye contact with her as I did so. As both my hands came up to about halfway, I thrust them forward, using the heels of my palms to strike Heidi in each shoulder joint at the same time. Her arms flew apart as she fell backwards. The gun went off, the bullet harmlessly heading skyward. As Heidi hit the ground, the gun was knocked from her hand and bounced away. Following Heidi to the ground, I sat on her chest with my knees holding down her arms. She struggled at first but soon gave up. And that was where I stayed until Inspector Allswell and the police from Whitby arrived a few minutes later. I felt very proud of myself, I'd only had a few judo lessons and they'd proved successful already.

By the time I'd finished giving my statement to Inspector Allswell at Whitby police station. I'd missed hospital visiting hours for that afternoon, and was fearful of not seeing Holly at all that day. So I asked the Inspector for a favour.

'Forgive me for asking Inspector, but could you ask one of your officers to drive me to Hull? My car is wrecked, and I'd like to visit Holly in the hospital this evening.'

'I expect that's the least I can do for you after what you've done for us.'

'Thank you, Inspector. But first, I must telephone Mummy and let her know I'm okay, and that I'll be home late.'

'I'll send you an officer. It's okay; take your time; when you're ready, just tell him where you want to go; Goodbye.'

Grubby and dishevelled from the day's events and with a bruise forming on my forehead, I walked onto the ward to glares of disbelief from the other visitors. After all, everyone else was nicely dressed. I spotted Holly sitting up in bed and waved.

'How are you feeling?' I asked as I sat down beside her bed.

‘A lot better, thank you. They are going to let me go home tomorrow. Did you get them?’ said Holly.

‘Yes. I’ve just come from talking to the police in Whitby. It was from there that Robin Steel and Heidi planned to leave the country. They were going to use a fishing boat to take them out to sea, where they would have transferred to a larger ship which would take them to East Germany.’

‘You told me that it was Robin Steel who arranged the murder of your Aunty Violet, but why did he get everyone else involved?’ asked Holly.

‘That was Heidi’s idea. She couldn’t dissuade Robin from killing Aunty, so she turned it to her advantage and helped him. Robin Steel and Faith Warlock met when he was in prison and she was a prison visitor. During one of their talks, he told her about how after an argument, Violet Birch had got him arrested and charged with theft. Faith then told him about her husband’s experience with Violet Birch. A strange coincidence them meeting like that; don’t you think? Faith had given up a lot to support her husband’s career in the church, and it all turned out to be for nothing because of Aunty. So Faith and Robin made a pact; together they plotted to kill Aunty when Robin got out of prison. Only, to save Robin and Faith from making a mess of the plan, Heidi helped them. However, it was Heidi’s idea to develop the idea further. With Faith’s help, Heidi discovered more people who had been harmed by Aunty Violet. Heidi’s idea was to implicate them all in the murder so she could blackmail them into helping her, through their business connections, integrate more of her East German spies into a normal British lifestyle. That’s where the Harrogate hotel and Henry Bunkhouse came in. His hotel provided the newly arrived East Germans with a job, giving them work experience that they could take to other hotels in whichever part of the country they were ordered to go.'

'Wow, you'll be famous and in all the newspapers for saving this country from a gang of spies and traitors,' exclaimed Holly, excitedly.

'Shhh; not so loud, anyway, you played your part in it too. Wait until the papers mention that. You'll be able to pick any part you like in Hollywood.'

We spent the rest of the visiting hour comparing notes about what had happened to us both. By the time my visit was over, Daddy was standing in the ward doorway waiting to take me home. It was late before I got to bed that night. I had to explain to my parents everything that had happened during the day. I only left out the part about Heidi holding me at gunpoint.

Wednesday.

I spent the day at home, thinking that I deserved the day off after all I'd been through. Jennifer had a spare set of keys; she would let the others into the office. After a long lie-in and a late breakfast, I was sitting in the garden with Mummy enjoying the sunshine, flowers and peace, when Rex turned up.

'I'm sorry to disturb you both but, I must speak to April.'

'You've got a nerve turning up after what you said in Whitby,' I snapped at him.

'Yes, I know, I've come to apologise and explain, if you'll let me?'

‘Well!’ I exclaimed, indignantly.

‘Do I need to leave you both alone?’ asked Mummy.

‘No, Mummy, stay.’

‘Some tea and cake would be wonderful if you please, Mrs Showers. What I have to say is for April’s ears only I’m afraid and by rights, I shouldn’t be telling her. It’s just that she must already have suspicions about me and my work by now.’

‘You mean that you’re a rat?’ I interjected.

‘April, that’s rude, apologise!’ snapped Mummy.

‘No, It’s alright, I understand. I know it must seem like I’ve betrayed you, that’s why I’m here, to explain, said Rex.’

‘I’d better put the kettle on while you two sort yourselves out,’ said Mummy.

So whilst Mummy disappeared into the house, Rex took the vacated seat in the garden.

‘I’m sorry for the way I spoke to you in the interview room, but I needed to get Robin Steel to open up and talk. If you haven’t guessed already, he’s part of a spy ring operating in East Yorkshire. Their job is to learn as much as they can about our military installations here and report back to East Germany and ultimately the Russians. You have helped me and your country to destroy one of those groups. By rights, you should be given a medal for what you’ve done for this country. You may even have saved it from war or at the very least top-secret plans from falling into enemy hands, but no one can know that these spies exist.’

‘What have East German undercover agents got to do with Aunty Violet?’

‘Everything and nothing.’

'What have you got to do with East Germans? Have you got a gun? Why are they here? This is East Yorkshire, not London,' I was getting more confused.

'I haven't been quite truthful about what I do now that I'm home again. I'm still kind of in the army and hold the rank of captain, but I work directly for the British Secret Service.'

'The East Germans want to know our military secrets. It's my job to find, stop them or use them to our advantage.'

'You're not trying to tell me that Aunty Violet was a foreign agent?'

'No. Her part in all this was coincidental.'

'What do these agents do?'

'Some work at Blackburn's Aircraft at Brough. Others have opened shops in Bridlington to disguise their actual activities. From Bridlington, they can easily pay visits to our missile base at R.A.F. Carnaby, or the R.A.F. airbase at Leconfield. We know who they all are and what they are doing. We intercept all their incoming mail and radio messages and read them before allowing them through. All their outgoing messages get intercepted and replaced with our own messages before they leave the country. We send them fake replies, supplying believable but incorrect versions of the spies original message.'

'Why don't you or the police arrest them?'

'We can't. That would tell the East Germans we have infiltrated their communications system. If they knew what we are doing, they would change their method of communication and their agents. It might take us years before we could break into their system again. No, it works out better for us if the East Germans think that it was you who discovered and arrested the gang for your Aunty's death. That way, we can keep their spying activities a secret and we don't spook any other East German spies operating in the country.'

'What about Inspector Allswell? First, he was in Harrogate then, he turned disappeared and later turned-up in Whitby.'

'The police loaned him to us once it became clear your murder investigation and my investigations overlapped.'

'Wait until Mummy hears that I uncovered a real live spy ring.'

'Oh, no, April, I'm sorry. That, you cannot do. As far as the rest of the world is concerned, nothing special has happened here. There are no spies. You know nothing about spies and I was never here telling you all this. Robin Steel will vanish, never to be seen again. He will become another missing person on a police list.'

'What about Heidi Steel and the others?'

'Heidi Steel will be turned into a double agent or she will meet the same fate as her husband. All the others will stand trial for murdering your Aunty and go to prison, including Natalie West and Faith Warlock. The hotel manager has already confessed and is willing to help us. You will enjoy the fame and notoriety of discovering who murdered your Aunty and go back to being a private detective looking for straying husbands and missing cats. I'm sorry, but we live in a hard world, there is no medal and no recognition for what you have done to help us. However, the country owes you a great debt and so do I. We won't let you down. I, for one, will keep a close eye on you. You never know our professional paths may cross again.'

'So you weren't following me because you like me, but because it's your job?'

'Yes. No. I mean, I was following you because it is my job, but more importantly, because, I do like you.'

'I don't believe you.' I put on my best hurt feelings expression.

'How did you know who I was investigating?'

'Holly read one of your files on the case when you left it on your desk and then passed the information to me.'

'So Holly is working for you?'

'No, I just used her to learn about what you were doing.'

'So you've betrayed Holly as well, and Holly has betrayed me!'

'No. It's not like that. She didn't know why I wanted the details of the case you were working on. I just said as a friend of yours, I was interested in how you were getting on.'

'So, I'm right. You've betrayed Holly, and Holly has betrayed me.'

'I'm sorry you feel that way. I'll leave you for now, hopefully when you've had time to think it over, you'll be able to make sense of it.'

When mummy returned after Rex had left, I struggled with the overwhelming desire to tell her that Rex was working for MI5 and how we had broken up a nest of East German spies and saved national secrets from falling into enemy hands. But I couldn't. She was happy enough knowing that I had discovered who had killed Aunty Violet.

She didn't need to know all about her sister's murky and unsavoury past life, she'd heard enough.

A few days later.

There's a wonderful photo of you in the local paper, April; along with an explanation of how you solved the case,' said Daddy as he arrived home from work.

'Oh, let me see,' said Mummy. 'I'll cut it out and start a scrapbook. You're becoming quite the celebrity in Driffield.'

'You're not cutting it up before I've had a chance to read it,' insisted Daddy.

'Nonsense, you can get another one tomorrow!' Mummy whisked the newspaper away to the kitchen to be disembowelled.

'What do you think of having your very own female Sherlock Holmes in the house?' I asked Daddy.

'April, come through to the lounge, I have something for you.'

I followed Daddy and sat on the settee. He chose his armchair next to the fireplace. I met your Aunty Violet's solicitor in the bank today, and he gave me this letter for you.'

After reading the letter contents I passed it to my father to read.

'So, the solicitors are happy you've solved the case and that you were not involved in Aunty Violet's death. You are the sole heir to her estate. You are a wealthy woman in your own right now. You have enough money to make you financially independent; you no longer have to work for a living. Won't your mother be pleased when she reads this? She always said you were Violet's favourite.'

'And I thought she hated me.' I wondered what Rex would say if he learnt about my inheritance.

'What do you think you'll do with all that money?' asked Daddy.

'I don't know; it hasn't sunk in yet.'

'There is her house, her art collection and her savings. You'll need to decide what you will keep and what you'll sell.'

Over dinner that evening, I was about to ask Holly to join my detective agency when she made an announcement.

'I've decided. I am giving up professional acting. If it is okay with you, I am going to stay here in East Yorkshire. You see, whilst I was working at the hotel in Driffield, I applied to the Driffield Academy for Girls to be their Drama Teacher and they've accepted me. The money I get from this film will buy me a modest house and my salary as a teacher will provide a guaranteed income'

'That's wonderful. I didn't want you to return to Hollywood. Now, we'll still be able to go shopping and have nights out together, just as though we are real sisters.'

'Yes, that will be lovely; and guess what? Rex has asked me out to the pictures tomorrow night.'

'That's nice, dear,' said Mummy as we all congratulated Holly on getting her new job and her date with Rex. But Mummy's shoulders sagged at hearing the news. She had a smile on her lips that didn't reach her eyes and I could see the disappointed she was feeling about Holly's date with Rex.

Now you can buy any of these books direct from the author.

The Mathew Fletcher Series

Friends and Enemies

The Enemy Within

Farewell to a friend

In need of a Friend

****

More books by Steven

The Firebird Inheritance

Follow me on Facebook

Steven Turner-Bone

or

Email: steventurnerbone@aol.com

or

For my webpage

https://steventurnerbone.co.uk